Lex Files

Celeste Castro

BELLA
BOOKS
2018

Copyright © 2018 by Celeste Castro

Bella Books, Inc.
P.O. Box 10543
Tallahassee, FL 32302

All rights reserved. No part of this book may be reproduced or transmitted in any form or by any means, electronic or mechanical, including photocopying, without permission in writing from the publisher.

This is a work of fiction. Names, characters, businesses, places, events and incidents are either the products of the author's imagination or used in a fictitious manner. Any resemblance to actual persons, living or dead, or actual events is purely coincidental. The publisher does not have any control over and does not assume any responsibility for author or third-party websites or their content.

Printed in the United States of America on acid-free paper.

First Bella Books Edition 2018

Editor: Ann Roberts
Cover Designer: Sandy Knowles

ISBN: 978-1-64247-017-8

PUBLISHER'S NOTE
The scanning, uploading, and distribution of this book via the Internet or via any other means without the permission of the publisher is illegal and punishable by law. Please purchase only authorized electronic editions, and do not participate in or encourage electronic piracy of copyrighted materials. Your support of the author's rights is appreciated.

Other Bella Books by Celeste Castro

Homecoming

Acknowledgments

My wife: My number one fan, honest critic, loyal supporter, and constant voice of reason. Thank you for the pep talks and spanks on the butt.

My sister and her husband (Lexy's people): Thank you for letting me use Lexy's name, her memory and her spirit for this story. I hope her heart lives on through *Lex Files*.

My brother: for imagining the Lake Lowell Ghost. That story scared the crap out of me, when I was a kid, not now, or anything.

Officer Richards and Mishka, Washington Department of Fish & Wildlife Retired: Thanks for the inspiration, sharing stories, and answering my questions. I told you I was writing a romance and you said, "I hope the wildlife officer is a big tough guy." I hope my tough *little* lady does you proud.

You: I hope you find a little bit of yourself in this story. I suspect that a few of you will find yourself identifying with Lexy, my furry and fierce canine tracker, who has a knack for deescalating tense situations with a simple look, shake of her booty or a gentle kiss. Thank you for reading.

Bella Books: Thank you for this incredible opportunity to get my story in front of such a wonderful community of loyal readers. Thank you for your support, phone calls, emails and guidance.

Sandy Knowles: Thank you for taking my vision for this cover and making it come to life. I love it and sincerely enjoyed working with you.

Ann Roberts: Thank you for your expert editing skills and making me feel like there was hope. P.S. Ann said this story was good, so there you go.

Melinda Faulkner: How dare you question every little detail of my story. Thank you for your pragmatic guidance and surfacing your concerns with…everything. *Lex Files* is much better, because of you.

Hannah Love: Thanks for spinning all the issues with my first draft so positively.

Elena Fox: My wildlife expert. Thanks for teaching me how to talk to birds.

Julianna Comstock: Thank you for taking beta reading seriously. I appreciate your honest, no-nonsense perspective.

Carla Chávez: Muchas gracias para tu ojos verificar mi Español. Claudo nessisto ayuda! Buena suerte salvar todo el munco en Puerto Rico amiga. (Aren't you glad I asked for your help? This acknowledgment is the worst.)

Treena and Sean: I feel horrible because I never thanked you for helping inspire my first book. When I said, "Hey, I'm going to write a book about Caldwell, Idaho." And you said, "Plop some lesbians in there and *maybe* we'll read it!" Good call.

Nancy W. Cortelyou of Saffron Writes: Thanks for your assistance in the development of my story and for pushing it to greater heights.

Alexis Rittenhouse: The business of writing can be complex. Thank you for your expert guidance in making it less complex.

Isabelle Simonet: Thanks for your words of encouragement. Helping me get in front of readers. Letting me talk *endlessly* about writing and for being my most vocal fan!

Jenny Holiday: Thank you for taking time out of your busy writing schedule to offer a manuscript critique. In addition to your valuable perspective on my story, I've learned the importance of making time to help other people.

Jessica Jones: Who else can say that Jessica Jones read their work? I can. Thanks Jessica!

Chris Carter: The way you left the last season of The X-Files was… My story would really turn things around for you.

SJ Brooks: Wildlife can be both awe-inspiring and terrifying. You may have read headlines this year about a rare and fatal cougar attack in Washington State. The person who died was my friend. SJ was the co-founder of the Seattle chapter of Friends on Bikes, an organization dedicated to fostering community between women of color who love to ride bicycles. I want everyone to know that SJ left a legacy of helping people feel included. The last time I saw them, they attended an event I coordinated. I needed friends to show up and they were one of them.

About the Author

Celeste Castro lives with her wife in the Pacific Northwest. She uses her life experiences to drive her writing.

Dedication

For Lexy.

CHAPTER ONE

Puff, Puff, Gasp

"Pass the joint, man. It's puff, puff, pass, not puff, puff, puff."

"Eye-am."

"Whatever. You took two hits."

"Whatever." Kristof took another massive hit and his face grew red before he handed it over. "'Ere. Asshole."

Marnie rolled her eyes and waited her turn. As their joint smoldered, so did their conversation devolving into silence. She closed her eyes, enjoying the high and the sun on her face, when a faint sound in the distance captured her attention. A whistling sound. That is, it sounded more like someone learning to whistle, and only a faint and high-pitched shrill noise could be heard.

Her curiosity pulled her to her feet. "Hey, do you guys hear that?" She looked into the distance. "Listen."

"I can't hear over Kristof hoarding the joint," Forrest said.

"Fuck off."

"You fuck off. There are no rules, man. You just smoke it."

"There are rules you need to abide by as a pot smoker in today's world."

"Shh. You guys…" She bit her lip, turned toward the trees, and then back to her companions. "You don't hear that?"

They were fighting over the small bit of black paper, stealing turns to inhale every last bit of smoke. "Seriously. Listen," she whispered.

Their faces contorted as their eyes narrowed.

"Is it like, hissing?" Forrest got up and pushed the roach into his pocket. He brushed off his backside as dried leaves, grass, and bits of gravel fell to the ground. "That's weird."

"Totally! Come on, brah, we gotta hunt that shit down!" Kristof jumped to his feet.

"Wait," Marnie pleaded. "You guys…"

"It's cool, Marn. We're in Lake freggin' Lowell in Caldwell You-Da-Ho," Forrest said. "There ain't jack to worry about."

They left her with stupid grins and raced each other toward the sound.

"Forrest! Kristof! Idiots!"

She yelled and gave up. Both of her male companions disappeared through the brush. One of them flipped her the bird. She flipped them one right back.

"Fuck it."

She trotted toward the direction the boys had taken, but the sound pulled her in another direction. She hesitated to go alone, but laughed it off. She wasn't scared, just curious. There was absolutely nothing to worry about around Lake Lowell, except for the Lake Lowell Ghost. A story her big brother used to tell her about an apparition in the form of a young woman with long white hair and a flowy white dress. She couldn't remember the details, only that her face was the last thing someone saw before their heart exploded.

Nope. Nothing to worry about.

A gentle breeze brought scents of new mint, alfalfa, and onion, classic Caldwell staple crops that received life from the Lake Lowell reservoir. As she made her way deeper into the brush, under the shade from the trees, different scents lingered about—musty wet leaves, damp mineral-rich earth from the nutrient-dense lake, and pot and cigarette smoke.

There was another scent. She searched her memories for something familiar with nothing to show except perplexity, confusion, and growing paranoia.

"Forrest?" she asked. "Is that you?"

Her words felt fat and heavy, the classic weed-induced cottonmouth compounded by fright and uncertainty—and a feeling she couldn't place. A hand to her chest calmed the building pressure. She clenched her teeth. Her jaw tightened. Unable to move. Rigid legs rooted her in place. The dark under the canopy of the trees cast shadows and animated tree trunks.

The ground was shifting. Bubbling, as if lava threatened. She wondered if their weed was laced with something. She'd heard stories of synthetic marijuana.

"Seriously assholes, you better not be fucking with me." She almost lost her footing. Something wet below. A look downward. A dark tar-like substance. Oil? Mud? Her white canvas shoes were now red, her feet wet, her toes slipping around inside and curling in response. The sensation hitting her at once. It was fight or flight. Or fall. She took off, but a tangle of branches and an exposed root brought her down.

"What the hell?" She worked herself on to her knees and inspected the substance on her hands. Blood?

It was definitely blood, but from where?

A dead deer. A totally destroyed deer. Its insides were on the outside. A mess of guts, gore, blood, and matted fur. Its stomach split from end to end. Its face appeared to be twitching and its eyes were still blinking, but that was impossible. The animal was dead, totally and completely, one hundred percent dead. But its tongue was moving and it was hissing like her cat did when she was being brushed, just a warning hiss, but a hiss it was, and how could the deer be hissing if it was dead and blood was spilling from its throat?

But the sound wasn't coming from the deer.

The hissing grew louder and evolved into words, the whispering of words she couldn't comprehend. And it was coming from above, no, behind her, all around, a vortex with her at the eye.

She tasted blood. "Shit." Her nose was bleeding. She raised her arm and used the cuff of her hoodie to stop the bleeding.

Out of the corner of her eye, movement. Deranged and distorted as if a lightbulb was dying. On and off. Dark then light. Over and over and over again. Something was there, lurking and hissing, whispering. It was growing louder, getting closer. It was everywhere and nowhere and she wanted to catch a glimpse.

"Marnie!"

Forrest and Kristof. Their shouts broke her free from the call of the hissing.

"What the fuck happened to you! Your nose. Your face. You're covered in blood." The boys looked to their feet. "Holy shit! It's everywhere!"

"Do you see it? Can you hear it?" She stood rooted in place, unable to move and wanting to run, but where? "There!" She pointed. "Lost! Can't see! Trapped!"

CHAPTER TWO

A Girl & Her Dog

"All right, girl. Hold. Only for a sec'." Officer Daya Soto exited her service vehicle and gave her work partner a pat on the head and a couple of scratches behind an ear. The tolerant colleague: a short-haired, medium-built, black-and-white canine named Lexy. Alexus Marie to be exact, named for the simple fact that Officer Soto had always loved that name. Other names the dog had been called during her three years included Lex, Lixi, and Lix, mainly because she licked so much, especially when she was happy.

Soto loved the look in Lexy's eyes at the onset of an investigation, a mix of eagerness and intrigue. She wondered if the feeling was mutual. Probably. Officer Soto was certain they communicated on a special wavelength and had tales to tell to back her claim.

"Mr. Simmons?" Soto positioned her Stetson, adding another few inches to her five-foot-four frame. The hat did its other job of shading her olive skin from a sunny summer day in Seattle. Her long wavy black hair was woven into a single braid, which she always wore while on duty.

"To some." He snorted. "But you can call me Larry."

"Officer Soto."

They shook hands. His was large and chubby, and he had an overly strong grip, but she gripped back just as hard if not harder.

"I'm sorry this happened, sir. My partner, Officer Tom Roselyn, is talking with your wife. Everything will be okay." Larry seemed more interested in working something out from between his teeth. She inspected her notes. "You said a *cougar* attacked your wife and then took off toward the Highlands?"

"Darn straight." He lifted his ball cap to scratch an itch, then resettled it.

"What color was the cat and about how large would you say?"

"It was a big ol' critter," he said, holding his arms out in front of him as if he were holding a wine barrel in his arms. "The thing came out of nowhere, scratched up the wife real good. Ain't never seen no cat do that before." A smirk appeared on his face. He settled his thumbs into his belt loops. How he managed to find his waistband under his protruding belly she didn't know.

"Nor have I. Cougars don't usually attack people."

His smirk disappeared when he noticed Lexy poke her head out of the backseat of the service vehicle window. He ceased to be concerned with the troublesome piece of food in between his teeth at the sight of the dog. "When did y'all get dogs on the force?"

"She's the only one like this," Soto said, making eye contact with her partner.

"Like what? Looks like a regular dog to me. A buddy of mine's got one, looks just like that. A cow dog I think, and real smart. Are you sure this isn't a cow dog breed, little lady?"

"Pretty sure," she confirmed.

"Well, then?"

"She's a Karelian Bear Dog."

"What kind of fancy newfangled dog is that?"

"Actually it's an old breed, a rare and specialized one known for hunting large game, moose, and bears to name a few. Oh, and large cats, which she can smell a mile away."

"They let women on the force and now dogs? I would think it would be the other way around." He gave her a playful swat on the arm and let it linger there. "In fact, I don't know why your six-foot-somethin' partner is talkin' to the wife and you're here talkin' to me." He stepped closer and smiled. "You're just a little bitty thang."

She suppressed an urge to take his meaty fat wrist in hers and twist it all sorts of awkward, if only to teach him to abstain from laying his hands on a uniformed officer. And he could wipe the lecherous look off his face at the same time. She eyed his hand and he took a step back.

But her looks deceived most people. She could bench more than the average man, and she was quick on her feet and acutely aware of her surroundings, which made her extremely effective in dealing with scared wildlife and out of control humans.

"Come on, you know I'm joking. Try smiling. It was funny."

He rocked back and forth on his heels as he did the one-two look up her body in that way so many men do—the look that said she had no business carrying a weapon, wearing that badge, or working in wildlife enforcement.

"I'll smile later when I know your wife is okay," she replied as she looked toward the wife and paramedics, who were tending to her wounds. Soto's longtime team member, Officer Tom Roselyn, was doing the questioning, but by the looks of it, he couldn't get a word in edgewise given her overly emotional state. "Sir, would you mind showing us the area of the attack? I want Lexy to get the cat's scent so she can start tracking." She clipped on the dog's leash and let her out of the cab. Lexy jumped out and danced around, sniffing the air, the ground, and waiting for her cue. "Come on, girl."

"Yap. It's over on this ways where it happened."

The partners followed, stopping on the way so Lexy could sniff out the bit of blood on the ground in the man's driveway.

"The little fucker. Now you know, I've seen it around here before."

Junk cars, an old RV, and fiberglass boat parts sat collecting mold and moss just like the house they were headed toward.

"The cat's been getting into other people's yards. You can straight-up ask anyone 'round here."

"I don't doubt that. It is summertime."

"Them cougars, bears, and other critters are a common occurrence around these parts this time of year." His comment sounded more like a question.

"Sure are."

She remembered untangling the moose that had wandered into the high school playfield earlier in the summer. The poor creature could hardly stand on her own by the time Soto and Lexy had freed her. There was footage of them all over the Fish and Game's Facebook page. The post had gone viral.

"Sir, I'm going to let her off the leash so she can go to work." Soto's eager partner whipped her head around, raring to go. "C'mon, girl. Find it."

Lexy snorted her response. As fierce as she was, having tracked down aggressive wolves, subduing massive moose, and treeing numerous black bears that were quadruple her size, Lexy hated large cats. Pinned-back ears and fur standing on end were her telltale signs that a feline was near. But the dog gave no indication the cougar had been anywhere close. She pranced around, sniffing her way with her tongue hanging out the side of her mouth. Freed from the leash, she darted toward the back of the property, running to inspect a rusty coiled chain, an empty feeding bowl, and a water dish green with algae.

"Sir, do you own a dog?"

His face contorted. "We used to. A while ago. Gave him away...Now, I said the cougar scattered on up to the Highlands. Why are you wasting time around here?"

It didn't take a specialty wildlife enforcement canine to tell her that he was acting suspicious. "Sir, let us do our job. She's got to get the scent." She spoke into her shoulder intercom device. "Roselyn, what's the happs on the wife?"

"I'm getting nothing out of her. She's not talking," he reported.

"Why not?"

"All she says over and over is that it was a cougar and it went to the Highlands. When I press, she freaks out."

The sound of hysterics came in loud and clear through Soto's intercom. She turned her attention back to Lexy, who scratched and sniffed her way around piles of junk in Larry's backyard. She eventually made her way to a door, which presumably led to a basement.

"Roselyn, come out to the backyard. I think we're about to have ourselves a situation."

"Copy."

Before Soto made it to the basement door, Larry was there yelling, "Get her away from there! Y'all can't go down there. I don't give nobody no permission to go into my private home! There's a cougar, a big ol' cat, that attacked the wife running 'round loose! You bunch of incompetent fake police are wasting my tax dollars."

"Excuse me?" Her hand moved to her Taser, a habit she'd developed. She rarely used the device since the mere act of reaching for it usually calmed people significantly.

"I guaran-fuckin-ty that it will attack again, and that'll be on you, lil' missy," he shouted as spittle dripped from his lips.

"Sir, you need to calm down. Got it?" she said, careful not to change her tone and upset him even more. Still, she kept her hand resting over her Taser. "You called us here to investigate an animal attack and that's what we're doing. If there's something dangerous down there, we need to investigate, so what's in the basement? My dog's going crazy."

"Nothing's in the damn basement. I told you. The goddamned cat scratched up the wife and headed up into the Highlands. Ya' know, that way." His belly shook when he pointed northward. "What's in my basement has nothing to do with you and it's my right as a property owner to protect what's mine."

"Soto?" Officer Roselyn made his entrance. "Is everything cool?"

"It will be," she replied, her tone steady.

"No! It most certainly won't be." Larry huffed his response. "Man, you gotta calm this little know-it-all down. She thinks I'm hiding something in my damn basement."

"Are you?" Roselyn asked and stepped closer into Larry's personal space. Roselyn's large stature helped in these situations.

"What? No! Why the hell would I?" Larry removed his ball cap and scratched his head aggressively.

"Sir," Soto said, "We are going into the basement. Every indication says the trail leads there. Either you let us in, or we will use force because we have probable cause. What will it be? You're the boss here."

"Like hell you will. I am a gun-carrying citizen!"

He charged toward the basement door. Whether he had a weapon in that sweaty waistband or not, Soto wasn't about to take any chances.

"Move out of the way, you damn dog," he gruffed, charging as fast as his massive belly permitted. She was right behind and grabbed his arm, swung him around, and dropped him, though not before he took a swing at her. Her quick reflexes helped avoid the brunt of his fist, but a loud crack and blinding light told her his elbow connected with her cheekbone.

"Whoa. You okay?" Roselyn rushed over to her. Lexy bared her fangs and gave a low growl, a warning that put most people's hair on end.

"Peachy." She touched her cheek with the tips of her fingers to assess the damage. No blood, but she felt swelling coming on. "God damn it."

"Get the fuck off me, you fuckin' whore!"

Larry struggled to no avail, cuffed in her signature compromising position. The more he moved, the more uncomfortable the cuffs became.

"Sir, you need to shut the fuck up and stay the fuck down." Lexy's complete focus was trained on him. "It's okay, girl. Roselyn, we're going in. Watch this piece of…" She took a deep breath. "Keep an eye on him."

"You got it."

Larry tsked, snorted and spat onto the ground, landing most of the viscous substance on her right boot. Soto rolled her eyes.

She turned the doorknob. "Locked." She so wanted to karate-kick the door open with her big black combat boot, but she reminded herself that she was a professional. "Sir, where might I find the keys to get in?"

He spat. "Fuck you."

"Roselyn, can you help us please?"

Roselyn hoisted Larry up to his feet and held him in place for Soto.

"This day keeps getting better and better," she said as she worked a hand into Larry's pockets, grimacing at feeling his sweaty rolls of fat as she dug out the keys—a memory she didn't want to revisit. Ever. Taking her frustration out on her flashlight, she clicked it on harder than necessary—with an expletive to match. In the background, she heard Larry making crude and sexual remarks about her to Roselyn. That was nothing new. Being taken down by a woman didn't usually sit well with the men around her mostly rural territory. She trudged onward into the basement through mountains of trash. Boxes and empty cans, tires, motor oil, and other toxic-looking fluids littered the space. She pulled out her leather gloves and covered her mouth and nose with the bandana she always wore around her neck. Then she proceeded through and over endless junk. Lex led the way, releasing dust particles and mushroom spores with every step.

A whimpering and a rattling metal sound pulled them deeper into the dark space, a trail of blood and recently disturbed dust on the ground outlining the way. Lexy made her way to a cage and barked several times before sitting down. She pawed the air a few times, her signal that she'd found something worthy of Soto's attention. A pit bull was inside, its muzzle bloodied, and full of scratches. He was scared and he was aggressive—not a good combination.

"Good job, girl. You found the cougar." She gave her partner a treat and a pat on the head. "Roselyn," she said into her shoulder radio, "get the county pit bull rescue on location."

"Copy," he replied as she and Lex navigated their way out of the dank and depressing basement.

"A pit bull?" Roselyn confirmed as he hoisted Larry to a standing position. "Let me guess. He's bloody and full of scratches like the wife? Best to come clean now, man, and quit wasting taxpayer dollars." He directed Larry toward Soto.

She Mirandized her charge, a speech she'd recited a few hundred times in her line of work where humans were always the culprits. She led him to her service vehicle and with Larry in the backseat, she closed the door with a bang. Then she let Lexy into the front cab to keep an eye on their suspect.

CHAPTER THREE

A Blast from the Past

The rhythmic knocking pattern belonged to only one person, and one person alone: Special Agent Winifred Ford's superior: Special Agent Johnny Rankin. At first she thought about ignoring it, but she knew he would enter regardless of her permission. "Come in."

She was deep in thought with all her focus on the fifteen-inch monitor before her. Ford glanced up from her laptop momentarily to see Rankin, her supervisor for the last twelve years, look around for a place to sit down, while holding file folders and two cups of iced coffee.

"A little help here?" he asked.

"Morning," Winifred said. She moved a pile of papers over for him, making way for the cups of coffee.

He settled on a dusty metal folding chair. "Morning? It's officially the afternoon."

"Is it?"

She turned her attention back to her monitor, trying to remember where she was going with her last thought. Out of the corner of her eye she couldn't ignore the production he was making as he thumbed through the folders, spreading papers out on top of her small metal desk. "Give me one sec."

"Any time *you're* ready."

"I'm trying to see if, no, that doesn't make sense, Winnie. Get it together." She picked up a ballpoint pen and twirled it through her fingers, back and forth, clicking the top over and over each time it arrived back to her thumb. Then, into her mouth it went, familiar teeth grooves already imprinted in the cheap plastic.

"Earth to Ford," Rankin said. "You know, you are encompassing every FBI agent stereotype at this exact moment." She gave him a look and he gave her a chuckle. "I'm only kidding. How can you see in here? It's so dark."

"I like it this way. I can *focus* better."

"It is really nice outside." He got out of his chair to open dusty blinds, letting light fill the room. A beam shone right at her eyes.

"Close it!" She waved away floating dust particles. "It's too fucking bright."

"It's a lovely summer day."

"There are two seasons in DC, muggy or frigid, and neither is particularly lovely."

He rounded her desk. "So, what has your complete attention?" He peered over her shoulder. "Ah, UFOs?"

"At least that is what they look like. But this light here," she waved her finger across the upper right part of the screen, "it's not right. And the angle of light there," she circled the area on her monitor, "tells another story."

"Fascinating. Who sent you these?"

"A legitimate source."

"Who, Briggs?"

"He's legit, Rankin. We go through this every single time. There has got to be something else I'm supposed to be focusing on."

"I see," he said, busying himself by emptying coffee cups and take-out containers that he tossed in her recycling bin.

"Please stop picking up after me."

"If not me, then who?" He popped the top off one of the cups. "There's mold in this one!" He tossed the last empty cup into the bin, which was now full. "This place is a sty."

"It is not." She went back to studying the images on her laptop.

"Yep," he tsked. "Every single stereotype. Jesus, Win, when's the last time you left your office?"

"I just got here." She glanced at her watch. "Holy hell." It told her she'd spent the entire morning tweaking out on UFO photos. Her stomach growled at being neglected.

"Special Agent Winifred Ford, I came into your office for a reason," Rankin said as he sat back down. "I would appreciate the courtesy of your attention, if for no other reason than I am your boss."

"Sorry." She dropped her shoulders and circled her head to the side, emitting a cracking sound. "I get sucked into these things, you know that." She pulled away from her computer screen to give him her undivided attention. "What can I do for you, Special Agent Rankin?"

"I know you're not taking any new cases, but I thought you might want to see this." He pushed the file folders toward her. "Reminds me of the case you investigated in Oregon."

"Which one?" She mentally ran through the investigations she had conducted there.

"Blue River."

"Blue River *Reservoir*?" She stared at the folder sitting on her desk, recalling the details of her most defining case—*the* case that set the stage for her checkered career in the FBI.

"What did the locals call it?" he asked.

"The Whispering. The Hissing. Aunt Betty from Beyond. It depended on who you asked and what they heard in its presence. The only thing in common was its unintelligible whispering and mauling of wildlife."

"Take a look." He pushed the file folder toward her. "It might be related."

Ford begrudgingly pulled out her reading glasses. They made her feel old, and worse, they were the opposite of chic. She sifted through the details that conjured bitter, stale memories of her infamous case. Chills prickled down her spine along with feelings of resentment.

"Well?"

She pretended not to hear him as she took a sip of her iced coffee, which was not a good idea. The acidic cold liquid did nothing to comfort her. "I'm not one for jumping to conclusions."

"The MO was pretty darn clear."

"At first glance, maybe. But these photos look like your standard circle of life shit," she said and closed the folder, pushing it toward him.

He pushed it back. "You don't think it's merely a coincidence that it's been exactly nine years to the date since Oregon?"

"To the date?" she said and narrowed her eyes.

"Look for yourself."

He pushed another file toward her. She knew this one by heart—a thick, mint-green file folder, the kind with four panels and two metal prongs on each page, holding hostage the evidence and proof of an impressionable agent. Its edges were worn, and tattered sheets of paper spilled out the sides. It also had a specific scent to it like walking into an antique shop. Memories of former owners. A place she didn't want to revisit.

"Such an amateur," she muttered. Then over her reading glasses she asked him, "Where is Deer Flat Refuge?"

She really shouldn't express any interest and lead him on. She was absolutely not taking any new cases—especially not this one. She was determined to take her imminent extended leave of absence.

"Caldwell, Idaho."

"Caldwell?" She tapped her finger on her lips.

"Southwestern part of the state. About thirty miles east of the Oregon border and about the same distance to Boise," he said.

"And Deer Flat?" she asked.

"It's a ten-thousand-acre wildlife habitat. Lake Lowell sits on the land, and get this," he said, tapping a single finger on her desk, "it's another manmade reservoir."

"Damn." She recalled the Blue River Reservoir built in the late sixties by the Army Corps of Engineers. "How many attacks are we talking about? What's the frequency?"

"Unknown, but it has the potential to do much more damage than Oregon due to the sheer size of the preserve. It's a significant resting place for wildlife in the winter."

"Any whispering?"

"Yes. Scared some kids pretty bad. We have their eyewitness accounts. It's all in there."

"And the locals?" She rubbed her temples and tried to ignore her growling stomach.

"Upset, going crazy, fighting. It's your classic small-town fear-mongering."

She nibbled at the tip of one of her perfectly manicured fingernails, reverting to an old habit. She took a deep breath. "What else?"

"Local authorities are bringing in an expert from Washington State Fish and Wildlife and a specialized K-9."

"There aren't specialized K-9 in Idaho?"

"Not like this. It's a one of a kind experimental program and by the looks of it, highly effective."

"What's it called?" she asked, bringing up an Internet search window while he fished out a sheet of paper from the folder.

"The Karelian Bear Dog Program."

"A Karelian Bear what now?" She typed into her browser. "What is that, like a huge-ass dog?" She pressed enter, bringing up stock images of black-and-white medium-built muscular dogs.

"No, this one doesn't look huge." He fished out photos from the crisp new file folder. "This is Lexy. This particular breed specializes in tracking large wildlife. An Officer Soto runs the program. They are lucky to get her on this case. She's highly sought after. A rare commodity." He pushed photos toward her, and she found the one of the dog.

"Good-looking dog." Ford edged the photo with her fingertip. The dog was sitting obediently complete with service vest. She pulled another photo from the stack. "Whoa! Look at those fangs." She held it up for Rankin to see. A large bear was cowered against a rock wall, and the same dog was keeping the massive creature at bay. Ford laid the photos side by side on her desk. "What's the *official* story?"

"An exotic pet someone let loose because it got too difficult to take care of."

"It'll take the enforcement officer a day at most to realize it isn't an exotic animal running wild." Flashback to the Blue River case. No traces of *normal* animal tracks, no traces of human involvement—only disturbed habitat, hallucinations, mauled and partially devoured wildlife, and a lot of blood. Add interviewing people for their recollection of the story only to get a sensationalized tale of the account they read about in their local newspaper. "And the unofficial story?"

"The Lake Lowell Ghost."

"Oh boy."

"Listen to these accounts."

"Do I have to?"

"It'll be worth it." He picked up the folder and cleared his throat. "Reports have confirmed several apparitions were spotted at Gott's Point."

"Probably fog."

"My sister and I spotted a bunch of teenagers wearing black clothing. They were leaving Lake Lowell late last night. They looked high on drugs and they had a bloody-looking bag, probably had black cats in it."

"Black clothes, bloody bag of black cats, try saying *that* three times fast."

"We were out early yesterday evening and saw what appeared to be a three-hundred-fifty pound wolf-like creature. It had red eyes and a red mouth and was darting around erratically."

"Three hundred and fifty pounds? Impressive."

"Here's a good one. On our walk this morning, we spotted cloven animal tracks, El Chupacabra? Or is the devil himself running amuck at Lake Lowell?"

"Okay," she drawled. "As tempting as this is—and you know I love a good haunt—I got six fascinating cases on my desk that need wrapping up before I go on leave, and this one isn't one of them." She pulled off her reading glasses, folded them up, and put them back into their velvet case. She closed both of the file folders and pushed them toward him with both hands. "Feel free to send Officer Soto all of my files."

"Come on! How can you say no to this?" He sported several lines on his forehead.

"How about I say yes and no. I'll make myself available for a phone call or two, if need be. How's that?" The look on his face told her he was not appeased. "They have a bear dog for crying out loud. Plus it really isn't worth my time or energy to be chasing ghost stories cooked up by local incompetents. Been there, done that. Besides, I'm knee-deep in the Burning Hand report. I nearly have it where I want it. I need to follow up on these UFO photos," she said as she motioned to her laptop. "I got shit I need to do. I leave in three weeks. How the hell am I going to wrap up six cases and investigate a seventh?"

"I know." He inched himself toward the edge of his seat. "But—"

"There are no refunds to Saint Martin. Package deal," she reasoned. "They got it covered." He folded his arms and narrowed his eyes. "Bear Dog—"

"Oregon was a long time ago, Ford. You took a couple of wrong turns. We didn't give you the support you needed. Paranormal Investigations was a new unit. It's come a long way. *You* have come a long way."

"You're right. I have come a long way, and part of that is I get to pick the cases I want—and this one is not one of them." He leaned in and she leaned back. "It's been nine years. What new information could I possibly offer that would help in any way whatsoever? They are better off starting from scratch."

"Look at the file again. Nine years to the month. Officer Soto and company look extremely competent. You could make a great team."

"A team? Really?" she scoffed. "I don't work well with others, you know this. Everyone knows this," she said, thinking back to the only partner she ever had on that freak show in Oregon. Being a team player wasn't what she was known for these days. In fact, people purposely avoided her, which suited her fine.

"Look. I get it. Blue River was bad," he sympathized.

"That's an understatement. They still call me Winifreak. Did you know that?" She dug her nails into her palms to refrain from breaking something or breaking a lot of somethings. She couldn't bring herself to look at him for fear of the latter. She picked up her trusty pen. The sound of clicking soothed her.

"Everybody knows that, and so what? You kept going year after year despite what happened. You," he pointed at her, "have continued to work the hard cases those other asshole agents are too chickenshit to even touch. And everyone knows that too."

She attacked her fingernail, biting through two layers of polish. She tore off a big piece and spit it out, realizing she'd made herself bleed. "Shit." This wasn't about missing her trip or not getting to take time off. The case in Oregon changed her at her core, made her paranoid at times, and clouded her judgment when she needed clarity.

"Getting scared is how you knew you were getting close. That's what Paranormal Investigations are all about. I never said it was an easy road," he said in a soothing voice.

"It hasn't been." Which was why she was weeks away from taking a three-month hiatus after going far too long without taking a proper one. Up to this point, *vacation* to her simply meant working remotely from a hotel room somewhere.

"With your background, Win, and having already faced it once before, you'd bring leadership and a critical perspective. You can have this thing solved in a week, two at the very most. If not, do what you can and turn it over. You won't miss your flight."

"Since when are we rushing investigations?"

"That's not what I am suggesting. It's just that Officer Soto looks like she's incredibly efficient."

She bore into him with a look that said he was probably right but with overtones of *fuck you*.

"Besides, if they screw this up, your name is tied to it, and you will have to get involved anyway, which will be even more difficult, because you weren't there from the get-go. Furthermore, you will have to solve it when it shows up again in some other place nine years from now. How old will you be?" He reached over for her calculator.

She pushed it out of his reach. "I'll cross that bridge when I get there."

"No, you won't. I'm pulling rank on you this time."

"Rank? Really?"

"You are the only Native American expert I got," he reminded her.

"If you recall from the last time, this isn't based in Native American spiritualism."

"Close enough that you are the subject-matter expert," he said, and she knew he was right. "Come on, take a look at what you got to work with."

Her curiosity won and she reached for the folders. She thumbed through the contents before clicking into the Fish and Wildlife website, muttering while eyeing Rankin. She pulled up the website again and scanned the *About* section of the Karelian Bear Dog Program webpage that described Officer Soto's program, including photos of Lexy with a huge black bear atop a tree, barking at people in cuffs wearing camo gear, and working with officers. She landed on a shot of Lexy next to a captivating woman with bronze skin and a jet-black braid holding a heavy-duty dart rifle pointed at a massive bear running out of a small cage and into the forest. A spark of recognition flickered in her mind. "This woman..." Her typing intensity shook her laptop as she clicked around the webpage. "Interesting. Very interesting."

"It really is an interesting case when you take a good look at it. This is a second chance that a lot of people would kill for, especially in our line of work."

"What's her name again? Her full name?"

He scrambled through the folder. "Officer Dayan-na-ra..." As he was stumbled over the Spanish name, she pulled the sheet over to see what all the fuss was about.

"Dayanara Soto," she said without hesitation. She was fluent in Spanish as well as six other languages. "Looks like she goes by Daya, so don't break your head."

"Well, that's not a name you hear every day."

"I think I know her," Ford mused aloud. "Or know of her, maybe?" She sifted through the compartments of her mind with nothing to show. She and Rankin stared at each other. She slapped her desk and startled Rankin. "Former Senator Juan Soto. She's his daughter, all grown up."

"Well then it's meant to be."

Ford pulled both of the file folders toward her in an act of ownership. "Send me a full background on Officer Dayanara Soto along with her entire team, whomever is going to be involved. I need to know who I can rely on, their backgrounds, anything and everything. I'll need information on the dog too. I need to know how the breed reacts, how they track. This one's temperament, images of her and Soto working together, videos, things like that. I'm serious. If after two weeks this case isn't solved—you heard it—I'm walking."

"You have my word. Thank you."

"Permission to exercise my authority above and beyond what is necessary."

"Please, don't."

They both chuckled at her comment. She knew it was among the things she excelled at. *Complete bitch. Difficult to work with. Stops at nothing to get answers.* All ways her colleagues described her. She was the best and the only paranormal expert the FBI had at the moment. Not to mention she also had the highest solve ratio, which was her biggest bargaining chip.

"Do what you need to do to solve this case knowing that you're about to go on leave for three months. Would you really leave loose ends for me to clean up?"

"Good point." She wasn't all bitch. She stood up on weak legs and closed her laptop, placing it in her bag. "I'm going to need extra backup on this one."

"You got Gorman, Ladd, and I'll give you Grady."

"Grady? God. I hate that guy."

"He's one of our best techs."

"And," she held out her hands, "I can scarcely tolerate him."

"I assure you the feeling is mutual."

"Thank you for giving him up." Her shoulders dropped an inch knowing she had the best, but most annoying in a little-brother-she-never-wanted sort of way, tech in the bureau. "What about on the ground?"

"I've already briefed local FBI. They are on hand for whatever strategic support and manpower you need. Call me for anything else you can't get locally, and I'll do my best to help."

"Thank you." She smiled at him as she slowly zipped up her bag, checking pockets she had already checked and looking around the room hoping something would jump out at her that would require her to stay. "I wish you could come with me."

"You got this."

"We will see about that." She sat back down in her chair and blew out a breath of air.

"Hey, look on the bright side," he suggested.

"What is so bright about this?"

"You can finally see if you're cut out for that dog you've always wanted."

"I was actually thinking more of a lap dog."

"Even a Great Dane can be a lap dog for the right person."

CHAPTER FOUR

Federal Bitch of Investigation

"Special Agent Winifred Ford. Federal Bureau of Investigation." Ford flashed her badge and then put it in her breast pocket. "I need to discuss the site of the latest attack. Grace Jewell is expecting me."

An overeager young naturalist in a khaki uniform hopped off a stool and stood at full attention. "The FBI? Wow. Can I see your, like, badge again?"

Ford looked at the girl's name plate. "Sure. Emma." Ford repeated the action slowly and held the badge closer to the young woman's face while staring her down. "The attack? Time is of the essence. There's probably a flurry of little animals being slaughtered as we speak."

"I hope not." The girl's eyes widened. "Do you really think so?" Ford only shrugged her shoulders. "Well, like, FYI we're not really using the word *attack*. We're being very particular about the words we're using and what we're saying. The kids are like sponges at this age. That and," she leaned in and whispered, "you never know who is listening."

"Right."

Ford took a deep breath and narrowed her eyes. She took a step back observing a horde of kids running in circles. A handful of chaperones turned toward her now. Her impeccable attire made her a beacon amongst the sea of naturalists clad in homogenous khaki jumpsuits and black rubber boots.

"We were expecting Officer Daya as well?"

"Yes. Officer Daya Soto and her Karelian Bear Dog, Lexy. Looking forward to it." Ford didn't try to sound enthused. She pulled her phone out of her pocket.

"Me too. She's great. She comes down here for classes sometimes. She's legit good with the kids," the young woman added. "Oh, my God!"

"What?" Ford jumbled her phone in her hands at the exclamation.

"Did you see that post of her and the moose? Oh my God, it was lit."

"Totally lit."

Ford agreed despite not knowing what the word *lit* actually meant in this scenario. In fact she had watched the post several times, at first, trying to gain an understanding of how Officer Soto utilized her service animal, which evolved into being captivated by the officer. Her movements, her hands, her light step, the care in which she treated the poor distressed animal. Ford could see that Officer Soto communicated with her work partner on a subliminal level. She shook away the feeling and used her wristwatch as a prop, hoping the gesture would send the young woman on her way.

"I'll go and get Grace." Emma took the cue and worked her way through the crowd of wild children running around the exhibits and other naturalists at work explaining bird migration patterns.

Ford studied the interpretive center noting the exhibits about birds of prey and riparian and wetland habitats. She realized she was visibly grimacing at watching the wild tiny visitors getting up close and too personal with a filthy-looking animal pelt display. She wondered how many different viruses lived on the dirty furs. A video straight out of the seventies was playing in a theater across the way on the opposite side of the building. There was another group of young students who stared at her while their chaperones elevated their voices to get them to focus on scat.

"Special Agent Ford? I'm Grace Jewell, executive director of the Deer Flat Interpretive Center."

"A pleasure." Ford flashed her badge again.

"Likewise," added Director Jewell, an older woman in a navy pantsuit. She held out her hand for an introductory shake. "So glad we can help the FBI with the investigation. I hope you will feel right at home working with us."

"We will."

"We?"

"My team," she said as a trio of FBI agents walked through the front door, loads of equipment in tow.

"Should we wait for Officer Soto?" Director Jewell suggested.

"Not necessary," Ford said. "First," she pursed her lips as she thought, "we'd like to get plugged in. There are a few critical things we need to set up and apparently there are keys we need in order to access parts of the preserve?"

"Of course. This way." Director Jewell led Ford's team toward a closed-off area. "The code to get through is zero-one-three-one." She punched in the numbers, the door made a buzzing noise, then popped open. "There is also a back entrance and a basement entrance, but not to worry, I'll show you everything and get you all the keys you need to get around here. Though, there should always be one of us around here during the day." The group followed her through the door and into the private administrative offices. "You can set up there." She motioned to an open workspace. "You'll have to share with our staff. It'll be cozy." A handful of naturalists snuck glances from behind their computers. "The staff shouldn't be too much in your way. They are in and out quite a bit during the day when they are teaching." A confused expression appeared upon Jewell's face as she watched the tech team unload their equipment. "You'll also have to share the area with Officer Soto."

"And the bear dog too, I presume?" Ford flashed a curt smile.

"Probably." Jewell forced a laughed.

"Why is the preserve still open to the public, Director Jewell?"

"Why wouldn't we be open?"

"Did it ever occur to you it might not be safe?"

"Of course it's safe."

"It's not very smart."

"Excuse me?"

"There is a horde of crazy kids out there trampling about the preserve, destroying—"

"I assure you they are not trampling about the preserve, Special Agent Ford. We have skilled naturalists who guide our guests around certain highly controlled areas of the property."

"Really? I spent the last hour walking about the preserve, no questions asked by the officers on duty."

"They must deem it safe if they didn't stop you."

"It's *not* safe," Ford said with a chuckle. "The center should not be open."

"Can we please take a step back?" She placed her hand on Ford's forearm.

"What part don't you understand?"

"School visits have already decreased significantly once the news started taking a strange turn…"

"So, you need the funding?"

"Yes, very much so. Yes."

Ford bit the inside of her cheek. "This puts me in a tough spot." She sucked air in through clenched teeth.

"What do you mean?"

"The center will be closed," Ford stated and joined her team in unloading the surveillance gear. "Effective immediately."

"You can't do that."

"Federal property, federal agent's orders. Besides, it's out of my hands," Ford said and took a CAT 5 cable that Grady handed her and plugged it into her laptop. "Perfect. Thanks."

"But, closing off access will only validate existing fears. We already have people sneaking onto the property after-hours thinking they're going to see Bigfoot or something, meanwhile disturbing habitat and our Sagebrush Rehabilitation Project."

"Grady, where are the power packs?" Ford asked. She snapped her fingers a couple of times to get his attention. He pointed in the general direction of a large pile of equipment.

"I can't tell you how important it is that we remain…Are you listening to me, Special Agent Ford?"

"We will issue a press release and get the area properly secured, not this joke of an enforcement going on out there."

"But we have a huge fundraiser coming up. A significant amount of our annual revenue comes from that event. We need that revenue now more than ever!" pleaded Jewell, jumping into Ford's line of sight.

"I really am sorry." Ford feigned sympathy.

"There has got to be some sort of compromise that can allow the heart of the preserve to be kept open…"

Ford felt a twinge of compassion at the woman's defeated expression.

"To at least let us continue furthering our mission somehow. We need this revenue." She held her hands together as if praying would help.

"I assure you," said Ford, enunciating each word and softening her tone considerably, "this is the only and fastest way. It'll be no more than a week to conduct the investigation. Maybe two. A real quick in and out."

"Two weeks?" Jewell wrung her hands together. "We're a week away from our trail groundbreaking ceremony, the new path around the lake. The city council, the mayor, they are all planning to be here for a press op, which is already behind schedule. Surely you noticed the large hole in the ground when you drove in here."

"I did—and what's a couple more weeks?" Ford held up her hands to silence the director's retort, "And don't worry about funding for that. The trail project is a federal project. I'll make sure the higher-ups know there will be a bit of a delay." She turned to her team. "Are you guys good?" Ford asked, as they were nearly done unplugging the building's systems to make way for their equipment. "Get the hotline set up ASAP and get started on that press release. And I want to see—"

"Excuse me!" Director Jewell finally took notice of her staff standing in a line with all their computers turned off. "Where will my team work?"

"You are closed until further notice," said Ford. "I really am sorry. Now I need to get out to the site before it gets any later. Perhaps we can talk and walk?" She shuffled her arms as if she were speed walking. "The sooner *we* get started, the sooner *we* can wrap everything up, and the sooner you can open the preserve again, got it?"

"I…I…" The director held her head in her hands. "This is unacceptable! You can't do this!"

"It's already done."

Ford was so hyper focused on the woman's throbbing vein in her neck that she didn't notice the newcomer standing in the room with them.

"Is everything okay Grace?" came a calming voice from behind her.

Ford turned to the source.

"Oh, thank Goodness, Officer Daya, it's good to see you. Please, you've got to talk to her." She gave Officer Daya a shaky hug. "She's shutting us down." Her chin quivered when she spoke.

"Likely for no more than a week, and I assure you no more than two," Ford said, taking in the woman who was booted and suited in a polyester officer's uniform complete with tool belt. Ford knew the officer was a small woman, but to see her in person, she looked even smaller. And true to the photos Ford reviewed, the officer's hair was tamed in a thick rope of a braid.

"The biggest two weeks of the year," Jewell noted, her face redder than before. "I won't have time to find another venue. The catering, it's all set."

"Out of my hands…"

"Grace." The officer stepped in between the feuding women. "It will be okay. We'll talk and figure something out. In the meantime, do as she says, close things up, send the classes back. Get your team together and talk about a remote work plan."

"But the event. I can't find a place…"

"I'll talk to my dad about using the vineyard."

"You will?" Jewell asked.

"I would be happy to," Officer Soto said.

"On the way to the site, yes?" Ford asked and studied Officer Soto. She was as captivating as her background report had indicated. Everything Ford had read about the wildlife enforcement officer was now right in front of her. Ford was a good foot taller than this tiny woman with a fine plump backside. Slender fingers shuffled a tan Stetson from hand to hand. Dark eyelashes batted to reveal concerned rich brown eyes. Ford grimaced at the nasty bruise on Soto's cheek, and she wondered who or what had done that to her. Otherwise, her olive skin was flawless—no makeup required—and she had the sweetest little dimple on the middle of her chin and full lips that Soto had moments ago licked, drawing Ford's eyes to them.

"Of course." Soto's eyebrows rose at Ford's heels and motioned to a supply closet. "Would you like a pair of boots? It's a bit flooded out there."

"That's not necessary."

CHAPTER FIVE

Splitting the Workload

"Come on, girl," Soto said as she slapped her thigh a couple of times.

"Excuse me?" Ford asked.

Soto looked at Ford's raised eyebrows. "Oh." She laughed. "Not you. Her." Lexy hopped free from a crowd of adoring children. Soto clipped on a leash.

"Oh." The special agent cleared her throat and watched the dog with narrowed eyes. "I'm Special Agent Winifred Ford, Federal Bureau of Investigation." She flashed her badge.

"Officer Dayanara Soto." She held her hand out for an introductory shake getting nothing in return. Washington State Fish and Wildlife. People call me—"

"Officer Daya. I know who you are."

"Is that right?" Soto asked and settled her Stetson upon her head.

"FBI. I was briefed."

"On what exactly?" Soto was curious about what tidbits the special agent would share.

"You've been an enforcement officer for eight years, most of the last four have been spent building your Bear Dog Program. In addition to enforcement, you do outreach and fundraising to support your efforts, which isn't really respected by a lot of people, males mostly. This is too bad and a little on the ignorant side, but for the record, I think it's impressive and your program should be replicated. Your, um…"

"Partner? Lexy?" Soto offered.

Ford jumped about two miles into the air when Lexy licked her fingers to say hello. She held her hand in front of her, and appeared unsure as to what to do with her now wet fingertips. "Your partner, Lexy," she said louder, "lives with you and you pay for her care out of your own pocket. You're from this area. Your father is a retired senator. He ran the Department of the Interior under the Clinton Administration. He lives approximately five miles from here at a vineyard."

"Goodness, do you ever breathe?" asked Soto before the redhead continued. She didn't have to be briefed on Special Agent Ford to know that she was *off* somehow and terribly annoying to boot.

"You wanted to be a teacher but something pulled you toward working with wildlife. Obviously your father's profession had something to do with it, but I imagine your mom passing away when you were young had something to do with it too."

"Okay. Got it. Enough." How dare this stranger bring up her mother's death within minutes of meeting, as if it were simply a fact of her life and not the agony that she had endured? "And what about you, Special Agent Ford? What's your complete life history?" Soto took an in-through-the-nose-and-out-through-the-mouth calming breath to help steel her emotions against this intense and strange being.

"That's classified," Ford replied. "Or is that a joke?"

"Didn't you read anything about me having a sense of humor?" Soto stared into her intense green and gray eyes.

"It wasn't in the report," Ford quipped as they made their way from the building, navigating swarms of energetic schoolchildren and concerned chaperones being corralled to their buses and sent home early.

"Moving on," Soto whispered to herself as a couple of unruly kids dashed in front of the special agent.

"Son of a bitch, fucking kids. Jesus H!" Ford wobbled on one of her heels. A slight popping noise elicited more swearing.

"Language," Soto said.

"Pardon me?" Ford sounded confused as she stopped to rub out her ankle.

"There are children around, if you haven't noticed," Soto said as a couple of chaperones gave them both sour looks.

"And?" Ford let out a single syllable laugh.

"They have a limited vocabulary at this age, if you catch my drift."

"Not my fucking problem that they're behind on their vocab homework." Ford enunciated each word and laughed at her own joke.

"Kiss your mother with that mouth?"

"Come again?"

"I said, it's not the kids who are lagging behind."

"Excuse me?" Ford placed a manicured hand to her own chest.

"Looks are simply deceiving." The comment seemed to strike a nerve. Red snaked its way up Ford's neck.

"What is so deceiving to you, may I ask?"

Soto took the opportunity to thoroughly inspect Special Agent Ford as her flecked green and gray eyes bore into her. Special Agent Ford was tall and lean and hadn't much of a backside to speak of, but made up for it with breasts that bounced beautifully when she walked. Long perfectly straightened auburn hair lay on her shoulders and cascaded down her back, every lock smoothed into place. The few strands that had come loose during their heated exchange, Ford kept tucking into place, as if even slight disarray wasn't an option. Soto wondered how long she took to get ready in the morning. She wore a formfitting black skirt, and what looked like expensive designer footwear. Her stark white silk blouse stopped where a gold belt fit around her waist, and a black blazer nearly concealed her service weapon. She was probably a couple years older than Soto's thirty-five years. "You're *seemingly* elegant."

"Judge a book by its cover much? And thank you, Officer Soto, for revealing your approach to investigation. It shouldn't be too complex working with you."

"I'm judging you more than by your cover, Special Agent Ford." Time to move on from this bizarre introduction. "You already know about this morning?"

"Of course. An elderly couple, bird watchers, heard some strange noises at approximately seven thirty before they found the scene." She consulted her thin gold wristwatch. "To my knowledge they haven't been questioned."

"Lucky us."

"I wouldn't call it luck, Officer Soto. No offense, but the local officers are a bit slow to respond."

"Don't hold it against them. It's a small town with limited resources."

"Too late. What's done is done, or not done, in this case." She again laughed at her own joke. Soto wondered if she was nervous. "Besides, I am mostly interested in tracking down a couple of kids, Larissa Larsen and Charlie Adler, the ones who had a close encounter. They sound like they might have more information than what is in the official report."

"Sure. Let's split up the workload. You talk to them and I'll visit the bird watchers, Mr. and Mrs. Richards. I know them from—"

"Officer Soto, these are incidences that closely resemble a case I worked many years ago. I'm sure you read the file or maybe you couldn't find the time?" Ford gave her one of those quick courtesy smiles.

"I read each and every line, Special Agent Ford, and no offense to you if you wrote the thing or not, but it was seriously lacking. A pile of nothing. I have a ton of questions." The flush of pink on Ford's cheeks, yet again, all but confirmed that Ford had crafted the inadequate files.

"Well, now's not a good time." Ford rubbed the back of her neck.

"It's as good a time for me as any. Why was it so heavily redacted? There wasn't anything useful."

"Sorry but that's classified."

"Is that going to be your answer for everything you want to avoid talking about? And thanks for revealing *your* investigative approach to me. We will get along famously," Soto said with a curt smile.

"Look, Officer Soto, I'm not quite sure how I will utilize your unique skills." Ford waved her pointer finger between the officer and Lexy. "But I expect to receive full support when *asked*."

"I don't need your permission to move forward with *my* investigation."

"This is a federal preserve and technically—"

"And technically, as a specialist in my field, I can proceed at my own discretion." Soto stared down Ford. "We didn't drive six hours for you to figure out what you are doing." She motioned to Lexy, giving her a scratch behind her ears before letting her off her leash so she could jump into the cab of the truck. "We will do whatever it takes to get to the bottom of whatever it is that is happening. This is a very close-knit community. This is my community, where I grew up. People are scared, animals are dying, and our backyard is under attack. We're under attack."

"And that's precisely why I'm here," Ford remarked.

"Paired with me, the top tracker in twelve states," added Soto as she coiled Lexy's leash in her hands.

"Only twelve?"

"I can only be in so many places at once," Soto rebuffed. "Did you need to make a public spectacle out of closing Deer Flat?"

"A spectacle? Let me ask you something, Officer Soto. What is the point of this place?" She spread her arm out to present the preserve like Vanna White presented a vowel.

"The point?"

"What are they are trying to do here?"

"It's a preserve. Dedicated staff helps people appreciate nature and take an active role in preserving it."

"So, there has to be nature here for people to appreciate, yes?" Ford ran her fingers through a low hanging branch of leaves.

"Of course." Soto wondered where this line of questioning was going.

"The last time I investigated a situation similar to this, countless marine and wildlife died. Whatever the fuck it was ate the reservoir out of house and home. Though, to this day, catfish thrive as does a large and very red algae bloom. I'm not a nature expert, but I know algae blooms aren't healthy to an ecosystem, or are they?"

"Of course not. Don't be an…" She stopped herself before she voiced something well deserved, but rude. Another deep breath was in order.

"So you agree? You think wildlife should be present for the preserve to be effective?" continued Ford as Soto felt an eye-roll coming on. "You understand my aggressive approach, don't you?"

"Why didn't you explain that to Grace?"

"To what end?"

"It's basic communication. So she can make better decisions about the future of her programming and her supporters, her big event coming up, the groundbreaking ceremony."

"That's not the FBI's problem."

"It is your problem if you want help from the locals. I assure you, keep up whatever shtick this is," Soto waved her pointer finger up and down Ford's body, "and the entire community will know who you are by the end of the day, and not in a good way."

"Are you threatening me, Officer Soto?"

"Do you feel threatened, Special Agent Ford?"

"You wish." Ford let out another fake laugh.

"Okay." Soto closed her eyes momentarily to collect herself. "We were both requested to assist in this case. You will need to communicate with me. I'm not going to sit around and wait for you to figure out how my abilities can further your next steps. And, if that means me conducting my own investigation, so be it."

"Fine." Ford bore her intense emerald and gray eyes into her, as if she was trying to make sense of a technical manual. In fact she thought Ford *was* the complex one. So much odd, pent-up energy hidden beneath a classy exterior. One that was tailor-made to hide unflattering parts of her personality. Despite Ford's first-class arrogant attitude, there was something deeper within that was intriguing.

"Fine," mimicked Soto as she took in the strange woman before her.

"How did that happen?"

"What?" Soto drew the word out an extra three or four beats. Ford's gaze dismantled her rational thoughts, making her tremendously self-conscious.

"That," Ford said again.

Soto's eyes widened as the special agent reached out to her—and she let her. Clenched hands and a stiff jaw released the moment she felt the redhead place a finger on her check to gently caress the area around the bruise.

"Um, I..." Soto's hand joined the exploration, and she nearly closed her eyes from the comfort of Ford's touch, but she maintained eye contact. "Got hit. Big fat man."

The sound of clipped barking broke the moment.

"I hope you threw the book at him."

CHAPTER SIX

Bugger Off

Ford was relieved to see the incoming call from Rankin. Someone she could be herself around.

"How's it going?"

"Fucking nowhere. I'm going in circles with a couple of old-timers, two backwoods bird watchers. No one is talking to me. Either they are playing stupid or they really are stupid!" Ford thought back to Officer Soto's warning earlier that day. "How anyone manages to get shit done in this ass-backward ignorant town is beyond me. Christ on a stick."

"Winnie."

He only called her Winnie when he meant business. "Johnny Rankin the Third," she said, countering with her own made-for-business name for him.

"Officer Soto's father, you know the former state senator and presidential cabinet appointee?"

"Yes, I'm well aware of who he is."

"He is a major benefactor of Deer Flat and an important part of that community. Apparently you have pissed off a lot of people and guess who they called?"

"How many guesses do I get?"

"Don't get smart with me. The man is on vacation and now he has to come home early to coordinate some sort of fundraiser or something?"

"On vacation? Oh, that must be nice. I wonder if he's anywhere tropical. I hear Saint Martin is—"

"The last thing he probably wants is people calling him complaining about a pushy federal agent."

"Pushy? Who cares? Why are you bothering me with this?"

"Because you've been there twelve hours and you've already worn out your welcome. What is this I hear about you shutting out Officer Soto?"

Ford conjured up a vision of the officer with her beautiful skin and those concerned eyes and that uniform fitting snuggly in all the right places. The utility belt, the Stetson, and the dog!

"Are you there?"

She cleared her throat. "I didn't shut her out." She put him on speaker, tossed the phone on the seat next to her, and went after a bottle of water, squeezing it too tight and spilling cold water onto her lap. "God damn it." The liquid seeped through her skirt and onto her skin in between her legs, bringing her thoughts back to Soto and how the officer made her feel there too. "Fuck."

"You okay?"

"I'll call on her when she is needed."

"You need her now. She is a valuable resource that you need to utilize. She grew up there, has countless contacts, not to mention influence. Use her and her partner. They have solved their fair share of complex and strange cases, so take advantage of what you have there. Because if you don't play nice, this is going to take you a lot longer than it needs to and I'm not going to back you up if you're not doing everything you should."

"Fine. I'll...I'll..." She reached for her chest.

"You will ask her for help and you will partner with her on this case. You have to change your approach, Win. You have no choice if you want to take advantage of your first-class ticket to Saint Martin."

"I gotta go," she warned.

"Yes, you sure do. Go and find her. It shouldn't be hard. It's a small town."

"I know where she is."

"Dare I ask how?"

"I put a bug on her."

"What? Win, really? You and I need to have a talk about how to attract the ladies, because that isn't the right way." He sighed. "You better hope she doesn't find out."

"As if."

"Be careful out there. Despite it being a small town, they have high-up connections so shape up." He hung up before Ford could get the last word.

"Christ."

She downed some water despite needing to pee badly. She shifted in her seat from the pressure, and the damp between her legs felt clammy and uncomfortable. A fitting analogy for her life to this point: a complete mess about to burst if she didn't change something quick!

The mere thought of working with Officer Soto set her terribly on edge. As much as she wanted to let her badge do the talking and skate through the investigation to her extended leave, Soto wasn't going to let that happen. From the get-go she had seen straight through her pushy federal agent façade: the woman who gets what she wants by being a complete bitch.

Ford acknowledged the truth. She couldn't breathe around her. She blamed the dog. Allergies.

CHAPTER SEVEN

Ginny's Diner & Gossip House

"Thanks, *Papá*. Yeah, I know. I'm at Ginny's. I will. *Yo también te amo. Claro*, I still have a key. And I know where the spare is hidden. *Bueno*. I'll see you when you get here. *Adiós*." Soto ended her call and placed the phone on the table in front of her. She loosened a couple of buttons of her uniform top and rolled out the creak in her neck, stiff from the almost six-hour drive. Add the clusterfuck in the form of a certain redhead at the preserve and voilá, a full-blown migraine. She popped a couple of pain relievers, chasing them with an ale.

"Isa!"

"I thought that was you!" The waitress plopped a rag onto the table and wiped her hands on the front of her apron. "Come here, kid!"

Soto stood and embraced one of her closest family friends. Her father's former chief of staff and now owner of Ginny's Diner—the only diner in town that had framed photos of famous people, heads of states, and political leaders with Isa in each of the shots. Isabelle, or Isa as close friends called her, was the trifecta of what Daya needed in her life growing up: quasi-mother figure, lesbian in a committed relationship, and a friend's ear at a moment's notice.

"Hi, Lexy! Can I?" Isa pulled a dog treat from her apron pocket.

"Of course."

She crouched, treat in hand, and Lexy gobbled it in seconds. "She straight up swallowed it whole, didn't she?" Isa said with a laugh. "What a good girl." She gave Lexy a good rub on the belly.

"It's like I never feed her." Soto nudged her pup's rear end softly with her boot.

"What the hell happened to your face?" Isa held Soto's chin in her hand and turned her face from side to side.

"The line of duty."

"It looks horrible."

"It looks worse than it feels," Soto assured her and caressed it again.

"So…" Isa looked her up and down again. "That video of you guys with the moose was awesome!"

"Oh God!" Soto threw her head back in laughter.

"It was great! You were badass wrangling that moose if I do say so myself."

"All part of the job. You look great too. This place is awesome! How is Ginny?"

"She's good. Off with her sister on a trip in France. She keeps sending me pictures of bread." Isa pulled out her phone and showed Soto the latest shot before sitting down and wiping off the table.

"I'm glad to hear it, and I can't wait to see her too. Looks like things are going well."

Soto took in the positive vibe: the people enjoying their dinner, young professionals taking advantage of happy hour pricing, a random hoop and hefty holler, a couple of waitresses teasing each other, and the people at the next table celebrating a birthday.

"Apparently we're known for our pizza. See that guy over there? That's Mr. Legg," said Isa. Soto followed her gaze to an older gentleman sitting alone in a booth. He had a plate full of pizza crust and was working on the last piece. "He's supposed to be grocery shopping, not chowing on a large pizza. In fact, just the other day, Mrs. Legg called looking for him, blaming me!"

Isa's laughter was a welcomed remedy for releasing the tension that had built in Soto over the course of the long day.

"Ginny's has all the makings of a happening diner," she added as she snapped her fingers a couple of times to the beat of the music.

"It's doing great, especially since we introduced evening activities, trivia, and dancing. You won't believe what a jukebox will do for a joint." She folded her dishrag in her hand. "So, how is Rae?"

"There is no Rae." Soto followed up the statement with a shake of her head.

"What happened?"

"Same thing that always happens. Didn't like that I'm gone a lot for my job. Didn't like that I carry a weapon. But this one went so far as finding me a desk job at the Seattle PD."

"Ick."

"I know. I tried, really tried to make it work, to understand where she was coming from, but she didn't offer me that same courtesy."

"I'm sorry, kid."

"It was one hundred percent for the best. I really don't know why I seem to attract the controlling ones." Ford's image float into her head.

"Attract or are attracted to?"

"Probably both I guess." Soto laughed and caressed her bruise again.

"Are you seeing anyone new?"

"That is the absolute last thing on my mind right now. Besides, this little lady," she said, motioning to Lexy, who was currently scratching her hindquarters, "is all the lady I can handle right now." Soto stretched. "It's been way too long since I was home."

"And it only took a shit ton of dead animals to get you here. What in the heck is out there?" Isa leaned in and whispered.

She twisted the rag in her hands. "What could it possibly be? Ginny's niece was out at the preserve a couple of nights ago and swears that a huge animal with red eyes and a bloody mouth was stalking her. Rumor has it that it's *La Llorana*."

"I assure you it is not The Lake Lowell Ghost," Soto said as she leaned in to add, "You want to know what I think it is? What I really think it is?" She waited for a couple to pass by their booth.

"What?"

"*Gigantism Phalangeriformes*," she whispered. "I've seen it before, but in rare instances." She watched her friend's eyes widen.

"Phala-what now?"

"It's Latin for giant-ass possum." She held a serious face as she watched Isa's concerned expression turn dumbstruck.

"You little..." Soto joined in her friend's laughter, throwing a straw at her.

"I'm sorry. I couldn't help myself. The look on your face." She leaned back into the booth. "I needed that."

"Seriously though, things are really tense around here. This morning a couple of guys got into a heated argument right over there." She motioned to an adjacent booth. "I had to break it up before they broke my dishes. People are freaked! It's not good. Have you read some of the stuff online?"

"Unfortunately."

"Any leads or at least an idea of what you are up against?" She watched Isa absentmindedly wipe down the table again.

"Not quite. I've read the case files, but I haven't been able to get much access to the site."

"Why the hell not?"

"Special Agent Winifred Ford, FBI."

"Is she the one who closed down the preserve?"

"Word has gotten around, I see."

"Indeed it does. That and one of my customers was volunteering out there this morning. Witnessed the whole thing. Rumor has it she is a complete bitch."

"Well, aren't you little miss small-town insider?"

"Hey, when you work in a diner, you overhear a lot. People are pissed. Boating season is on hold, the fundraiser is all screwed up, as is the trail project." Isa ranted and Soto couldn't argue with her. "So is she really that bad?"

Soto blew her hair out of her eyes and touched her cheek yet again. "Well, she has a unique way of handling things." She shifted in her seat.

"Are you sure you don't want any ice or anything?" asked Isa. "It looks like it's bothering you a lot."

"I'm fine," she said and folded her hands on the table. Ever since that strange encounter at the lake, her throbbing cheekbone made her think about Ford caressing her cheek rather than the guy who cracked her with his elbow.

"I heard it was mayhem when the FBI agents arrived."

"Mayhem. Yeah, that's a good name for her." Soto replayed their introduction again while she twirled the empty beer glass on the table. She'd been trying to shake the thoughts away all day without success.

"I can't believe she closed things down, especially with the fundraiser around the corner."

"Her justification for it makes sense. Her delivery is…She lacks basic communication skills. That and she's so damn cocky and intense. She's…" Soto struggled, not quite sure how to interpret what the hell happened during that strange encounter at the lake. "She had to do what she had to do. In a strange and chaotic way." Soto wondered why she was defending the annoying and pushy federal agent. She was her biggest roadblock at the moment.

"I suppose. Thank goodness for the vineyard. I mean, shit, we need the catering business just as much as Jewell needs her funding. Everyone owes your pops big time."

"He's really stoked about it. Hopefully it doesn't complicate things too much for you."

"We'll need to add a few more staff, but we're up to the challenge. Ginny also has to come home early. That federal agent is cutting a lot of people's vacations short." Isa shook her head. "It'll be fun, though, and it's beyond me why Grace never thought to hold the fundraiser there in the first place, with those never-ending bottles of great wine to keep the bids going! It's perfect." They laughed together and then Isa said, "Hot damn, who is that?" Soto started to turn around. "No. Don't look now." She didn't have to look to see who Isa was referring to. She could feel it, could feel her. "She's a looker."

"At first glance, but once she starts talking…"

"Oh, is that the federal agent?"

"Probably." Soto glanced quickly over her shoulder. Ford was scanning the diner.

"She doesn't look that pushy to me."

"A lot of people look good head-on. It's the side profile where you learn the most."

"Are you trying to tell me I need a chin tuck?" Isa said and pressed the backside of her hand under her own chin. Soto's laughter drew onlookers. "Table for one?" Isa asked of the approaching redheaded woman.

"No. I was looking for…" She gestured toward Soto. They held each other's gaze.

"The best diner in town?" Soto asked.

"Thank you, Officer Soto," said Isa. "Get you guys anything? Another beer perhaps?" Isa asked.

"I'm good. Thanks, Isa, but I'll take the check," Soto said. She watched Ford shifting a leather messenger bag between her hands.

"Your money is no good here, kid."

"Please bring me the check."

"Hush," said Isa. "And for you, Officer…"

"Special Agent Winifred Ford, FBI." She flashed her badge. "Nothing for me, thank you."

"I'll get you a menu," Isa said despite Ford's declaration.

"Not going to be here that long," she added, but Isa didn't hear the response before walking away.

"Did you have a productive talk with Mr. and Mrs. Richards?" Soto asked, already knowing the answer, having fielded multiple calls from the elderly couple.

"It went well."

"That's great." She shifted in her seat to pull her wallet from her back pocket. "Sounds like you're getting on then." She stood as did Lexy.

"Are you leaving?" Ford asked and her eyebrows furrowed.

"I need to get her home. She's tired." Soto cupped her dog's head between her hands. "We both are after this overly long day. Seriously, though, try the pizza. You ready to go, girl?" Lexy gave a snort.

"Wait," said Ford. "I got off on the wrong foot with Director Jewell, the witnesses, with you. I could use your help and your expertise on this case. Both of you." She motioned to the animal that had momentarily acknowledged her and then lay back down.

"Okay, let's talk." Soto sat back down. "Will you have a drink?" She waved her empty beer glass in the air to attract Isa's attention and Ford signaled she didn't want one.

"I don't like alcohol very much," Ford stated, surveying the room.

"Have a seat then?"

Ford tossed her bag into the booth and sat down. She folded nearly perfect manicured hands on the table in front of her. "Thanks."

The momentary sense of calm turned as the agent let off more nervous energy by tapping her fingers on the table repeatedly, as if playing the jazz version of "Jingle Bells" with her right hand. Soto noticed a jagged nail not like that earlier in the day.

"Of course," she said as she looked around for Isa, hoping the arrival of her beer would soon rescue her. Clearing her throat, she asked, "I'm sure you know about the mauled carcasses that were found about an hour ago?"

"Negative. God damn it. Another reason why I need your help. No one is telling me anything. Is it recent?"

"No. Enforcement happened onto the remains. The pathologist thinks it's a couple of days old at least. But on the plus side, it gives us another plot point in the grid we're establishing."

"You've started planning?" Ford asked and crossed her arms.

"I meant it when I said we would go at it alone." Soto and Lexy exchanged glances.

"I didn't doubt that you would."

Ford smiled and Soto wondered if it was genuine. She didn't think that such an icy interior was capable of exuding such warmth.

"And I knew you would come around," Soto replied, pleased that this interaction was off to a better start than the previous one. Isa delivered a fresh beer along with a glass of water and a menu for Ford. Soto hoisted her glass in the air. "Cheers." Ford didn't raise hers and instead leaned into the booth and closed her eyes. Soto took the opportunity to study her features— long eyelashes, pink lips—capturing a vulnerability she hadn't noticed before.

"Not that I had any say in the matter." Ford reanimated, startling Soto. "The locals pretty much forced me to come around." This spoken with a more forced smile than before. "So, we need to get in rotation on the *night patrols*." Air quotes around that last bit. "If you can call two dudes sleeping in a truck from dusk until dawn night patrols."

"We're planning to kick off tomorrow." Soto took another drink of her fresh ale. "I'll send you the maps and notes."

"Thank you. My team will be ready."

"Who exactly is on your team?"

"A bunch of tech guys. I'm expecting more enforcement tomorrow. We got twenty-four seven monitoring at the reservoir's major entrances, high-risk sneak-in points, kill sites and other areas of interest. We should have intel to review as soon as tomorrow morning, provided the public doesn't interfere with the cameras. Hoping the team can stop public contamination and neutralize the area so we can figure this out."

"How many on your team?"

"Triple what we have now with more any time we need them."

"Impressive." Soto took another drink of her ale and stifled a yawn.

"More like adequate. I'm assuming you have a team as well?"

"I've arranged for volunteers, trackers, local contacts with work dogs, hounds and labs. It's enough to get us going. We'll need more for shifting in and out, depending on how long this takes. But I got what I need to get started."

"Send me those names. I'll need both first and last names, addresses, names of spouses. Tonight preferably."

"What? No." She laughed at the request.

"Why not?"

"I don't have their permission. Besides, you can meet them tomorrow. You can ask them yourself."

"Fine. I'll get it the hard way." Her right-handed piano playing resumed.

"You do that," Soto replied, exhausted by the push-pull. Changing her tone, she said, "Let me know what you find out. I'm especially interested in one of the ladies that is coming. She has real potential to be an expert tracker. Her name is Debbi Crawly. If you're really going to investigate my people, let me know what you find out about that one, because she is…" She blew out a short breath. "Wow." Soto watched in delight as Ford blushed a bright shade of red that climbed up her neck, colored her cheeks and to the tips of her ears. Soto wondered why she was so embarrassed. Either she was really *really* into women or really *really* uncomfortable by the idea of two women together. She leaned toward the former explanation thinking back to the way she looked at her at the lake, the way she caressed her… She stopped herself from touching her bruise.

"And the plan?" Ford crossed her arms and shook her hair off her shoulders.

"Monitor, track, and see what turns up, how it gets around, and establish a pattern. Then trap it if it can be trapped."

"That's assuming it's a wild animal and not something entirely different."

"Entirely different?"

"You should prepare yourself for the idea that this may not be…How should I put this? Of this world?"

"I'm not sure exactly what you're referring to, but at first glance, it seems like your standard exotic animal on the loose."

"Exotic animals on the loose don't kill upward of thirty animals in two weeks."

"Sure they do. It's not uncommon. From experience, I can say that thirty animals killed in two weeks is totally plausible. And to make it friendly, I'll wager two dollars it is indeed an introduced species on the loose."

"Two dollars?" Ford laughed. "I'm not a betting woman."

"No drinking *and* no betting?"

"That's right." Ford stared her down. "Some people call those virtues, Officer Soto."

"I wouldn't know." The comment got an eye roll from the redhead. Soto ignored it and took a long pull from her frosty glass. "Oh, that's good. Nice and cold."

"Let me ask you this. How do you explain the absence of track marks?"

"It's getting around via some other means. Those means, I can't explain—yet."

"Why isn't it consuming what it's killing? Surely that's a big red flag for you?"

"Likely it's stressed out. It's not in its natural habitat. Introduced species sometimes mask their scent by covering themselves in the blood of native animals."

"That's a lot of blood," Ford said and leaned into the table, adding, "how do you explain the reports of whispering?"

"The same way I would explain why the majority of the community is blaming the Lake Lowell Ghost and the Beast of Deer Flat. Lake Lowell is a river run-off collection point. There are feet upon feet of sediment and foreign matter from the Boise River, which is a tributary of the Snake River, which is a tributary of the Columbia River. This wouldn't be the first time we've found something down there that doesn't belong."

"No offense, but you have no idea what this thing is, and frankly, neither do I, and I spent significant time with it. Until we know for sure or have decent leads, I'm saying you should open your mind a little."

"And all I'm saying is let's see what actual evidence we gather and what turns up in the traps before we jump to the most irrational of conclusions."

"Fine." They said in unison. Deep breaths, also taken in unison.

"Will you please fill me in, high level detail, on the Blue River Reservoir?"

"High level is all I got. I spent almost two weeks processing scenes, dealing with local assholes and logging stolen equipment. We had no reliable backup whatsoever. My support was tied up with another higher priority case." Ford scratched her forehead. "My unit gets whatever resources are left over, which at the time, wasn't much."

"What unit?" Soto asked.

"Paranormal Investigations."

"Paranormal? So like the *X-Files*?"

"Kind of." Ford forced a laughed, like she had heard that comparison one too many times.

"Amazing." Soto suspended taking another drink of her beer, realizing she was probably drinking too fast. She looked at Ford in a new light. "And exactly what does your unit do? All I got to go on is the show from the nineties. You know Mulder, Scully, Smoking Man." She felt her face flush at what she was about to say, but proceeded anyway. "Which, if I can be honest, you bear a striking resemblance to. Seriously, put on a trench coat and..." She wiggled her finger in front of her.

"I'll take that as a compliment, assuming you think I look like the female of the three people you just mentioned." Ford's cheeks bloomed pink yet again. "My unit, Officer Soto, unlike what you may have seen on TV, is simply an investigation into..." She tapped her fingers on her lips. "Things that don't quite fit into any of your usual categories. Swap missing person for missing memories, drug lords for little green men, UFOs, things like that. But very much like the show. The cases are weird. Strange. Unexplainable at times. Not taken seriously most of the time. Easy to sabotage and can sometimes cause you to second-guess your entire existence on this earth."

"Trying to make sense of the unexplainable. Sounds like you have a special gift."

"I wouldn't say it's a gift."

"An attraction?"

"Like a moth to a flame." She flashed another one of those warm smiles, this one moving past their booth and illuminating her half of the diner. "At least it was at first." Her smile waned at that remark.

She wasn't going to ask her to explain even though it was clear Ford was holding back. "What makes this case fall under your purview?"

"The fact that no one else wants it."

"You're kidding."

"Wish I was. But when you look at it closely, the fact that this thing ravaged an ecosystem, disappeared without a trace, is back after a nine-year hiatus, and add the gruesome nature of it…It has all the makings of a paranormal investigation."

"Unexplained and completely fucked?"

"Pretty much."

They both laughed at the comment.

Lexy got up and gave a good stretch and a yawn to match. "I do need to get her home and get her rested." She followed her dog's lead and stood up to stretch. She felt a tightness between her legs as she sensed the other woman's eyes run the length of her body. "What else do you need from me?"

Ford suddenly sat up straight. "I'll need help with the kids who had the close encounter." Ford pursed her lips. "And Mr. and Mrs. Bird Watchers. It didn't actually go so well."

"I know. They told me all about it."

"Shit. Well, as you can see, I'll need your assistance whenever I have to deal with the fucking locals."

"We will take the Birdwatchers together first thing in the morning. Then head out to the high school for the kids."

"Thank you." Ford got up as well.

"Where are you staying?"

"Hotel Quiet something. It's in Meridian. You?"

"I'm at home. At my dad's."

"Lucky you."

"How do I get a hold of you?"

"I have your number. Here's mine," Ford added, before Soto could get in a smart-ass response.

She took the card from between Ford's fingers.

"See you tomorrow," Ford said and headed out of the diner.

"Thanks," Soto said to no one in particular. She put the card in one of her several pockets, downed the remainder of her beer, placed money on the table, waved goodbye to Isa, and headed out the door. She let Lexy off her leash and gave her a good rub before she trotted off to do her business. Moments later, Soto opened the cab door, the dog jumped in, and promptly curled into a ball in the passenger seat.

"What are you doing, girl? It's your turn to drive. Yes, it is. You're so cute and popular. Everyone loves you and all the tracking dogs wish they were as bad ass as—"

The dog perked her ears into points.

"I'm sorry about earlier."

"Gaaa!" Soto grabbed her chest and whirled around. "Shit! You scared me."

"Sorry." Ford ran her hand through her hair and laughed it off. "It's me."

"Holy hell." Soto fanned her face. "But hold that thought. One moment. I need to…make sure. I got my…" Soto's voice trailed as she reached for something in the cab. "Sorry about that. I had to make sure Lexy was situated and settled. You good, girl? Okay. Yes." She shut the door. "What about earlier?" questioned Soto, as an entirely too-loud nervous laugh escaped her lips. She shrugged it off despite feeling like she was onstage with a hundred people watching, the spotlight illuminating her every action.

"About earlier, by the lake. I'm not sure what I was thinking…"

"Placing a tracking bug on me?" suggested Soto.

The special agent closed her eyes and muttered something unintelligible under her breath.

"I can't say it was the smoothest come-on I've ever experienced from a woman."

"I guess I'm a little rusty," Ford admitted, forcing a weak smile.

"A little bit." Soto reached over and gently tapped the agent's forearm, and then slid her hand to her fingertips, grabbing hold. The gesture forced eye contact. She inched Ford toward herself. "And it's okay."

"I am really sorry." Ford came willingly. "I didn't mean to—"

"Caress my poor bruised cheekbone? Forget about it."

"Did it hurt?" Ford's tone dropped as if she were talking to a child.

"Terribly."

"I'm really not sure what compelled me to…"

They stood a breath apart.

"It looks worse than it is." A storm was brewing in the pit of Soto's stomach. One more inch and their bodies would be touching. "No hard feelings, okay?"

"So we're good?" Ford cleared her throat, snapped out of her trance, and took a step back.

"Peachy."

And with that Soto watched Ford turn and walk toward her rental—complete with her own tracking bug on her messenger bag.

"And that's how you bug a woman, Lexy," Soto said under her breath as she climbed into her truck. She chuckled and closed her eyes and leaned into her headrest. She felt tired and wired all at the same time, though it wasn't the investigation that consumed her thoughts. Not the strange nature of the attacks or the sensationalized accounts. Not the alleged three-hundred-and-fifty-pound creature and not having a clue as to what was out there causing damage. It was Ford, all Ford, and nothing but Winifred Ford that started to consume her thoughts. The woman reminded her of an orphaned wild animal, the one she would sometimes find alone, lost and starving, wanting love and attention, but without the voice or the words to express it. Soto would need to approach the new creature in her life the same as if working with a wild animal, gently and with intent.

CHAPTER EIGHT

Mr. and Mrs. Birdwatcher

"Lucky for you, we know Officer Soto," Mrs. Donna Richards, aka Mrs. Birdwatcher, said to Special Agent Ford, crossing her arms. "You were very rude yesterday." The elderly woman looked Ford over from head to toe.

Ford managed to find the voice of her supervisor lingering amongst all the rage inside herself. "Sincere apologies and *I'm* willing to overlook—" She felt a slight tap on her elbow. The connection stopping her immediately as she turned to see Soto shaking her head slightly. Ford would need to pull out every form of restraint she knew to get through the next hour. "My apologies." She felt her ears getting hot.

"Mrs. Richards, Mr. Richards, thank you so much for agreeing to speak with us again." Soto embraced the elderly couple. "How's Michael?"

"Driving trucks again, works for Navajo, even got a lady friend to ride with him."

"Sounds like he's doing real well." Soto turned and gave Ford a little smile. "Michael and I grew up together." Then turning back around, she said, "We only have a few questions and we will get out of your hair." She followed them into their living room, Ford quickly behind.

"Nonsense," said Mr. Richards as he slumped into a comfy-looking armchair, his wife following suit in its matching one. "Does anyone want ginger tea? Donna doesn't like it much, but I love the taste and it's good for my digestion. Learned that from the AARP."

"No, thank you, sir," Ford said and looked toward Soto, who indicated she was fine without having tea.

"Well, how about after this, I show you the nesting pairs we got out by the trail? They are the cutest things, third year they have returned. You will love them, Daya. Yellow warblers! And my do they chat up a storm," said Mr. Richards.

"I bet they are darling little creatures. I would love to see them."

Ford couldn't help but smile at Soto's enthusiasm for, well, birds.

"I also got an article I cut out of the latest issue of the *Atlantic*, hoping you can give it to your father. I'm interested in his take on it. Landslide integrity solutions," he said as he placed his hands on either side of his armchair, fixing to push himself up.

"Get the article later, Wilbur," Mrs. Richards said as she patted his hand gently. "The ladies need to get started."

"It will take me two minutes, Donna. I know exactly where it's at."

"Do you?" she questioned with a tone that said she doubted him.

"As a matter of fact, I do, but okay. Let's not forget and let's not forget about those birds too. We can go now if you like?" He started to get up again.

"I would love to see them," Soto said. Ford shot her a wide-eyed look that said *you better not fucking go look at fucking birds.* "But let's get to it. We've got a lot of work to do to get to the bottom of this. I promise I'll stop by before I head out of town." She nodded to Ford to begin.

"Walk us through the morning of the attack," Ford commanded, but immediately changed her tactic when Mrs. Richards crossed her arms and pursed her lips. "Please."

"That's better, dear," answered Mrs. Richards. "Wilbur and I got up at five o'clock like we always do."

"No, it was five-fifteen. I remember because the Jon Joseph Show was on the radio and I remember him talking about that ballot measure, increased transit—"

"That was Monday, Wilbur."

"It was yesterday, Donna."

"Okay," Soto chimed in. "So let's say you woke up between five o'clock and five fifteen, no later than five thirty. Can we agree on that?"

"Yes," the couple said in unison, both nodding. "That sounds about right," Mrs. Richards confirmed.

"And you were on the trail by five forty-five?" Ford asked.

"Oh, no, dear. Have you even been out there? Goodness, it's a good twenty-minute walk from here to the lookout, and then another, oh, about thirty to the lake. And Wilbur needs to eat before we go out to maintain his blood sugar."

Ford closed her eyes and drew in a deep breath through her nostrils. "So six-fifteen?"

"Around six thirty. I only know because we got these new walking bits or fit walks. The kids gave Wilbur and I one for Christmas." Holding out her wrist, she added, "Though come to think of it, we don't know where Wilbur's is. He loses everything in his old age. Can't retain anything these days. Got the doctors worried."

"I know exactly where it is, Donna," he said, slapping the arm of his chair. "I told you it's in the shop so I can count my steps when I'm working on my projects."

"You're supposed to wear it all day. That's the point," she emphasized, tapping the face of the one on her wrist. "I got ten thousand steps this week already."

"Okay," Ford resumed as she rubbed out a growing kink in her neck. "So, you know you were out on the preserve by six thirty because of your Fitbits?"

"Sure. We're making good time these days too. Will's even lost a couple of pounds this month, though you wouldn't know it. He puts them back on at the MacDonalds."

He shot her a look. "I go there for the coffee grounds. They give 'em out for free, does wonders for my flowers out back." He motioned to their flower garden through the sliding glass doors. "Aren't they splendid?" The elderly couple looked out the window and started talking about tulips.

But it wasn't the garden that drew Ford's attention. It was Soto's attempt to stifle laughter. Tiny creases at her eyes and her hand at her mouth trying to cover her smile. Ford took a moment to drink in the officer while the couple argued. She started at her black work boots scuffed with mud around the edges. There was a deep gash in the leather of her right boot. She wondered what animal Soto might have been investigating at the time. Her uniform fit her in all the right places, unusual for polyester. Her thumbs were hooked on her tool belt in a quintessential cop stance. Ford lingered at the insignia on her chest and then at her full breasts—until she got caught. She clicked her trusty pen and shuffled the pages in her notebook and pretended to jot a note.

"I find the receipts in your jeans, Wilbur." A comment that shut him up. "You were saying, dear?" Mrs. Richards asked, causing all to turn their attention to Ford.

"Bear with me here. Uh, let's see, where exactly on the trail were you when you felt something was off?"

"Our favorite spot."

"Which is?"

"Trio Lane, dear. Where the warblers are nested. Daya, you should see them. They are there by the hundreds."

Soto gave a nod.

"Not by the hundreds, darlin', but a whole mess of them have returned this spring," Mr. Richards corrected.

"I bet they are splendid little things, especially the hatchlings," Soto agreed.

"I bet they are cute as pie." Ford shot Soto a look. "Can we continue? Pretty please?"

"So we was up on by the marsh when I heard whispering. I remember it because we had just passed the Willis's property on our way in, and he had his irrigation going. It's been such a dry winter and spring. He's been irrigating his property more than usual, we all have. I'm surprised the reservoir isn't completely dry already. Well, I thought that it sounded like his well was working hard to pump, like it was tryin' too hard." Mr. Richards turned to his wife for confirmation.

"Like something was blocking the pipes," she added. "And we don't think nothing of it. Mr. Willis isn't quite known for keeping his property shipshape. Besides, we're making good time so we proceeded to the lake. We were only out there for, gosh, twenty minutes, and we heard that sound again. Like a whispering or hissing." Mrs. Richards focused straight ahead when she said her next piece. "You'll think I'm crazy."

"I won't," Ford assured her.

"This can't get out. We got a lot of friends in this community." She shifted in her seat. "They'll think I'm losing it."

"It stays in this room. You have my word," Ford said. Soto gave hers as well.

"I heard actual words, or, maybe it was me thinking I heard words." She squinted as she continued, her eyebrows knitted. "I felt woozy and nauseous. I had to lay down when we got back, so it was likely in my head."

"What kind of words?" Ford pressed.

"I can't quite tell you what exactly." She looked out the window and shook her head. "I had a horrible feeling like when Wilbur had his mild heart attack last year. I felt it too, Daya, right in my chest, like I was having sympathy pains. I felt that same sort of sadness and fear all over again."

"She said something too," Mr. Richards interjected.

"I did?" The color drained from the poor woman's face and she held her fingers over her lips.

"You said you were trapped and couldn't see."

"Why didn't you tell me?"

"I didn't remember until this moment." Their confused looks turned to ones of fear and concern. Mr. Richards shook his head and alternated focus between his wife and Ford. "Do you think we're crazy?"

"No…" Ford reached within herself for comforting words and found she didn't really have any, so she settled with, "you're not…crazy."

"We've never seen anything like that in all the years living here. We understand the circle of life and have happened upon dead critters all the time, but not this." The old man rubbed his temple. "My wife of sixty-two years nearly passed out. Had to stay in bed all day." He placed his hand upon hers for comfort. "What do you think it is, Special Agent Ford? Rumor has it you've seen it before and that perhaps you almost trapped it in Oregon."

"There are a lot of rumors going around, and we're still working that out, Mr. Richards."

Her gut reaction told her this was related, but she needed more evidence, more eyewitnesses, more proof. "I know this is difficult, Mrs. Richards, but what else do you remember? What did you smell or feel? Any other details you can communicate will help us tremendously."

"I remember the poor animal was in a bad way, skinned and chewed up, spit back out. Blood everywhere." Her voice was almost a whisper. "Whatever this is, it's not killing for food. It's killing for sport."

"I'm so sorry you had to see that, Mrs. and Mr. Richards." Soto's words warmed the room significantly.

"And what time did you find the scene?"

"It was close to seven thirty or so. I was so shaken. We both were. We walked home as quickly as we could given Donna's state, and we called over to the station first thing when we got inside."

"The cops reported the call in at seven-fifty," Soto confirmed.

"That sounds about right," the couple agreed.

"Is there anything else you can tell us?" Ford wanted to squeeze every last bit of information to avoid any follow-up visits. "Think about the day before, the night before. Did anything around here feel out of the ordinary?"

"Actually, we didn't really see a lot of birds out that morning, which was strange given their activity the past couple of days. Oh, how they chatter so. You can hear them a mile away." Mrs. Richards folded her hands and placed them in her lap.

"But the coyotes were unusually vocal the night before and unusually quiet last night. Not sure if that means anything, but there it is." Mr. Richards gave his armchair another slap.

"Thank you. This helps a lot," Ford said, jotting down the last of her notes. "And you know the preserve is closed for the time being, right?"

"Yes, we heard. Dumb decision if you ask me." Mrs. Richards shot her yet another disappointed look. "Especially with the fundraiser comin' up and all."

"It's a security concern more than anything," Soto interjected. "We want to get to the bottom of this as soon as possible, and we can't risk outside influence or tampering into the investigation. Besides, it's not safe. I'm sure you can agree."

Their eyes seemed more alert, as if it was only at that moment it registered to them that this thing was in fact dangerous.

CHAPTER NINE

Detention

After the Richards' interview, Soto thought Ford would be more at ease than she was. From the moment they arrived at the high school for their next task, talking to the kids who had the close encounter, Ford was unusually quiet and spoke only two words to her, both of them single syllables. She also bullied her way past the ladies in the front office, a resource officer, and then the principal of the small school, insisting that a federal agent working on a federal investigation, didn't need an escort to the kids' classroom where they were at present waiting for the school bell to ring the end of the period.

"Well?" She tried again, trying to make eye contact—any sort of contact—without success. Basic communication was all she was looking for at the moment.

"Well, what?"

"Maybe we could talk about the Richards's story, or what we want to get from the students? Or…" Soto could tell she wasn't listening. "Basic investigation sort of stuff like rainbows, unicorns, frogs?" When Ford ignored her and stared out the window, Soto changed her tack and tried again. "What are your thoughts so far?"

"I have too many thoughts to voice in…" Ford tapped the face of her watch as her justification "…the five minutes we have until the bell rings."

"High level overview?"

"Later." Ford stood her ground, focusing on the door of the classroom, as if her superpower was seeing through solid matter.

"Whatever."

Soto groaned and headed toward the framed class photos of the graduating classes of years past. She took another step, and then hesitated as she watched her canine partner holding steady, looking strangely at Ford, until she was given an awkward pat on the head. She envied her dog for getting a response. Soto's frustration was continuing to build. She tugged gently at the leash. "Come on, girl." Her dog obeyed and joined her on the trip down memory lane. Soto was, after all, at her alma mater, home of the Jaguars.

"Sweet relief," said Ford, as the ringing of the bell gave life to everything around.

At once a horde of students emerged for brief freedom between classes. They walked every which way, as if in the middle of a crosswalk scramble. A few held lingered looks at the strangers, but the majority of the students walked with practiced precision to their destination—all the while looking at their phones.

"Where are they?" Ford asked as the last of the students filed out of the classroom and into others. Only anxiety-ridden love-struck couples and a kid picking up the spilled contents of his backpack were left, and then the slamming of doors and lockers, another bell rang, and that was that.

"Damn it." Soto watched as Ford beelined into the classroom and ignited. "Where are Larissa Larsen and Charlie Adler? They were to be in your class. By law you are liable for their whereabouts."

"I'm assuming they skipped class. Students do that from time to time." The teacher turned from erasing the white board. "I'm sorry. Who are you?"

"Special Agent Winifred Ford. FBI." She flashed her badge. "Judging by their attendance records," Ford rustled the sheet of paper attained from the registrar, "they skip a lot of your classes. Do you teach a boring topic or are you boring?"

"I'm insanely boring." He smirked. "If you'll excuse me…" He tried to step around the imposing agent.

"I'm not done here, sir." Ford blocked the man. "Do you have any idea where they could be?"

"Hey, whoa. Sorry, I have no clue," he said.

"You're around them several hours a day."

"I'm around them one hour a day."

"Times five days a week, through the school year. Are you are saying you don't know anything that might help?"

"Maybe try their social media?"

"Don't you think I've done that?"

"Sorry. I need to grab lunch and prep for my next class." He successfully slipped around her and out of the classroom, stopping abruptly. "Oh, hey, Daya. Hi Lexy! How are you guys doing? What brings you to town?"

"Hey, Kev," Soto said.

"That's Mr. Barnett to you." The two embraced. "Can I?"

"Of course."

He acknowledged the service animal with a scratch behind the ears. "Your moose-wrangling post was so awesome." He laughed. "I showed it to my students. Really rad."

"You did not." Soto alternated Lexy's leash from hand to hand.

"They loved it. I got a couple of them excited about wildlife enforcement now. Will you be home long? A few of us are getting together this weekend for a bonfire. Want to come on by? Suzanne and Matt will be there, and Heidi. They would love to see you."

"Would love to see them. I haven't seen Heidi in forever. Love that lady."

"You should come."

"Maybe I will, but at the moment, Special Agent Ford and I are investigating the attacks at Deer Flat. We're kind of focused."

"Oh, yeah. I should have known that." He threw his hand in the air looking between the two women. Ford slapped the folded paper in the palm of her hand. "Any ideas on what it is?"

"Not yet. But it's important that we talk to those kids. Where do you think we could find them?"

"Deer Flat."

"It's closed," Ford interjected.

"And? That's not going to stop these two."

"What about their parents?" Ford continued.

"Normally I would say that's a good start, but in this instance," he arched his eyebrows, "they aren't really the involved type."

"How so?" asked Ford.

"The boy lives with the girl and her dad works long hours at the meat-packing plant, and when he's not working, Dad's at his girlfriend's place. Charlie and Larissa are on their own. Come to think of it, I'm not sure I've even met the father before. Wait, have I?" He focused his gaze on the ceiling and to a flickering iridescent light. "I can't recall. Isn't that bad?"

"Yeah, that is bad and so not important," Ford quickly countered.

"They gave formal statements, several of them. Isn't that of any use to you?"

"The statements are total crap."

"And we have more targeted questions," Soto jumped in, shooting her a look, though Ford was either oblivious or ignoring her.

"Are there any other places we can try? Do they have jobs?"

"Actually, yeah. Larissa works at Taco Time."

"Which one?" Soto asked and pulled out a notepad from one of her uniform's several pockets.

"Um, Caldwell, I think. Oh, actually Nampa, yes Nampa," he said and held up a finger.

"Which is it?" Ford asked.

"One of those two locations."

"And the boy?" Ford asked.

"Centennial Golf Course."

"Thanks, Kev. This is very helpful and we appreciate your time," Soto said.

"Of course."

"If you can think of anything else that would be helpful, that is if you can find time from teaching to help save a few innocent animals and maybe an entire ecosystem—"

"Please let us know," Soto interjected. She placed her hand on Ford's shoulder. Touching Ford was the only action she had found to get her to stop whatever she was doing.

"Seriously though, check out their social media stuff. They have everything on there, photos, blog posts. The two had an up close and personal encounter and weren't shy about telling all."

"We will look again," Soto assured.

"I really do have to go. Learning doesn't stop, boring topic or not." He readjusted the materials in his arms. "Always a pleasure Daya and…?"

Ford gave him her card and he gave her a look.

"Seriously, Daya, come to the bonfire."

"I will if I have time. Text me."

He headed down the hallway and into another room. The retreating clicking of heels down the hallway brought her back to her work. "Ford," she said to no avail, trying to catch up with her. "Agent Ford."

"Officer Soto?" The agent finally stopped and turned to face her.

"Did you have to be such an ass? What gives? One moment you're barely tolerable, the other you're…"

"Barely tolerable?" Ford threw her head back in laughter. "And the other moment I'm what? Hmm?"

"There's no need to push your way around here," Soto said in a gentle tone, one reserved for out of control things. "We can get what we need by asking nicely." She felt like she was talking to a child.

"Oh, I know. I'm familiar with manners and etiquette. I'm seemingly elegant."

She was a grudge holder. Soto so wanted to walk the hell away, abandon the case, and head back to Washington State.

This feeling of defeat was as foreign to Soto as was the woman in front of her. But giving up was not an option. The case already had a high-powered scope thrust upon it. Soto felt her cheeks burn. "This isn't a game for me."

"It's not a game for me either. It's an art, really. Look, Officer Soto—"

"No, you look Special Agent Ford. It's important that I maintain the relationships I have here, got it?" Only she got nothing but those green and gray stormy eyes piercing into her. "For Christ's sake." She sighed heavily and removed her hat to run her hand through her hair, rubbing at her temples, a migraine threatening. Ford was seriously bad for her health. "We should split up, given that we need to report to the preserve in a few hours. Lexy needs to get more rest and I have to pick up a few things before tonight."

"Fine with me. I got what I needed," retorted Ford, causing Soto to nearly lose her cool, but her dog nudged her head against her leg and brought her out of the moment.

"Thank you, girl," Soto said to her pup, giving her a rub behind the ears while focusing on some in-through-the-nose-and-out-through-the-mouth breathing.

"Since you're such a big social media star, moose wrangler, how about you scour the kids' social media accounts again? And I'll take point on tracking them down to see what I can get out of them. How does that sound?"

"Fine with me," Soto said. "Are you able to talk to the kids on your own without pissing them off to where I'll only have to help you again tomorrow to get their stories?"

"We'll see," Ford said as she walked away.

"They could be our best witnesses so far." Soto's elevated voice echoed down the hallway.

"I'm great with kids," Ford said, leaving Soto behind with only the clicking of her heels and a swagger in her wake.

CHAPTER TEN

Staffing Changes

The ringtone, a recently purchased Salt-N-Pepa jingle, signaled a much-needed break for Soto who'd spent the past couple of hours enduring hundreds of posts and tweets centered on food, clothing, shoes, makeup, politics, and the Kardashians. Comments and opinions were impressive for a small-town girl who attracted higher-up attention from the likes of staffers in the mayor's office. She was glad for the interruption until she saw the DC area code.

"It's Ford."

"Yep." Soto thought she had calmed down, but hearing Ford's voice, that demanding and haughty way she spoke, made her channel her go-to method of calming herself, deep breaths from her diaphragm, to get through the phone call.

"The girl called in sick, and the boy had the day off so—"

"Yeah, I know."

"What do you mean, you know?"

"I called Taco Time and the Centennial Golf Course minutes after you walked out of the high school."

"Why the hell would you do that?"

"Can you blame me for wanting to warn them they would be getting a visit from a person who has a certain knack for berating people to get what she wants?" Soto asked, hearing commotion in the background.

"It's not my fault everyone around here is so damn sensitive. Thanks to you I got absolutely nothing. They wouldn't even talk to me, and believe me, I tried. Jesus H! They might have had something of value to offer. Did you think of that?" Her tone elevated.

"They didn't have much else to provide, at least not from my conversations with their managers."

"Did you *see* the expressions on their faces when you questioned them? Did you also talk with every one of their co-workers, Officer Soto?"

"I got enough information to know their places of employment aren't where we should be focusing, Special Agent Ford." Soto kept her tone calm despite Ford's growing agitation.

"Why the hell didn't you fucking call me?" Ford's voice was strangely calm. "Jesus Christ."

"I got sidetracked." Soto leaned back in her desk chair in her room at her dad's house. Payback was fun, she mused. "Larissa's social media is quite riveting. Did you know there is a Kardashian brother?"

"You let me fucking waste my time!" The cursing continued on the other end of the line.

"Surely you didn't spend the *entire* afternoon running around the tiny town of Caldwell?" Ford tried to get a word in, but Soto cut her off. "Besides, you deserved it."

"Deserved what, actually? You have no idea how precious my time is!" screamed Ford, so loudly Soto had to pull the phone away from her ear.

"What's *my* time worth? Half of yours?"

"I have two fucking weeks to solve this fucking shit small-town case."

"Why two weeks?" Soto asked and looked at a wall calendar.

"I'm going on leave."

"Oh, a vacation? Well then, why didn't you say so?"

"It's not that type of vacation, okay. I'm fucking short on time. Let's leave it at that!"

"Let me help you then. Let's work together, pool resources, share information, be partners on this," Soto suggested. "How isn't it obvious that I can help—"

"Goddamn it!" Ford shouted while Soto braced herself for round two. "Just let me work at my own discretion! As I see fit."

"As you see fit? You seeing fit means being a bully, and I'm not going to let you bulldoze your way around *my* hometown."

"You have no idea who I am or where I come from to be telling me how to approach this investigation," Ford shot back.

"I may not have read a comprehensive report on you, Ford, but I know enough to know that you're a self-centered egotistical bitch who uses others to get what she wants."

"I'm doing the best I can here," Ford whispered.

"Pissing off my contacts and throwing your badge around to get what you want," Soto lobbed back, nearly falling out of her chair. "That is your best?" She let out an exuberant laugh.

"I…"

"What does a *bad* day for you look like?"

"It's…"

"That was a rhetorical question."

"Look," Ford said.

"No. You look. I won't be able to work with you if you keep this up."

"I didn't think you were a quitter, Officer Soto."

"I'm not the one who's going to quit." She felt her dog's wet nose in her hand. It gave her courage. "I know a guy who knows the guy who can get a new agent on the case *today*."

"Good luck with that. Federal property—"

"Jurisdiction has nothing to do with this. I simply do not have the energy to investigate this case and babysit your bullshit at the same time. There are a hundred other FBI agents and only one Karelian Bear Dog handler in all the land. Who do you think will prevail?" She took a breath before she continued. "But it doesn't have to go that route, Ford. How about let's be civil? Let's respect each other's time, each other's contacts, each other. Is that so problematic for you?" The silence was so loud Soto wondered if Ford had hung up on her, but her phone's display confirmed the call hadn't ended. "Can we start there?"

"Shit," Ford said.

"Apology accepted."

"That wasn't an apology."

"For you it was."

"It's the case," she whispered. "It feels like Blue River. I'm not dealing with it very well. There," Ford admitted. "You happy?"

"No, I'm not. This sounds difficult for you," Soto said in a gentler tone. "Tell me about it."

"Let me collect a bit more evidence before I…"

"Yes?" Soto tried to help Ford along.

"Put myself out there."

"But it could help the case."

"Maybe, maybe not," Ford admitted. "Give me a bit more time to formulate everything."

"I'll give you whatever you need, Ford. All you have to do is ask." Soto took Ford's silence as her understanding. "And no more of this hot and cold business."

"You'll have to settle for lukewarm."

"Deal." Soto felt the tension start to ebb. She took a deep breath.

"Did you learn anything more from social media?"

"To date, the Lake Lowell Ghost is outranking the three-hundred and fifty-pound Beast of Deer Flat in the town's whodunit," Soto joked, which elicited a warm laugh on the other end that she hoped was a good sign. "Also, did you know you can add kitty litter to terrariums to help them stay mold free?"

"I did know that. Anything else?"

"In addition to calming the stomach, ginger has several other uses like—"

"Yeah, it's great for headaches. Anything of value to the case, Soto?"

"Something tells me that Charlie and Larissa weren't the only ones there that day."

"Explain?"

"Please," Soto suggested.

"Pardon?"

"Explain, please. Goodness, we talked about this less than a minute ago."

"Are you really going to require that I wear a Little Miss Manners hat twenty-four seven?"

"I think it'll be good practice for you."

"You don't know what demanding is."

Soto failed to hold in laughter. "Oh, I think I do." Silence on the line. "So, there's a backpack in a handful of the photos that doesn't seem like it belongs to Larissa or Charlie, at least not according to their other photos."

"Isn't that interesting?" Ford mused. "Send them to me, will you? Please?"

"Already done," Soto said as she clicked a key on her laptop. "I'm thinking we go back to the school and try to nail down the owner of this backpack."

"Provided it belongs to a student at that high school and not some random person."

"Lake Lowell is the local teen hangout. Starting with the two high schools in the area is a good first move. It should be fairly simple to rule out. It's neon green with a mushroom patch on it."

"I'll get my people on that right away," Ford promised.

"Thank you. And in the meantime," Soto said, "I say we let Charlie and Larissa go about their business and see what sort of new evidence shows up online. Something doesn't feel right. I want to see what they are feeding their followers. Between you and me, these kids seem like total tools."

"I can't wait to grill those little shits."

"And I can't wait to see you do that." Her comment got a warm laugh from Ford. "Well what do you know, there is one point we can agree on."

"Oh I'm sure there is more."

Ford's comment, or the way she said it, made Soto nervous. "Where are you?" Soto asked after clearing her throat.

"At Deer Flat. Looking at useless footage from last night!" Ford's volume increased again, causing Soto to pull away the phone from her ear again. She was reaming someone named Grady about camera misplacement. "Get here as soon as you can. Please."

"I got one errand to run and then...Really?" she said to a dead line. She popped another aspirin and made a mental note to stop by the store for some headache-helping ginger chews. In bulk!

CHAPTER ELEVEN

Night Watch

The setting sun gave way to her most cherished feelings about her hometown. The forthcoming sunset with its hues of red and magenta was a smoldering fire in the distance. Smells of watered fields, damp dust, mint, alfalfa, and onions hung in the air, and a light dew settled. A full moon, low on the horizon and inching skyward, would provide the perfect amount of illumination. The preserve's luscious full trees took on another appearance at night that might cause people to look over their shoulders at the faintest movement of their massive limbs, thinking their brambles and leaves harbored odd creatures when it was simply the awakening of wildlife. Other people, but not Soto.

"I'm excited too, girl." Lexy's whining, chattering, and overall restlessness gave her enthusiasm away. "We're almost there."

She gave her partner the go-ahead and watched as the dog made her way toward the trail and the group. Soto cracked a smile as Lexy happily danced around Agent Ford for her attention. Ford stumbled over her words, repeating the word *intel* several times in a row, trying to proceed and ignore the dog, but finally giving up. She crouched to pet Lexy with her full attention. She was whispering things to her, but what? Lex would never tell.

"Come on, girl. Leave the nice lady alone."

Ford gave her a shy smile as she rose and pulled herself together. She was likely still embarrassed about Soto's scolding earlier, but she continued with her briefing to a crew that had grown significantly. What had been a handful of local law enforcement and Idaho Fish and Game employees, was now an honest-to-goodness effort with her infusion of federal agents complete with radios, black clothing, and heavy-duty tranquilizer guns strapped to their bodies. Ford, on the other hand, had a handheld dart gun secured to her leg and wore jeans with what was without a doubt a tailor-made blazer on the top. Her hair was in a low bun and she wore somewhat sensible shoes.

"In addition to twenty-four seven boots on the ground at the entrances and the hot spots we've identified, we have tech, also known as Grady and company." She motioned to her colleague, who gave a wave. "He will take point on monitoring from home base. Should something get by us, should a motion camera be triggered, should a member of the public report anything through the hotline, he will dispatch the appropriate ground crew to investigate."

She took a deep breath and turned toward Soto and said, "For those of you who do not know, this is Officer Dayanara Soto." She spoke her name with near perfect Spanish enunciation. Soto wondered what other hidden talents she possessed. "Officer Soto is with Washington State Fish and Wildlife. And you have already met Lexy." Laughter circulated through the crew as Lexy made her rounds sniffing at outstretched hands, fishing for scratches and prancing around like the belle of the ball.

"Don't let her fool you," Soto interjected, "she's pretty darn fierce. And please call me Daya."

Soto shook hands with a short stocky guy, not much taller than herself. He favored black clothing and black Chuck Taylors.

Even his glasses were black framed. He also wore a black beanie. even though it was summer and kept a full beard. "Are you the Grady Ford was berating earlier?"

"The one and only." The comment drew more laughter and she shook his hand.

"Sorry, that was probably my fault," Soto said. "We were in a heated conversation." She found Ford's eyes on her.

"A pleasure, and it was her fault. And I'm used to it."

They all were used to it as evidenced by the snickering and sounds of agreement from the agents.

"Moving on," Ford said while rolling her eyes. "Officer Soto and I are working together to manage the investigation. She comes from one of the largest and most diverse regions of the Pacific Northwest, a sprawling six-county jurisdiction of thick, forested lands and marine habitat. She is also from the area. Her expertise is a valuable resource for us."

The introduction threw Soto off guard. She wasn't expecting such a buildup.

"Anything you want to add?"

"Like Agent Ford's plan, mine is also quite simple. I assume you received and studied the plot maps and notes and received the proper darts for taking down a large animal?" A round of nods confirmed her question. "Can I?" An agent handed over his gun, she inspected it and was satisfied. "More dogs and expert trackers are on their way and at your disposal. Work together. Each handler is different, so I'll let them outline how they like to work. In general, let the dogs guide you. Their sense of intuition is very different than yours and mine. If you get lucky and dart something, do not lose sight of it. Tranqs are powerful. If not properly monitored, one shot could kill. If darted, an animal's instinct is to hide, so do not lose track. It can take hours for the darts to have an effect." The agents nodded their heads showing they were on the same page. "Once we establish a pattern, we have a few plot points from the kill sights so far, and we'll determine where best to deploy the traps. Any questions?"

More nodding heads and chatter amongst the crew indicated they were ready. Soto made her rounds as well, shaking hands with the team and making introductions with the people she would work with for the duration of the investigation.

Ford handed over a large box of radios for Soto and her team. "We will be on channel twenty-one."

Ford seemed different to Soto. If it was possible to look less uptight, she did. "Thanks for the introduction," Soto said as she took a radio from the box, affixed it to her belt, and adjusted the coiled line around to her shoulder intercom.

"I figured it would be nice for the two people who don't already know you." Ford placed the box onto the ground. "What the hell is that?"

"The quintessential sound of the hound dog. Don't you love it?" The approaching hounds were yodeling and howling as if someone's unruly twelve-year-old had found a trumpet to play.

"Not particularly. They sound like they're injured."

"They're just happy." She shot Ford a look, enjoying the expression on her face, especially after a pair of hounds ran toward them and danced around the agent, creating a whirlwind of paws, tails, and tongues.

"Hey, hey, whoa!" Ford waved her hands in front of her.

Soto grinned at the special agent's attempt to ward away the dogs. The more she tried, the more determined the rambunctious pups became for her attention. She backed up, almost falling backward over the box of radios. Soto caught her before she landed on her backside.

"Easy now," Soto whispered, helping Ford upright. "You good?" A nod told her she could let go.

"Leave it!" The owner's call was all it took for the dogs to fall into line. "Daya! Hey." The newcomer waved as she approached. "It's so good to see you!" She extended her hand toward the recovering agent as she caught up. "Hi. I'm Margo Crawly." A tall Latina woman with wavy black hair extended her hand for a shake.

"Special Agent Winifred Ford, FBI. Thank you for your assistance."

Soto watched her scan the woman's body. She was sure she was checking her out.

"And these guys are Dexter and Debbi," Crawly said.

"Wait. Debbi Crawly?" Ford asked.

"That's right. Debbi and Dexter. Sue me. I'm into that serial killer show, *Dexter*.

"Wait. The dog is Debbi or you're Debbi?"

"The dog is Debbi."

"I see." Ford crossed her arms, turning to face Soto. "You're right, she *is* a good-looking…dog, Soto."

She enjoyed seeing Ford flush at her little joke from the diner. Enjoying it a little too much and already looking for the next opportunity to mess with her and get her to lighten up more.

"Go on, kids, shake the lady's hand." The dogs did as they were told and lifted their paws in unison. Instead Ford gave each of them a brief pat on the head and then wiped her hands on her pants.

"Come here, you!" Margo gave Soto a big embrace. "You look great!"

"So do you and look at them!" Soto crouched on the ground and gave them as much equal attention as she could, given their excitement, licks, and head bumps. "Last time I was here, they were so little."

"They are all grown up now."

"Thank you for being available on such short notice," Soto said as she stood.

"Thank you for pulling us in. It's a curious and messed-up case, isn't it?"

"We've never seen anything like this before," Soto said and motioned to Ford. "She has, though."

"Any idea what we are up against? It's got to be something introduced, right?"

"No idea that I can communicate at this time." Ford's simple responses seemed to work for her. Thus far she hadn't berated this contact, likely because Soto thought she was smitten with her.

"Well, we are happy to serve and figure this out. This your first time working with Daya?"

"Affirmative."

"She's great. You'll love her." Margo turned to Soto. "We've worked on what, six or seven cases together?"

"At least." Soto nodded.

"The things we've seen, huh?"

"God yes!"

"Hey you still owe me that date."

"And here you are!" Soto noticed Ford's narrowing gaze upon Crawly. She couldn't discern if she was into the woman or jealous of her. Ford's actions all but confirmed her romantic preferences.

Soto greeted more volunteers and even more dogs, hounds and various shades of Labradors. At first glance one would think it was a typical day at the dog run if it weren't for the fact the dogs were highly specialized trackers. They wrestled and frolicked and said their hellos through sniffs to each other's back ends.

After introductions were made between the teams and between the dogs, and after they were briefed on the plan, the teams went into the night to their assigned zones. Soto would pair with Ford. As the heads of each division, they needed to stay together, work with Grady, and deploy assistance as needed.

"You ready, girl?" Soto gave Lexy the go-ahead to get going. The dog didn't need to be told twice and took off. "What about you?" Soto asked and justified another reason to look at Ford from head to toe. "Those are mildly better," she said, pointing to Ford's footwear.

"You jealous of my sensible shoes?"

"A little," she replied as the two headed down the trail, not knowing what the night would bring.

CHAPTER TWELVE

Average White Van

"Good luck out there," Soto offered to the departing shift on their third night of patrols. "Hopefully tonight's the night we'll get lucky."

"And maybe even dart something," Ford added.

They sent their groups out to the field, but nothing of significance was collected or observed. The only noteworthy thing was a one hundred eighty-degree pivot in Special Agent Winifred Ford's attitude and sense of humor. Soto had witnessed her work through the five stages of grief at suffering a deep gash in a beloved pair of designer shoes. And Ford's short responses evolved into more meaningful conversations. Soto even managed to pull out bits of what happened in Oregon. Ford proved intelligent beyond measure, she had a prescient-like intuition and was thoughtful in her approach to everything. Soto respected the hell out of her abilities.

"So your guys have the perimeter secured?" Soto asked at the two o'clock hour as she and Ford made their way to an old white VW van found by Lex. The vehicle was hidden in the natural overgrowth within the preserve.

"Grady." Ford radioed to home base. "We got an occupied vehicle parked on preserve property. Stand by and note our location."

"Copy," came his scratchy voice on the other end.

"Let's see what we got." Ford approached the van.

Soto observed the fogged up windows. "It looks like a couple of kids enjoying themselves."

"Well the enjoyment stops now." Ford rapped her knuckles loudly on the window of the foggy van, eliciting swearing and elevated voices, and then scattered movement inside, rocking the van from side to side. She shot Soto a look. "What's so funny?"

"*You* are." Soto didn't try to hide her growing smile.

"What? Why?" asked Ford, interrupted by the van occupants, two teenage girls, rolling down the window.

"Sorry, we were right about to leave."

They were both still adjusting their clothing. Ford waved her light into the van, illuminating a makeshift bed, blankets, and clothes strewn about.

Her light focused back onto her subjects. "You know the preserve is closed, right?"

"Um, no?" they said in unison. "We lost track of time, I guess," said the one in the driver's seat.

"*I guess*. It's been closed this past week, so either you have been here for over a week, or you trespassed. Which is it?" The girls froze. Ford flashed her badge, which seemed to reanimate them. "FBI by the way. You're on the scene of a highly controlled investigation." She motioned to Officer Soto with her tactical light.

"Hey, girls." Soto gave the girls a wave, thinking she recognized the blonde, the one in the driver's seat from Ginny's diner.

"FBI? Shit. We didn't know that the signs were, like, for real. Seriously we will leave right now. My parents will kill me if they find that I've snuck out. I'm supposed to be grounded!" the passenger said.

"Why the hell did you say that? They are cops!"

"Save it. I'll need to see your identifications and vehicle registration, please." With the documents in hand, Ford headed toward the back of the van.

"What are you doing?" Soto asked.

"What do you mean, what am I doing?"

"Haven't you ever seen women making out?" A laugh escaped.

"Jesus." Even in the light of the moon, Ford's cheeks burned red. "Did you really ask me that?"

Soto shook with laughter. "What do we got?"

Ford turned the documents over in her hands inspecting them with her flashlight. "This one's got a good four years on the other."

"It looks consensual."

"Four years, though? This one, Missy Vance, she's a kid. Seventeen years old." Ford tapped the two identification cards in her palm.

Soto studied her intently. The all-nighters were getting to her. The moon was illuminating Ford in all the right ways. And the way she walked when she was tired was more of a swagger. Soto shook away the feelings creeping in.

"No, I get it," Soto said, "but tell me you haven't been with an older woman before, huh?"

"Who hasn't?" Ford replied, surprising Soto with her comment. Ford gave her a smile and lingered a look at Soto's lips. "I'm just giving them a scare." She pushed off from leaning against the vehicle. "People need to respect the fact that the preserve is closed and under federal investigation," Ford said loudly. "Word needs to spread. I'm not fucking around," she said even louder.

"Come on. Send them on their way. Lex is getting antsy," Soto said, blaming her dog for her own feelings.

"I will." She found her radio. "Grady, I need an escort out of the park. Turn the lights on, keep the sound off, and send a female please."

"Copy."

"Pretend that you're going to call their parents but don't." Ford radioed over. "Give them a really good scare, god damn it."

CHAPTER THIRTEEN

Norma Jean

Ford groaned and continued thumbing through the intel, muttering under her breath to avoid fueling the gossip that was at an all-time high after their arrival onto the scene and their pattern of breakfast at Ginny's. "There have been attacks every night in this area for the past couple of weeks." She vigorously traced several circles around the location on the map with her pen. "And the last three nights, nothing, not even a fucking rabbit." She dropped the pen onto the map with a thud.

"Attacks have likely shifted, given the high concentration of us in that particular area," Soto said, eyeing Ford's food.

Ford pushed her untouched plate toward her. "For being about five-foot-something you eat like *you're* the three-hundred-pound Beast of Deer Flat," she said, smiling.

"So I've been told." Soto stabbed the sausage off the plate. "So my hunch is hunting here is getting too difficult. The wildlife are on to it. We are on to it," Soto said in between bites. She took a long pull from her coffee mug, wiped her mouth on a napkin, and pushed both plates out of the way.

"So you think it's simply migrating?"

"Yes. But I don't imagine it will migrate very far. Blue River is tiny compared to Deer Flat. There's too much wildlife here for it to up and leave to search for another food source. It mirrors the typical behavior of the hunter and the hunted. The constant shifting of strategies on both sides. It's a game of wits, really. One side anticipating the other's next steps…"

Soto and Ford locked eyes, Soto beat her to her pen. Ford gave her a sweet smile and pulled another one out of her bag.

"If we keep at it, I think we can force it here." Soto circled an area on the map.

"Well, I don't have another week to play a damn chess game. Something's got to give. Soon." Ford rubbed her temples and closed her eyes. She opened them and found Soto taking her in. She held her ground and took the opportunity to study Soto in return. Her hair was out of sorts, a tangled black halo wanting out of its braid. Soto leaned into the booth and folded her arms.

"What is it?" Ford asked. Soto shrugged her shoulders. "It kind of feels like you want to ask me something," Ford nudged, twisting a napkin between her fingers.

"I'm thinking."

"Do you have to think so loud?" She tore the mangled napkin in half.

"Besides having inadequate resources, what happened the last time you chased this thing down? I need to know your theory. It could help us put this investigation on the fast track."

"My theory?" The last time she'd faced this thing, she almost lost her credential. "I didn't have time to formulate a theory which was the least of my…" Ford ran her tongue over dry lips. "I'm sorry. The time zone change has finally caught up with me." She stifled a yawn and reached for her pen. Tap, tap. She bounced the point of the pen against the table.

"The time zone?"

Tap, tap, tap.

Soto placed her hand atop Ford's before she could tap the pen again. The action stilled her fidgeting. "For an FBI agent you suck at deflecting."

"Excuse me," came a third voice that made the two jump. Soto pulled her hands back and put them under the table. A man wearing overalls and black rubber irrigation boots interjected, "Are one of you Special Agent Ford or do you know where I can find an Officer Soto?" He looked over his shoulder a few times.

"I'm Special Agent Winifred Ford, FBI. What can I do for you?" Ford asked as she flashed her badge.

"And I'm Officer Daya Soto." She stood and shook the man's hand. "Please have a seat Mr...?"

"Roger, call me Roger. Thank you." The man took Soto's spot in the booth, and Soto joined Ford on the other side. Ford sat up straighter and eyed Soto's movements.

"What can we do for you?" Soto asked.

"My horses went nuts last night. They wouldn't calm down. I'm not sure what it means, because save for a major storm, they don't spook easily. Well, I take part of that back. They are Arabians, which are chock-full of personality. And by personality I mean they get into the strangest sorts of trouble and talk a good talk too, if you've ever owned one, let alone several. Like when our family gets home from running errands or whatnot, as soon as they see the motion trigger lights poppin' on, they go nuts prancing all about and chattering. Show-offs, the lot of them. I'll tell you, our youngest one ripped up the lining straight out of one of the water troughs we have. Dragged and kicked it all about the pasture like a soccer ball. He couldn't have been more proud of himself."

"Roger?" Ford started tapping the pen again. "What can we help you with?"

"I think that whatever is out there in the preserve was on my property last night."

"And where is your property?" Ford asked. She pushed the map in front of him.

"Deer Flat, lower embankment. It's the Nelson Homestead." He leaned in and circled an area on their map with his finger.

"That's a long way to migrate." Ford got a nod of agreement from Soto. "So aside from your horses being spooked, what makes you think something is out there?"

"Because it killed Norma Jean. One of our horses. I am one hundred percent sure that it was the devil creature." The man reached across the table and got a napkin from the dispenser. "Pardon my reach. We're torn up about it." He blotted his eyes.

"Roger, I'm so sorry," Soto said. She pushed the dispenser closer to him.

"What makes you think it's related?" Ford asked, curious that Soto would take the man's account at face value.

"I have only heard stories about how, uh, unnatural, the attacks are. Norma," he was welling up again, "she is pretty torn to shreds."

And there it was.

"Sorry." He wiped the tears away and blew his nose. The sound drew onlookers.

"It's okay, Roger," Soto said in that soothing way that caused Ford to want to curl up next to her and ask her to read to her.

"There's more. Something strange." He looked around the diner and leaned in. "When we went to check on the rest of the horses this morning, they were all in different stalls. Cindy was in Cinnamon's stall, Dewey was in Comanche's. I mean these particular horses get out from time to time and they are real smart, smarter than the average breed, but to be up in each other's stalls all locked up and secure?" He shook his head. "It doesn't make no sense at all. None of it. I watched one of those unsolved mystery stories before where this exact thing happened, where horses were being terrorized, and they come to find out that the barn was situated over some vortex straight to hell."

"Wow," Soto said and scooted closer to Ford, their thighs touching. "I think I saw that episode too," she whispered. Ford looked to their touching legs, then to Soto. The spooked look on her face compelled her to touch Soto's knee and give it a gentle squeeze.

"Is this musical stalls an ongoing occurrence?" Ford inquired.

"Well, no. But I heard the Richards had an up-close encounter with it and described it to be a ghost or a paranormal presence. Isn't that your background, Special Agent Ford? The paranormal, UFOs, and the like?"

"Well, yes. But…"

"So then you agree? You think it's paranormal? Because the guys on the farm seem to think so."

"Before I answer that, have you talked with your neighbors?"

"Closest neighbor is three miles away. Only time we talk is if a heifer gets out or if the wife's made one pie too many."

"Do any of them have teenagers?"

"Of course they have teenagers, real good kids too, always happy to lend me a hand on a big job. Now, you're not saying, you don't think one of my neighbor's killed our horse do you?"

"No. But I think maybe one of the neighbor kids might be a little too caught up with the news of the week and maybe played a prank and switched the horses. I'd check that out first before jumping to the conclusion that your property is sitting over a vortex to hell."

"So unrelated?"

"Probably."

His sorrowful look took on a different expression. "God damn it." He slammed his fist onto the table. "I dare them to come onto my property again. This time I'll be ready with my shotgun, scare the living daylights out of them and make them think they're headed straight to hell."

"Hold on, Roger. Let's take a deep breath," Soto said. The man complied and the sorrowful look returned to his face. "Where is Norma Jean now?"

"She's where we found her." He sniffled and dropped a few more tears. "She must have managed to get out of her stall in the middle of the night and did what she always does."

"And what's that?"

"Oh, she loves rolling around in the patch of sand on the north side of our property. She rolls over and over and then shakes herself all about like she's doing the hokey pokey. Don't you know it? She especially loved rolling in that sandy patch right after a bath. Drove my wife crazy after spending so much time washing and brushing her to have her roll around first thing."

"Is your family home now?" Ford asked.

"Yes. Everyone's there. Got the farmhands keeping watch, got her covered as best we could. I called the hotline right quick and then made my way out to the preserve. They said you might be here for breakfast."

"Sir, by official order, we're going to set up surveillance on your property tonight." Ford grabbed her phone and started to text furiously.

"I was hoping you would say that. Thank you both so much. Scared my wife and little ones bad. It was my youngest out doing his chores this morning that noticed she was gone. He found poor Norma Jean. He's only eight, and…to see a mess like that. He ran the whole way home, shaking so badly. She was going to be his 4-H project."

"I'm sorry, Roger." Soto gave him a sympathetic smile. "That's not a sight for anyone, let alone a little guy. We can talk to him if you think it will help."

"He's not talking."

"Oh, I think he will talk to me," she said as she motioned to Lexy. "I have a secret furry weapon. Lexy, say hi." The pup raised her weary head.

"Hello, girl," Roger said as Lexy gave him a brief lick on the fingers before curling back into a ball under the table. "He'll love her."

"I'll come over this afternoon."

"I appreciate that and thank you." Roger waved goodbye and left.

"Can you get the bill?" Ford said as she motioned to their table and scooted herself toward Soto, letting her know she needed out. "I'll take care of it next time. And you need to be on point to talk to the vet. I'll send Norma Jean over for the necropsy as soon as I get there," she added. "We got a lot of work to do, so rest quickly and head over."

"Perfect," Soto replied. "We can also finish talking about that other thing too." To which Ford just waved her phone in the air.

CHAPTER FOURTEEN

The Bat Cave

Soto opened the door to the preserve. "You are never going to believe what's trending on a certain teenager's Twitter account," she said, looking at her phone before realizing no one was around to hear her. Zero-one-three-one gained her access to the workroom where she found something interesting: a cot in the corner of Grace's office.

Judging from the scattered clothes, Ford had tried on a couple of different tops before making her choice. Photos and file folders and an assortment of pens littered the space, a suitcase was in the corner, and a smattering of shoes was strewn about. She watched Ford from afar as she put her toothbrush into a small bag, her still-damp red hair now a dark auburn. "Oh. Sorry." Soto snapped out of her trance and turned to give her privacy, but not before noticing Ford wore a black lacy push-up bra. Not sorry she thought.

"Officer Soto," Ford said as she hurriedly slipped on the chosen top.

"I thought you were staying in Meridian?"

"It's a total pain to get to. So I moved in. Everything is here: a shower, albeit cold, a kitchenette, the team." Ford motioned to the cots in other offices. "It's closer to you, uh, the work, and all the action. Hey, Lexy," Ford said as she held out her hand for Soto's partner to provide her standard greeting.

"I am sure Grace won't mind, given your mutual understanding," Soto said with a laugh as she thought back to Ford's rocky introduction. "Your hair…"

"What about it?" Ford asked as she ran her fingers through the damp auburn locks.

"It's wavy."

"I didn't have time to straighten it."

"I like it," Soto said, smiling.

"Um, thanks," Ford replied, leading the way to the main floor.

"Impressive." The space was totally transformed. "It feels different in here without its regular patrons."

"You mean the parents and teachers chasing snot-nosed hyper kids?"

"It's certainly calmer in here." Soto walked over to the mini-theatre. "Is that what I think it is?" Her eyes were fixed on the images on the screens.

"Live footage. Tech has taken over, literally. They've tapped into the AV system, which makes it easy to see the big picture." Ford yawned as she stretched. "I scarcely slept. I couldn't stop watching."

"A bat cave."

The usual nature videos that played on loop on the large screen in the mini-theatre now featured six different live feeds. The video installation on the wall that had played the clip of Theodore Roosevelt's executive order establishing the federal preserve now featured Deer Flat's northernmost entrance. The center's dedicated screen for news and information now featured aerial footage. "Is that…" Soto looked back and forth between the image and Ford.

"We have a drone." Ford crossed her arms and rocked on her heels. "And what you are seeing is Grady and company prepping out at the Nelson's Homestead."

"Grace won't like that. Drones are prohibited on the reserve."

"Federal preserve, federal drone."

"They scare the wildlife. No wonder it's been so quiet."

"We just got it today and it's top of the line, totally silent and nearly invisible. Not like the amateur crap the public can buy."

"Fair enough. I'm not in the mood to argue." She took a seat on the lowermost level of the stadium-like seating to take it all in.

"Any word from the pathologist?" Ford asked, joining Soto in the darkened area, sitting a couple of levels up.

"She's performing the necropsy as we speak. The MO looks pretty spot-on."

"Yeah, no shit. We could tell that when we got there. Anything else useful?"

Soto frowned. "You are extra patient today."

"I'm fully rested." Ford smiled and gave her a wink.

"Thanks for the heads-up," Soto said, rolling her eyes. "She mentioned a ton of lake sediment was left at the site."

"Is that strange?"

"Yes and no. Sediment around the preserve isn't anything strange. However, it shouldn't be at the horse pasture. That's what's strange."

"Could it have come up with the irrigation?"

"Roger doesn't irrigate his pasture. When you investigated this thing before, did it ever venture into populated areas and attack domesticated animals."

"Not that I am aware of."

Soto twisted in her seat to face Ford who was looking at her nails. "Were people attacked?"

"Negative. People were not attacked."

"Did you see aliens? Seriously, my mind is running wild. According to your schedule, we have, what, six days to sort this out? And like you, I don't want to be here longer than necessary."

"I do need to fill you in, but the guys will be back soon." Ford looked at her watch. "We need to map out tonight's plan. We're going to change things up a bit." Ford stood and looked at her phone and made her way from the benches. "I need to review the plans. I'd love your help with that."

Soto got up and motioned to the live feed. "They look like they are knee-deep in whatever they are doing at the Nelson's, I mean according to the drone footage. So we have an hour and a half? I think we have ample time to look at the revisions *and* talk about the Blue River. It doesn't take a seasoned investigator to know the case files we got were missing information. If it's relevant to the case, Ford, I need to know. Besides, it's only fair, given you know everything there is to know about me and then some, I imagine."

Ford groaned. Lexy snorted as Ford plopped herself down next to Soto who added, "I'll quit right here unless you fill us in right this second."

CHAPTER FIFTEEN

The Elwha in Common

"The Paranormal Investigations was a new unit and I was under a ton of pressure to confirm to the higher-ups that they made the right decision to both fund the program and put me at the helm," Ford said. "And boy was I cocky."

"Sounds like my first few cases with my new program too." Soto gave Ford her undivided attention but Ford focused on the live feeds instead. Soto scooted closer to her.

"And this case hit my desk." Ford hung her head, turning her attention to her fingers. "People got hurt and I almost lost my credential."

"Oh. I'm sorry."

"I never thought in a million years, let alone nine years to the month, that it would show up again. That is, if it's truly related." Ford searched for her trusty pen to abuse. "I had nearly forgotten about it." Her whisper was almost lost in the cracking of her knuckles. "Actually that's a lie. I think about it all the time, and it's bringing up a lot of stupid stuff. But it's not the kind of stuff that will help advance this case."

"Let me be the judge of that," Soto said. She placed her hand on Ford's, stilling the abusive treatment of her joints. "If anything, it will help us better understand your mindset. Lex and I can't fully communicate with you until we know where you're coming from." The canine's ears perked up at the mention of her name.

"That goes back a long way," Ford warned.

"We're all ears." Lexy waddled over to join them.

"To give you some context, I grew up in Forks, mostly."

"Washington?"

"Yep. My mom and I spent our time between Forks and the Klallam Reservation. She was dating a Klallam guy off and on. Long story short, mom OD'd when I was seven."

"I am so sorry," Soto said as she inched even closer to Ford. "I know how that feels to lose..." She moved her legs against Ford's. Gray and green eyes met hers. "I'm sorry."

"Thank you." Ford conjured a smile and started chewing on a fingernail. "She died with a hundred-dollar pull-tab lotto locket in her hand. Wasn't that lucky?"

"What about your dad?"

"Nonexistent. The only other family I had, lived a world away in Virginia. They took me in, but it didn't work out. I went into foster care. I wasn't there long. I was adopted by a very wealthy family, an older couple. I was their only child. They pushed me toward anything and everything that I showed an interest in, which was my profound interest in the Klallam. It had an immense impact on my life growing up. When I started middle school in Virginia that first year, I insisted my classmates call me Red Mama."

"And did they?"

"No." Ford focused on her hands. "Any opportunity we got, my adopted parents brought me back to Forks for vacations or cultural explorations. We would visit with tribe elders, my mother's gravesite. They made generous gifts to the Klallam Nation. There are several building on the rez in our name."

"They sound like wonderful people."

"They were. I didn't know at the time, but my interest in Native American culture and their support would lead me straight toward Paranormal Investigations. One of my first cases brought me full circle back to the Klallam. A series of disappearances at the Elwha River. I investigated it years before the dam would be demolished."

"My father worked on that legislation when he was in office," Soto said. She sat up suddenly. "It had a tremendous impact on me as well. In fact, we were there for the initial demolition."

"I know you were and so was I. For all three of them to be exact."

"What?" gasped Soto. "Why didn't you tell me that when we first met?" She faced her.

"It's not like we actually met each other and shook hands or anything. I just remembered that you were there. You were a kid, really."

"A kid?" Soto nudged Ford's bobbing foot with the tip of her boot. "I was new on the force, only a few years away from creating my Bear Dog Program. I was on duty *and* packing a firearm. That's hardly a kid."

"At the time I thought you were a kid."

"I didn't think you were *that* much older than me, Special Agent Ford."

"I'm not *that* much older than you."

"How old?"

"That's classified." Ford laughed at her own response.

"I know that you're old enough that you need, but aren't quite used to, using reading glasses. Forty, forty-one? That's significantly older than me."

"I wouldn't call six years your senior *significantly older*." Ford reinforced her statement by nudging the tip of her high-heeled pump against Soto's boot.

"So you thought placing a tracking bug on me a much more fitting first introduction?" Soto couldn't keep a straight face. "Seductively, I might add."

"I proceeded how I felt would be most effective," Ford said as she now stepped lightly onto Soto's boot.

"That's not how you attract the ladies."

"Isn't it?" Ford said as she held Soto's gaze and bit her bottom lip.

As much as Soto wanted to explore that topic, Lexy's rattling dog tags brought her back to the task at hand. "Can we just… Can we focus?" She shifted in her seat and took her braid in her hand, ruffling the tip against her palm. "The case. The Elwha. Time is of the essence."

Ford laughed softly. "This case comes to my desk. Disappearances that were happening around the ruins of an ancient labor camp that housed men who worked on the dam back when it was being built in the early nineteen hundreds. Sometimes hikers, anyone who neared the ruins or got remotely close to the area, would disappear. When they were found, they learned they were missing for days at a time with no recollection of being gone or how they spent their time. This particular case…"

Soto never believed in ghosts, hauntings, or the paranormal, but to hear it from someone who specialized in it? She didn't know what to make of it. She ran her fingers through Lexy's fur, grounding her in reality.

"You okay?"

"We've been out there several times, as have several of my fellow officers," Soto said. "It's a little creepy." She rubbed her arms to temper the chills.

"It's nothing to be scared of. I mean not compared to some of the shit I've seen…"

Ford obviously sensed Soto's growing paranoia and scooted closer to her. "Sometimes I forget that other people don't deal with this on a day-to-day basis like myself. You okay?" she asked, leaning against Soto.

"I'm fine." Soto conjured a smile. "Please continue."

"So, this particular labor camp was built directly on the site where hundreds of Klallam were murdered and buried. Biological warfare. Small pox infected blankets to reduce their numbers, to silence their opposition to the dam. And, there was also a makeshift jail that housed the holdouts who refused to leave when the government took over their land for the dam. They were arrested for poaching salmon on their own land. There isn't much documenting the horrors that happened there, but through the accounts of elders, the labor camp had a sordid and sad history. Freak accidents, disappearances, violence, and unexplained phenomena. At the time the federal government blamed the occurrences on worker accidents, job abandonment, and Klallam sabotage. The last thing they wanted to do was acknowledge mythology or paranormal activity."

"What was causing it?"

Ford shrugged. "I can't say."

"Classified?"

"No. I simply can't explain it definitively. Sometimes, in my line of work, all you can do is document its existence and move on knowing it's out there."

Soto looked to the camera feeds. "Is that how a lot of your cases end?"

"Not all of them." Ford reached over and gave Lexy a pat on the head when the dog adjusted her laying position. "Some of them are complete misunderstandings, but since then, I've been all over the US researching similar types of cases and other types of unexplained phenomenon."

"So, fast forward to Oregon. Blue River."

"I thought it was going to be another chance to research Native American revenge. But what I found there was much more malicious, and to this day, I don't believe it's related to Native American spiritualism." She fished her phone from her back pocket and brushed off the screen.

"What specifically makes you think it isn't related?"

"It was darker, angrier..." Ford turned her phone on and scrolled through her messages, but the jingling of dog tags as Lexy got up for a shake, brought her back. "It was personal..."

"How? I don't understand?"

"It made people, made *me*, see things that weren't there and say things that..." Ford looked to the ceiling and tapped her fingers against her lips. "I can't describe it." She held her hand out for Lexy. The dog gave her fingers a lick. "It's similar to what happened with Mrs. Bird Watcher. How she relived painful memories."

"It sounds related."

"I wouldn't jump to that conclusion yet." She placed her phone back in her pocket.

"It sounds pretty spot-on to me."

"Despite my personal time constraints, I'm not going to proceed full steam ahead based on the account of one eyewitness. And, I've gotten further on this case than I did the last time, so I really don't have anything new to offer. It's been so long." She groaned and rolled her neck out and stood, reaching for her phone yet again. "Ready to talk about tonight's strategy?"

"We're not done." Soto stood too, placing her hands on either side of Ford's shoulders and sat her back down. "And this thing will ring or buzz or flash when someone wants to get a hold of you." She reached for the phone, setting it out of view. "So then what?"

"I took a lot of wrong turns in Oregon. Stupid wrong turns, including taking part in a ceremonial sweat lodge ritual that went horribly wrong."

"How wrong?"

"A few of us experienced medical complications. Charges were brought against the facilitator. I spent a couple of days in county lockup in their psych ward."

"The psych ward?" Soto straddled the bench to face her.

"As in psychiatric ward," Ford confirmed. "These hunters, a dad and his kid, a little guy probably about eight or so, found me wandering in the wilderness the morning after it happened. They almost put a bullet in me, so I was told later. I was nearly nude, rambling like a madwoman about the whispering and revenge and...What didn't help is that the dad, probably in an effort to spare his poor kid, basically threw me in the back of their pickup along with fresh and very bloody game for the drive into town. When I arrived to the police station...Think Carrie on her prom night, think bloody, very very bloody..."

"Jesus." Soto rubbed her temples.

"I told my side of the story to the authorities. Needless to say, they thought I was crazy. I insisted I was a federal agent with the FBI but couldn't provide proof. I remained in their custody until Rankin, my superior, came looking for me a couple of days later when we failed to report in."

"We who?"

"We, my team. Not important. The point is I fucked up, everything was fucked up, a total mess…"

"I can't imagine," Soto said. She placed her hand on Ford's knee and gave it a squeeze. She felt there was more to the story but didn't want to push her too far, too fast.

"It was bad. Bad for the Bureau. I was on probation for a long time after that. My supervisor pulled a lot of strings to keep my unit alive and me on the force. I'm still shocked that I remembered as much as I did to draft the report for the case file. The stuff I pulled out from the case files that you got revolved around the fallout of what happened due to my serious lack in judgment, trusting someone I barely knew to facilitate a ritual in a sweat lodge."

"What did you think you would gain from participating in a ritual?"

"In my line of work, sometimes answers are found in strange places. Places you wouldn't normally think to look. Needless to say, I didn't find what I was looking for this time."

"I am so sorry that happened to you. But…" Soto drew patterns with her finger on the bench in the space between them.

"You can ask me questions."

"Do you think the experience at the sweat lodge could have skewed your understanding of what you were pursuing? Extreme factors can cause people to hallucinate and manifest things that aren't there. I see it all the time when we're called to locate lost hikers and injured hunters."

"Of course I have. And I wish it was something that simple. But I stand by my experience, and as a result, I gained a nickname that follows me to this day."

"Tell me."

"Winifreak. Sometimes they call me Winafraid, or they'll call my unit Paranoid Investigations. Pretty clever, right?"

"More like cruel. I've been called a name or two, especially by those who believe women shouldn't be in law enforcement."

"It's been difficult." Ford let out a humorless laugh. "Actually, it's been hell."

"So the scheduled time off probably looks pretty good right about now."

"I've got three months coming to me in about six days. I'm not sure how I'm going to manage…"

"I'll do whatever I can to help solve this case sooner rather than later." Soto placed her hand on Ford's knee again, but this time let it linger there longer. "Want to know what I think?" She continued before Ford could reply. "I think it takes a determined and fearless person to keep going despite what has happened."

"Thanks." Ford wore a huge grin, especially as Soto scooted in closer to her.

"You're fucking good at what you do. Can't say I agree with your line of questioning sometimes, but you're talented beyond measure."

"Thank you."

"And you know what's different this time? You have Lexy and me to back you up and corroborate what happens." Her furry partner was smiling at them both.

"That means a lot, Soto." Ford placed her hand on top of hers to hold it in place. "A lot has changed since then. I'm not that same impressionable agent anymore, that's for sure."

"But you're still cocky as all hell."

"Some things get better with age."

Soto nodded in agreement. "Thank you for telling us. I know it wasn't easy. And it explains why you were so tense and high-strung when you first rolled into town."

"Hate to break it to you," Ford chuckled. "That's how I am. I've been that way since I was a little kid."

Soto turned her phone on. "So, I want to show you what's trending today on Larissa's Twitter."

"The Nelson Homestead? How is that possible?" Ford read the post. "Word on the preserve. Lower Embankment is haunted #LakeLowellGhost 10 #350BeastofDeerFlat 9 #believe." They watched a black-and-white, old-fashioned GIF of a woman wearing a *Little House on the Prairie* style night hat, trembling in her bed. She pulled the covers up to her chest over and over. "Those little shits!" Ford exclaimed.

"It has fifty-seven likes and as many retweets. And get this, it was posted around midnight last night. But there is no mention of the mauling, and she hasn't tweeted anything new since, which is strange given how…Oh shit!" Soto showed Ford her phone again.

"What? Please, please, what?" Ford reached over to get a better look at what was displayed on the phone. Her hands wrapped around Soto's, bringing the screen closer to her.

"The tweet. She deleted it!"

"Tell me you took a screenshot of that," Ford pleaded.

"Of course I did." Soto stood and began pacing, Lexy in step with her, dancing about. "I bet those little shits were out there playing a practical joke on the Nelsons. They didn't secure Norma Jean properly."

"She got out and our culprit had an easy target. The mauling was something they didn't plan for, hence the deleted post. Those kids are fucked."

"What a break! Lucky us," Soto said. "Poor Norma Jean. She was a beautiful horse." Soto reached into her pocket and fished out a ginger chew, pulling it from the wrapper with her teeth. "I know you said these were good for headaches, but they don't quite cut it." She fished out a couple of pain relievers too. "I need water."

"You take a lot of those," Ford said as she stood.

"In case you haven't noticed, you're a little difficult to work with." Soto sat back down and rolled her head from side to side.

"Are you blaming me?" Ford said as she headed toward the kitchenette.

"One hundred percent."

"I heard that." She returned with a glass of water.

"Thanks." Soto chugged the whole thing.

"Thirsty?"

"Very." She leaned and stretched her back. "I could really use about ten more hours of sleep right now too."

"Tell me about it." Ford sat heavily back on the bench.

"Wait, what did you say?" Soto popped to her feet, startling both her partners.

"Nothing. I was agreeing with you, sleep sounded—"

"No, the other thing you said."

"I asked if you were thirsty." Ford ran her fingers over her lips and scrunched her eyes.

"That's it." Soto gasped. "Oh, my God." Soto rushed to the front desk and rolled out a map. "Tacks, I need tacks." Soto held the map against a bulletin board, covering children's artwork. "It's so obvious."

"What's obvious?" Ford joined her with tacks in hand, reaching over Soto to secure the paper to the board.

"Thanks." Soto stepped back and rubbed her chin as she assessed the image. "It *is* migrating and it *is* headed west toward the lake, which happens to be toward the Nelson Homestead, which I think isn't a simple coincidence. It needs to load up on water."

"Do animals do that?"

"Yes. Think about it. What's the first thing you do when you go on a trip?"

"Pack?"

"Exactly. Wildlife are intelligent and I've seen migrations like this happen before under threat of a predator or impending natural disaster. The preserve is under threat. Predator and prey are on the move."

Ford rummaged the desk for a pen. "But how is it traveling so quickly and undetected? The homestead is...seven miles from the grid we were monitoring?" She traced a line along the route. "Through neighborhoods and roads, somebody would have spotted it." She circled the area in question. "We would have heard about it." She dropped the pen onto the desk and sat down. "Right?"

"Maybe," Soto whispered and joined Ford by leaning against the desk. "Your phone."

"What about it?"

"I think it's…" Soto eyed the object in Ford's hand.

"Oh." The cell phone flickered a series of colors. "Ford. Did you now? Well, well, well. We're on our way."

"What was that?"

"That was Tech. Charlie and Larissa were pulled over on preserve property. Guess where."

"The Nelson Homestead?"

"Affirmative."

"You want to play bad cop?" Soto asked.

"Yes please."

CHAPTER SIXTEEN

Good Cop, Bad Cop

"The fact that we were on preserve property doesn't prove a thing," said Larissa, as she sat opposite Ford. Soto, along with Larissa's father and a uniformed officer, Officer Meg, watched from the other side of the two-way mirror. Soto and Ford were about to play good-cop, bad-cop—an especially effective technique for breaking cocky teenagers.

Soto observed Ford as she worked the room. Every one of her actions seemed intentional. She swaggered around as if starring in her own western film. One foot in front of the other, ready at any time to sling her weapon, or in this case, her trusty pen.

"Aside from us trespassing, which I totally admit to, we seriously got lost and made a wrong turn," continued Larissa. "I stopped to ask for directions and that's when we ran into those FBI guys. It doesn't prove anything, so get off my grill."

"You know what?" Ford pivoted on her high heels, and continued to slowly amble around the small, almost too cheery, interrogation room at the town's juvenile detention—complete with framed photos of wild animals, panthers and wolves touting patience, courage, and teamwork. She tapped a finger to her lips. "You are totally right. It doesn't prove anything."

"Uh, yeah. I know. I just said that," Larissa said. "Jesus. It's kind of obvious as fuck."

"But you know what does prove something?" Ford's voice elevated a false curiosity.

"I couldn't care less." She looked at her nails and then inspected the tips of her hair as if she was searching for split ends. She jumped when Ford slammed her hand on the table. "Size-eight Gucci combat boots."

"What are those?" Larissa snickered, overtly displaying her white tennis shoes as she crossed her legs "And what the fuck do you know about shoes?"

"I know good shoes." Ford lifted and pointed the toe of one of her heels and wiggled it around in a circle. "These are Valentino Rock Stud Pumps. They retail for about nine hundred and fifty dollars. I own several pairs of them. They aren't the most comfortable of shoes, but they sure do look sexy, right?" Ford's lips curled into a smirk. "Right?"

"Whatever."

Larissa attempted to lean back in her chair, but Ford had strategically placed it against the wall before the suspect arrived. The girl stiffened as Ford sat down and scooted her own chair closer and closer to her, each movement punctuated by the harsh grinding of the metal chair legs dragging on the concrete floor. Ford folded her hands before her next question.

"When I checked out your social media for the first time, I said to Officer Soto, 'damn this girl has got class. Her family must be loaded. And the poor thing.'" Ford furrowed her eyebrows, pursed her lips, and said in a high-pitch baby voice, "'She witnessed firsthand the brutal mauling caused by the Lake Lowell Ghost.'" Ford dropped the baby voice and pointed at her. "Or are you Team Beast of Deer Flat?"

She slid her phone across the table that displayed the screenshot of the deleted tweet. "The more I combed through your Twitter *and* Facebook *and* Instagram, and learned more about your shoe hobby…"

Larissa's smile slid down her face in an attempt to feign humor.

Her father turned to Soto and said, "She looks scared shitless."

"She'll be okay." They turned back to the unfolding scene on the other side of the two-way glass. "I won't let bad cop get too out of control," Soto assured.

"I realized that your taste in shoes is the only interesting part of your pathetic little life," Ford continued.

"F-fuck you," Larissa mumbled.

"Where did you get the money to buy shoes like that? Because I know your daddy doesn't make that kind of money at the meat packing plant. No disrespect to him and his profession. I've heard of doting daddies before, but this—"

"I have a job," she blurted.

"Oh, yes. Taco Time. What are you, part owner? 'Cause six hundred dollars on shoes is pretty steep."

From behind the glass, her father offered an explanation. "Her mom sends her money. That's likely where she got it."

"We know. We're just using it as a way to get her to admit to other things."

"It's none of your fucking business," Larissa said to Ford.

"Your shoes are every bit my business, kid. Where'd you get the money?" Larissa remained silent. "I asked you a question. Where did you get the money to buy such expensive shoes, and why on earth would you wear them to play horse whisperer at the Nelson Farmstead?"

Ford slapped down photos of shoe impressions, the designer name clearly imprinted in the dirt. The girl was as pale as if it were the Lake Lowell Ghost herself talking to her about designer footwear. Ford reinforced her point with another photo of Larissa wearing the exact same shoes, the photo taken from one of her social media posts. Larissa was shaking, on the fringe of tears.

Ford slapped down a series of gruesome photos, of mauled animals with missing faces and voids where their bellies should have been. "Tell me, Larissa, does this look like the work of the thing you stumbled onto a couple of weeks ago?" The girl focused everywhere but the horrific images. "Does it? You were there, weren't you? Are we on the right track?" Larissa's chin quivered and her nose turned red.

Soto headed for the door. "My turn, Dad. Homestretch," she assured Larissa's father as she headed out to play good cop. She swung the door open, the action jarring the teen, but not Ford.

"Whoa. Ford. Seriously. Larissa's had enough." Soto reached over and placed her hand on Ford's shoulder. "Hey," Soto said as Ford grabbed her by the wrist and turned her abruptly. They were inches apart.

"Fucking get your hands off me. I'm not done." Ford gave Soto a wink, a little smile, and squeezed her hand before dramatically letting it go and turning back to Larissa. "Are we hot or cold, huh?" She slammed her hands on the table, jarring the girl once again. "Come on, kid, throw us a bone here!" Ford shouted as she turned, as if to exit. She ran her hand through her hair, locks of red hair came loose in front of her eyes. Turning back to Larissa, she said, "I asked you a fucking question."

She went for another shot, but Soto stepped in front of her and placed her hand upon Ford's chest, feeling the hurried thump of Ford's heart on the palm of her hand. Soto gave her a soft caress, this orphaned wolf pup with stormy emerald and gray eyes. She lingered a look upon Ford's lips as Ford pushed off and headed out the door. "This is bullshit!"

The slam was so hard the teen yelped and the room's several framed photos rattled against the walls. Soto stared at the closed door, wishing she could see through the thick metal. Was Ford just as hot and bothered and breathless on the other side?

"My stories get likes!" Larissa yelled and then stood up.

"It's okay, Larissa. She's gone," Soto said as she gave the girl a can of soda while slowing her own breathing brought on by Ford's performance. "We can relax. Now sit back down."

"What the fuck is her problem?" Larissa asked with tears in her eyes. "She's annoying as fuck." The girl leaned in toward Soto. "Is she coming back?"

"Maybe. I don't know. I've never seen her like that before. What happened?"

"Nothing happened. She kept grilling me about money and selling stories and my blog posts."

"So you admit that's where you got the money? Selling stories? Because your daddy is right outside and he's real pissed. He wants to know where you got the money too. And guess what? So does Officer Meg."

"Fuck Officer—"

"I'd be really careful about what you say next. Both of them are looking at you right now through that two-way." She pointed to the glass with her finger and winked. The girl's head whiplashed around to the mirrored wall.

"I'm honestly not selling stories. That's not how blogging works."

"So how does it work?"

"Likes and retweets—and my stories get them, okay. Seriously, ask Charlie. He knows."

"Oh, we did." She pointed with her thumb to the door behind her. "Didn't Special Agent Ford tell you?"

"That fucking asshole. What did he say?"

"Everything. That you guys made up stories. How did he put it? Oh yes, that it's fake news."

"I have an image to maintain, okay. I'm going into journalism. Jesus, what's the big deal?"

"Well…" Soto chuckled. "First, lying on a police report is a serious crime in and of itself. Add fabricating stories on social media. You can pretty much kiss that profession goodbye."

She sat up in her chair. "What do you mean? Why?"

"People believed you, Larissa, and made decisions because of what they read. Do you have any idea how dangerous that is? My partner and I are trying to conduct an investigation, and your made-up stories have caused quite the stir around here—gossip, bickering, speculation. That makes our job a hundred times harder. And then there's this alleged trespassing and animal cruelty thing that happened."

"We didn't mean for the horse to get killed. Jesus. We were joking."

"Oh, so you were there?" Soto reached for a pen and paper as Larissa realized she'd outed herself. Soto lay down a handful of horrid photos of the poor mauled Arabian. "Because of you, this lovely creature, who never did anything wrong in her entire life, whose name was Norma Jean by the way, died in the worst way possible." She pushed the gruesome photos toward the girl. "And a kid found her, a little kid. Can you imagine seeing something like that when you were eight? That would have freaked me the hell out when I was a kid. Hell, it freaks me out now."

A solitary tear dropped from Larissa's eye, though Soto would guess her tears were from self-pity. She had gotten caught and her moment of fame was over.

"So here is what is going to happen." She returned Larissa's phone to her. "You're going to leave posts on all your social media accounts telling your followers that you are full of shit."

"What?"

"Well, you don't have to say it in those exact words."

"No..." She groaned and genuine tears appeared.

"And then you will give me your phone and I will reset the passwords for each of your accounts, got it?"

"When will I get it back?"

"Oh, it's evidence now. You'll get it back sooner or later, but the judge will determine how long it will be until you can use social media again and under what circumstances. But that's the least of your concerns. You know my partner in there? I can assure you, you're on her list." She emphasized that last remark. "So Larissa Larsen, who else was at Lake Lowell that day when this story broke? And whose backpack is this?" Soto slid over a photo of the green backpack with the mushroom patch on it. She leaned back in her chair and crossed her arms behind her head.

"That's Marnie Starr's backpack. She's in my class. She was at the lake with some guys when we found the mauled deer."

CHAPTER SEVENTEEN

Rest & Revelations

"They're both facing long legal battles, that's for sure. Future court dates, hundreds of hours of community service," Ford said as she finally sat down, the cool of the metal chair a welcomed sensation after the heated interrogation room.

"Not to mention monies owed to the courts, the blogs, and to the Nelsons," Soto added as she filled out the documents needed to formally press charges.

"I should have eased up a bit. Do you think I was too harsh?"

"You were perfect. Did you see the look on her face when I told her that Charlie had ratted her out even before we interrogated her?" Soto pushed the forms to Ford for her additions.

"I thought she was going to attack." Ford rubbed the area on her chest where Soto had held her back from one last go at the girl.

"You okay? You look miles away."

"Fine," Ford said as she feigned stretching her neck. She found her pen and started working on the documents. "Teenagers are total tools. Why anyone would want one is beyond me." She tried but failed to avert her eyes from watching Soto undo the top two buttons of her uniform top to rub out her neck muscles. "It's damn stuffy in this stuffy, too small stuffy room." Ford picked up the file folder to fan herself. "And when does everything end with the phrase *as fuck*?"

"Yeah. That's a new one."

"I kind of like it, as fuck." She took a sip of cold water to temper her rising heat only to have it dribble down her chin and onto her silk blouse. "Damn it," she said while fishing a Kleenex from her bag, dabbing the wet area. She looked up to Soto, averting her eyes from the wet spot that was forming between her breasts. "You certainly had that one wrapped around your finger. And what was that about my list?"

"That scared her pretty good, didn't it?" Soto giggled. "You kind of scared the crap out of me when I walked in on your little show."

"I totally had you."

"You totally did." Soto's eyes seemed to settle on her lips. "You're bright red by the way."

"Sorry." Ford again fanned herself with a file folder and cleared her throat. "It's hot and it's not very often that I have so much fun in my line of work. All I do is yell at Grady, which isn't that fun anymore."

"He's extremely patient."

"More like he's had a crush on me for five years."

"And you don't like him back?"

"Uh, he's not my type." Ford tapped her pen on the back of Soto's hand. "Surely, I have made that clear?"

"You have." Soto cleared her throat and rubbed her neck. "I work with this one guy. His name is Tom, too. Tom Roselyn. Technically we have different territories. But we work together a lot. I've been training him for a bear dog of his own as soon as we get the funding. We're always having fun, cracking jokes, playing pranks on each other."

"I bet you are all sorts of fun," Ford whispered while enjoying watching Soto's reaction, her squirming in her seat, and the hitching of her breath while she traced her fingers with her pen.

"One time he, uh, got me good…" Soto whispered. "We were on assignment—"

"What kind of assignment?" Ford asked, this time ditching the pen to instead touch Soto's hand with her own fingertips.

"I don't remember…"

She continued tracing Soto's fingers and smiled at the effect of her touch. The tough moose wrangler looked like she couldn't handle a kitten at the moment.

"You don't remember anything?" Ford asked and watched Soto licking her lips. What she wouldn't give to taste them with her own. The thought sent a hard shiver through her body straight between her legs, especially when Soto turned her hand over and intertwined their fingers. "Well…"

"Well what?" Soto's look was still focused on the intertwining of their fingers.

"Am I distracting you, Officer Soto?"

"Your hands are so soft… Mine are…I work outside."

Ford's phone vibrated against the metal table. "Fucking Jesus! Ford." She stood and turned to take the call. "Good. Fucking fantastic." She placed her hand over the receiver and turned toward Soto. "Marnie," she mouthed and returned to the call. "I'll bet. As soon as possible. Now. Why not? I thought kids stayed up late?" Her wristwatch said it was past ten o'clock. "Oh. Then tomorrow? Night!" She threw her unoccupied hand up into the air. "Fine. It'll have to be. I'll see you on the preserve in a few—" She glanced at Soto, who beheld her with a lusty look. "Did she now? Would have been nice for my partner to check with me before making that decision." Her voice elevated. "Okay then." She clicked her phone off, set it on the table and sat back down. "Marnie's parents said she had been sick these past couple of weeks. Now they know why. The kid's eager to talk to us, but we can't see her until tomorrow night. She's at her grandmother's house."

Soto shifted in her chair. "Fuck." She rubbed her temple.

"It won't put us too much behind schedule. We have plenty to do between now and then," Ford said. "But funny thing." She slapped her hand on the table. "Grady said you called tonight off?"

"Had to."

"Why? We're closing in on it."

"I knew Larissa would take some time. And Lex needs a night off."

"Can't you borrow another dog?"

"That's *not* how it works." Soto shook her head. "And my volunteers' dogs need to rest too. And you're right. Now that we are closing in on it, thanks to Larissa, we should let it think it's comfortable. Hone things back a bit in the area. Besides, there's no moonlight, which makes it difficult to work."

"We have state-of-the-art infrared vision devices, Officer Soto."

"Do you have goggles for our dogs?"

"I thought animals could see in the dark."

"It doesn't work like that either. There's a fog rolling in, which will make it difficult for animals and humans to manage the terrain. So I made the call."

"Fucking fine." She stood and stretched. "I guess that means one thing."

"What's that?"

"Reviewing intel." She stifled a yawn.

"A few of us are getting together. Nothing formal, some volunteers and a couple of people that I know are headed to a bonfire at Kevin's place."

"Kevin?"

"The teacher you berated."

"Oh, sure. Nice guy. Who else will be there?"

"I don't know, people."

"Will Crawly be there?"

"Want me to text her for you." Soto said with a smirk.

"I have her number."

"You're welcome to join."

"As tempting as it sounds to take a night off, I still have agents in the field. They might need me."

"What's a couple of hours?"

"I want to monitor the Nelson Homestead closely tonight. Besides, probably not a good idea with my deadline."

"My goodness. Yes, let me help you. Sorry, I wasn't thinking."

"No, you go. Seriously. You and Lex should rest up for tomorrow. I need you both bright-eyed and bushy-tailed." She made her way toward the door.

"Same to you. Get some rest tonight too. Take it easy, okay?" Soto suggested. "See you tomorrow."

"Tomorrow."

Ford gave her a nod and made her way out of the room then down the hall and out the doors. The cool night breeze didn't do anything to lower her fever.

CHAPTER EIGHTEEN

Holding on for Deer Life

She wondered what Soto was doing. Was she sitting on a log warming herself by the fire? Maybe sipping on a beer? Was Lexy curled in her lap or was that vixen Margo Crawly curled in her lap? Perhaps they were talking about dogs, or planning a date, a little action before… "Earth to Ford."

"What?"

Tom Grady stood in the doorjamb of Grace's office scratching his beard. "I've said your name like fifty times. What the hell has you so captivated?"

"Work. I'm kind of fucking busy here." She motioned to the monitor, and then noticed that her screensaver had kicked in. She pawed at a random key to wake it up.

"Yeah, you look *really* busy." He walked into her makeshift office, skirting the cot that took up much of the space. "What is that?" he asked. "Are you drawing?"

"Jesus H." Ford slid the sheet of paper under a stack of folders and stood to block his view.

"Let me see it. It looked good. Was it a dog?"

"What do you need, Grady?" she asked, placing her hand atop the pile of folders and leaning against the desk.

"I thought you might like to know that a bunch of cameras went offline at Gott's Point. Third time this week at that particular spot."

"Did you see anything beforehand?"

"Negative. Gorman and Ladd are booting up. You in?"

"Fuck, yeah. I'm getting nothing done here." She grabbed a radio from the cradle and clipped it to her jeans. "Where are the repair bags?" she asked, slipping into a lightweight jacket.

"By the boots." He motioned to the naturalists' supply closet. "Use a pair of those this time."

She beelined to the closet. "They're so hard to walk in."

"*Those* are hard to walk in," he said, pointing to the damaged pair of heels she had set atop one of Grace's filing cabinets.

"Those were such good shoes. A crying shame."

"I know. It'll be okay." He settled behind his monitors in the bat cave. "Radio when you're on location. I got eyes on you," he said, referring to the drone he operated with a joystick.

"We will," she said.

"Be careful. It's dark out there."

"Roger that."

"I bet you wish you had a dog right now."

"That would be nice."

"And a certain dog handler too? Huh Ford?" he added.

"Shut up, Grady."

Ford radioed home base. "How does it look now?" She blew her hair out of her eyes, wiping her forehead with the back of her hand.

"Better." Grady's voice scratched over the radio waves. "Can you make out why these cameras keep going offline?"

"If you properly secure them, we won't keep having to fix shit. It's a fucking wind tunnel here."

"We wired it in place last time."

"I'll add more wire," Ford said. She placed the radio on the ground and got to work, pulling a coil of wire and clippers from her bag. She gave the camera a hefty push to test it. "That isn't going anywhere now." She picked up the radio. "How does it look?"

"Perfect," Grady confirmed.

"What's next?" She hefted the strap of the heavy workbag over her shoulder.

"That's it. You guys got them all. Come on back."

"Copy," the trio said in near unison. "Last one to the truck buys coffee tomorrow," one of the techies said, causing a series of chuckles over the radio waves.

"And not that shitty kind," Ford added.

A short quarter-mile trek to the truck felt longer in near darkness. She thought back to Soto's warning. The nonexistent moon and the cold and heavy fog rolling in from the lake made it difficult to see. It was white and thick and smelled like minerals. It covered the ground and made it difficult to traverse.

"Hold up," Grady radioed. "Ford, are you still on location?"

"Close enough. What are you seeing?"

"You're not going to like it."

"Just tell me already."

"The camera you just fixed is totally obstructed. And…it's back offline."

"What in the bloody hell?" She looked over her shoulder.

"What was that about properly securing it?"

"Quit trying to be funny, Grady. It doesn't suit you," Ford said, getting a laugh.

"Radio when you're there."

"Copy."

She made a U-turn and headed back toward the troublesome camera that she knew for a fact she wired in place. Flashbacks of Oregon streamed into her consciousness. She had spent hours fixing cameras. Back and forth she wandered with no real purpose or idea of what she was surveilling. The only differences between now and nine years ago were better equipment, more boots on the ground, dogs, and the top tracker in twelve states.

"I'm on location."

"What's it look like?"

"Sitting on the ground along with the wire I used. Damn, this is fucked." She picked up the camera and wiped mud off it. "I'm leaving it as is. More wire isn't going to help whatever the hell is going on here." A blinking red light signaled it was back online.

"Er ack oline bu…"

"Grady. Repeat." It sounded like he made another attempt, but she couldn't discern it.

Rustling in the distance drew her attention. She dropped the workbag, clicked on her tactical flashlight, and whipped around, sure that someone was watching her. "FBI. You're on the scene of a highly controlled investigation." The response: more rustling, crunching underfoot, branches and brambles parting the way for something's grand entrance. She heard a wind growing in the distance, making its way toward her, and finally reaching her, blustering her hair about. "Grady, do you copy? Gorman? Ladd? Over."

"Ford, holy shit," Grady said loud and clear. "Are you seeing that? A shit-ton of deer on the move."

"Negative. But I hear them. I'm going to check it out. I want to know what the fuck they are running from."

"Wait for backup."

"Too late," she said and unclipped the dart gun strapped to her leg, which gave her a small amount of courage.

"Ford! You're going to get trampled out there."

"Already in pursuit," she said before the onset of a tingling down her spine. "Get the drone over my coordinates. I want some fucking footage, Grady. Gorman, Ladd, get your asses over here. I'm headed west."

"Copy" was the last reply she heard as she took off toward the sound. She stumbled over a downed log. "Damn clunky boots." She also couldn't see shit thanks to a veil of thick, white fog at her ankles. She got up and peered into the distance. Her knee was wet. Whether it was blood or mud she wouldn't know until later. Another garbled transmission, then nothing, then static. "God damn it." She inspected the handheld, tuning in to other frequencies. It was no use. Her radio was going haywire when she heard the telltale sound of something familiar. A whispering, a clicking, Aunt Betty from Beyond. She wasn't going to wait for it to invade her mind. The situation called for full pursuit, anything to catch a glimpse and confirm whether or not it was the same presence from so many years ago.

She headed toward the whispering and rustling sounds without reservation. Tears wet her face as branches and brush scratched her cheeks. Feeling a presence behind her, she turned to witness an opaque mass floating inches above the ground then dissipating into it. "There you are."

From behind, a force pushed her hard, knocking her to her knees, taking her breath. She gasped and coughed, then worked her way back to her feet. A lone deer leaped by. "Fucker, get out of the way!" She reaffirmed her grip on the dart gun.

The whispering returned, closer this time, facing her head on. She inched backward until she went feet first into a crude and jagged hole in the ground. She grasped for anything to keep from falling, but sliced her fingers and hands on the slippery gravel and razor-sharp rocks. "Fuck!"

After a painful struggle, she managed to work herself onto her elbows, her dart gun within reach. She wanted it and could feel the cold steel in her hands when the whispering surrounded her, made her dizzy, cold and nauseous. "No…Shake it off, Win…"

Her vision clouded, forcing her to rely on her other senses. She smelled blood, could taste it in her own mouth. She heard the desperate sounds of a creature in distress, a creature that was dying, being ripped apart, and she couldn't see a damn thing. It was gasping for air and losing the fight. There was gnawing and crunching, and the unseen entity growled and hissed. The ground trembled as the thing shook its prey and she felt blood spatter on her face.

Then it was over as quickly as it started and her vision returned. She gasped when she felt it. A force against her body. It kick-started her anxiety when she felt it brush against her as it retreated into the pit she now dangled over.

Grady's voice came through her radio a few hundred feet away. "I see you, Ford! I got eyes on you!" His words were lost among memories of her childhood, trembling in the kitchen when she found her mother, wondering why she wasn't moving and Ford thinking she should grab that winning pull tab lotto ticket and run away.

"Hang on!" Grady yelled.

"I will, Mom," she said with tears running down her face.

CHAPTER NINETEEN

The Other Ten Percent

"So you were fixing cameras when you heard it?" Soto asked Ford, pacing as she took in the story with the rest of the team seated in Deer Flat's kitchenette.

Ford's temper flared from Soto's interrogation but she held back. She hadn't seen Soto in plainclothes before. Well-worn blue jeans hugged her plump backside. She wore a crisp white tank underneath a loose-fitting lightweight jacket. Her work boots were hastily tied. Long and wavy jet-black hair reached mid-back. Soto ran her fingers through it for the third time since she'd arrived to get the lowdown of Ford's close encounter.

Ford started to recount her experience yet again. "Like I said—"

"You could have gotten seriously hurt out there," Soto said. "All of you. You guys have no fucking clue how dangerous it is out there, especially on nights like tonight. This area is full of sinkholes, pockets, dangerous terrain, not to mention the damn creature—creatures—whatever the hell it is, is still at large. What the fuck?"

"Burn it off, Officer Soto," said Ford. "Get it all out."

"There isn't anything to get out, Special Agent Ford!" Soto headed over to the sink, filled a glass and popped a couple of pills. She turned and leaned against the sink, sliding her hands into her pockets. "What part of *we're taking it easy tonight* didn't you understand?"

"My team doesn't *take it easy*. In case you haven't noticed, we monitor intel twenty-four seven. We can't monitor the sites if we can't see anything, and if we can't see anything how the fuck will we know what we're up against?" She slammed her hands on the table. "So you're welcome! We fixed twelve cameras while *you* were taking the damn night off!"

"I didn't realize so many cameras had gone offline." Soto rubbed her temple and worked on her neck.

"Well now you do," Ford added.

"Why were you alone out there?"

"I wasn't alone. We were on site with Grady on surveillance."

"Ow!" Grady yipped. "Jesus, Win. Did you just kick me?"

"Fucking back me up," Ford said.

Soto looked pointedly at Grady. "Were you physically with her when she decided to chase down whatever the hell she was chasing down? Were you with her when the creature ripped apart another animal right in front of her?"

"Is there some sort of impression I give off, Officer Soto, that makes you think I'm not capable of watching my own back?" Ford yelled.

Soto ran her hand through her hair again and muttered something to herself. "There's a reason why we partner with dogs on night patrols," she said, sitting down opposite Ford, folding her hands in front of her.

"You would have done the same thing if you—"

"The difference is I have a partner! Oh, my God. What don't you get?" Soto popped back up, opened the door to the fridge and then slammed it shut. She picked up Ford's muddy dart gun and checked the safety and then the chamber. "What the hell was your plan if you had darted it? Were you planning on chasing the thing down all by yourself? I thought we went over this. It can take hours sometimes for tranquilizers to take effect. Were you not at my briefing when I talked about how dangerous it is to dart an animal and lose track of it! You're lucky they found you." She waved her hand in between the special agents.

"Actually, we knew her location the whole time," Grady finally chimed in.

"You're not fucking helping," Soto insisted. She turned her scorn to the men. "And what the hell was it doing all the way out at Gott's Point again?" She looked at each of the agents before sitting back down. "Well?" No one had a ready answer. Soto sighed dramatically while fishing a ginger chew out of her pocket. The ginger chew rattling against her teeth the only noise in the room. "At least you wore proper gear." She motioned to Ford's footwear. "What happened to your other boot?"

"If you're done freaking out, Officer Soto," Ford said, "we will tell you what happened." She held Soto's gaze. "Are you capable of listening?"

"Yes."

"I think we figured out how the creature is getting around."

Soto crumpled the wrapper and shoved it in her pocket. "How?"

Ford recounted the story of falling backward into the pit. "It must have been man-made because it looked like I busted through an old plank board. I almost got a glimpse. I heard more than I saw." The blood on her clothing and on her hands told the rest of her tale.

"Were you scared?"

"Um, no." Ford glanced over at her team members. "But the bigger question is what's down there?"

"It looks like an old well, at least from what we saw," Grady added.

"That's odd. Usually when wells are decommissioned, they're capped, filled with rock," Soto said. She pulled out her phone and began texting. "We're not going to do anything about it tonight, not until we've had a better look. I got a land expert I'd like to consult in the morning." She looked up from her phone. "Got it?" The room was silent. "Are you listening?"

"Yes. Yes, we understand," Ford said. "Triple enforcement at the location. I don't want anyone even remotely close to it." Gorman and Ladd left to work on the request.

"We got images," Grady said and handed Soto an electronic tablet. "Check it out. It looks like years of growth concealed its existence for who knows how long. Something recently scratched through—"

"Hold up." She took the tablet and placed it on the table. "How hurt are you?" she asked Ford. "Is that mud or blood on your knee, or is it left over from your run-in with the deer?" she asked.

She placed a hand on Ford's knee to examine the rip in the fabric and the gash underneath. Ford promptly waved her hand away, immediately seeing the hurt in Soto's deep brown eyes.

"I'm fine."

"Here, Win." Grady handed her a bag of ice.

She looked at it scornfully. "What the hell, man. There's like three ice cubes in here." She held it to her knee, struggling to find the best position for it.

"That's all there is."

Soto eyed the measly bag. "Come with me to the vineyard. You need a good night's sleep and way more ice."

"I'll be fine here. I need to sleep it off." Ford motioned to her cot. "I'll be good as new tomorrow." She avoided the knowing glances of her teammates. Grady and company continued to give her a hard time about her growing infatuation.

"Not if you sleep on that tiny camping cot."

"It's extremely comfortable." Ford shifted in the chair and creaked her leg out.

"You said it was a shitty cot," Grady chimed in.

Ford gave him a look she hoped communicated he was more of a pain than her throbbing knee.

"Quit being stubborn, Ford," he continued. "They probably have big fluffy beds and meds and a lot of crushed ice over there.

If you don't want to go, I'll go. I twisted my ankle pulling you out of the damn hole."

"I'm fine," Ford said, trying to laugh at his joke, though her voice was shaky. She couldn't imagine being anywhere near Soto overnight.

"Winnie, for fuck's sake, listen to the lady. Go. Get some rest tonight," Grady pleaded. "So you're not a complete bitch tomorrow. Again."

"Fine." Her legs felt weaker than before, and it wasn't due to nearly falling down a well and getting scratched to shit on her way down. "Thank you, Officer Soto."

"You're welcome. Now go pack a bag and we'll get you cleaned up," she said. Ford groaned as she stood.

"So can you pull up the footage for me, Grady?" Soto tapped the tablet on the table.

"Sure." He grabbed the tablet, swiped around, and handed it back to her.

"Fascinating." Soto rubbed her chin and looked closer at the images, noticing that Ford didn't look scared—she looked scared shitless holding on for her life with an unseen culprit doing serious damage to another living creature a few feet away. "Damn." Soto's heart sank as she watched Ford reaching for her weapon while clawing on to the edge of the splintered board, talking to herself, yelling to an unknown assailant. Then she stared into the void while blood sprayed around her.

"Is she crying?"

"She said she got blood in her eyes. Stung like a son-of-a-bitch-whore is what I think she said."

"Does this have audio?"

"Just imagery." He looked over his shoulder. "But I can tell you what she's saying."

"What?"

He laughed. "Probably fuck this and fuck that."

She smiled, knowing he was probably right. Ford limped her way back from Grace's office. "Ready?"

Soto stood, shoved her phone into her back pocket, and jingled her keys in her hand. "Thanks, Grady."

"You guys going to be okay?" Ford asked her team as she approached with her bag in hand.

"We're fine."

"You know where to find me if you see anything."

CHAPTER TWENTY

Liberties & Lotions

It was past two in the morning when they pulled into the Soto family estate, a vineyard, tasting room, and private event venue located along the Snake River Wine Region. Set atop a plateau, stunning backdrops painted the beauty of the Marsing Valley. Expansive farmland patterned with orchards and rangeland and jagged cliffs added to its authenticity.

Lexy danced about and bobbed her head up and down when Soto and Ford walked in. Per her standard greeting, she licked Ford's fingertips in exchange for a pat on the head. The furry mistress led the way through the house and up the stairs to one of the estate's guest rooms, pushing her nose squarely against the door.

"Hold, little lady." Soto opened the door but the dog parked herself in front of them. "Sometimes I think she has forgotten all of her training." Anyone wanting in or out of the room would need Lexy's permission, or rather would need to step over her. "Really?" Soto gently nudged the dog with her bare foot and crouched down to give her partner a good rub on the tummy.

"Sorry." She looked up to see Ford smiling at them. "Do you mind?"

"Of course not, I love that she's right there," Ford said, stepping over the dog. She leaned over to drop her bag at the foot of the bed. "Oh," she whimpered, and creaked her way back up.

"You okay?" Soto asked, flipping on the light, taking Ford in from head to toe—scratches on her face, mud on her jeans, her hair a tangled bird's nest.

"My back's all locked up," Ford moaned.

"You'll feel better after a hot shower and sleep." Soto pointed out the room's main attraction, the bathroom. "The towels are clean. I'll bring you an icepack when you're ready."

"Thanks," Ford said as she removed her coat. "Where should I put this?" Bits of dirt fell onto the hardwood floor. "Sorry. I should have changed out of this mess before coming here."

"Oh, um." Soto lingered her response. "Put it here." She picked up a small wicker basket. "Put the rest of your stuff in here too and put it by the door. I'll run a load a little later. I have things I need to wash too."

"I owe you."

"Big time." The sound of crackling wicker let Soto know she was hugging the shit out of the small laundry hamper. She placed it onto the floor. "Okay. So the bathroom."

Ford pointed toward the closed door. "Is right over there."

"I'll bring you ice and something else that might make you feel better, but after your shower."

"I can't wait."

"But don't rush. Take your time."

"You've been more than kind." Ford's smile was a brilliant welcomed treat after the madness of the evening.

"It's nothing, really. I want you here." Soto snaked a hand up her neck, the tension building again. "*Mi casa es tu casa.*" She turned abruptly almost running into her dog. "Shit, Lex." She braced herself against the doorjamb, stepping over Lexy to exit the room.

"Holy fucking hell," she muttered as she ventured down the hallway, passing her bedroom. Backtracking. Feeling as though she was reliving a childhood crush. Her most basic actions felt like she was floating in zero gravity. What was up? What was down? Every direction was right *and* wrong. "What am I doing?" she whispered as she stood in the middle of the hallway. "Why did I invite her here? The poor woman is in pain, she's hurt. After all, I'm trained in first aid, even certified."

It was official. She was talking to herself. The rattle of the water pipes startled her. When had her innocent flirting turned into caring? Seeing Winifred Ford hurt after her close encounter? Seeing her frightened? Or was it because Ford texted her at all hours, wanting to know her thoughts on an image that intel had captured. It always evolved into hours of texting when they were supposed to be resting.

Lexy's nails meeting the wood floor signaled it was time. She retreated to the kitchen returning with an icepack in hand. Standing outside her guest's door she was hesitant to knock, but shook the feeling away. "First aid that's all." She rapped on the door. "Can I see you?" Soto bristled at her choice of words.

"Come in."

"An icepack."

Soto held the frosty blue gel pack toward Ford, stopping short of giving it to her as she was taken aback at the transformed woman sitting at the desk in the room. Ford had been reading something. She removed her glasses and set them on the desk. Color had returned to her cheeks. Her hair was drying in a thick, fat, damp auburn braid. She wore thin yoga pants and a fitted cotton shirt.

"Thank you," Ford said, and arranged the pack on her knee. "I put my clothes right over there." She motioned to the basket overflowing with the evidence of her evening fiasco. "Sorry they're muddy."

"I've washed worse in my line of work. Sometimes I'm in the field for days at a time, so as you can image, I get pretty rank. You probably didn't need to know that. You good? Do you have everything you need?" She tapped the edge of the desk.

"Yes. Thank you. I'll be very comfortable. I'm sorry about tonight. That I interrupted the bonfire."

"I didn't go," Soto said.

"Why not?"

"By the time I got home, I was beat. I didn't feel much like socializing." She leaned against the desk, lifted a pen out of a cup and let it fall back into the holder. "Plus Margo was there. I didn't feel like seeing *her*."

"I see." Ford bit her lip. "For what it's worth, I really am sorry. So much for relaxing."

"It's okay. This is my priority. You are my priority, the case, and your agents too, of course. Thank you for calling me over to the center and telling me what happened. I can't wait to see what's down there." She ran her hand through her hair.

"Me too," Ford said. "I *really* wanted to dart the shit out of it and get a glance. Something. Anything! I was so close. Closer than I've ever been." She hesitated. "It was really stupid of me to chase whatever the fuck that was without proper backup."

"I would have done the same thing. I'm sorry about losing my temper. I can be a total bitch sometimes." She met Ford's gaze.

"I deserved it."

"No, you didn't," Soto admitted. "I don't like seeing you hurt."

"Yeah, that sucked."

"I also probably shouldn't have asked you if you were scared in front of your agents," Soto said as she took a seat on the other side of the desk.

"Totally okay."

"Were you? Scared?" Soto asked, hoping to get at what Ford may have seen as she dangled in the hole. The drone captured her experience in vivid detail, her curled fingers digging into the soil, the movement of her lips as she spoke to an unknown entity.

"*Un poquito.*" Ford demonstrated with her thumb and pointer finger that she held about an inch apart.

"Very nice pronunciation, Special Agent Ford." Ford smiled but avoided eye contact. "What is it?"

"I'm still a little on edge that's all."

"Why?" Soto asked, leaning in.

"We've been taking a lot of liberties with each other. It's not something I usually do. At all."

"Me either. I'm sorry if I—"

"No. That's not why…Don't be."

Soto nodded, glad in a roundabout way they had acknowledged the facts between them. "So, are you sure you didn't break anything?"

"Affirmative." Ford demonstrated by taking a deep breath and extending her leg out a couple of times. "Just sore." She winced.

"Here is something else that might help." She removed the lid of a small tin, offering it to Ford.

Ford took a lingering whiff. "What is it?"

"Homemade salve."

"Oh," Ford moaned as if she discovered the meaning of life. "That's your secret."

"My secret?"

"The way you smell." Ford took another long pull in through her nose. "It's delightful."

"Thank you."

Soto turned her focus to the lid in her hands, twisting the brushed metal over and around in her fingers. "When you deal with wild and sometimes out-of-control animals, you get the brunt of their inability to vocalize how they feel, which often times results in bruises, bumps, and sore muscles."

"Do you think I'm an out of control and wild animal?" Ford asked, her eyes closed as she inhaled the scent again.

"Sometimes," Soto whispered. She continued focusing on the lid between her fingers. "I didn't think the scent was that noticeable."

"Of course it's noticeable. Besides, it's my specialty to notice every little detail about someone's entire existence, about your existence."

"Right. You were briefed." She played off Ford's comment as a joke, for fear of acting upon her desire to show her every little detail. Restraint was difficult, especially as she watched Ford rub the salve between her long and slender fingers. "We sell it at the tasting room. It's rosemary and lavender with eucalyptus to cool...sore...muscles."

"Let me pay you for it."

"It's on me."

"Is it now?"

Soto swallowed hard. She would have to barricade herself in her room for fear of sleepwalking right into Ford's arms.

"Let me know if you need anything." She hesitated at the look on Ford's face. "What is it?"

"*Your* bruise."

"What about it?" Soto touched her cheekbone and headed for the mirror.

"It's nearly faded."

"I hadn't noticed." Soto realized she spoke the words as she made eye contact with Ford through the mirror. "I've been too wasted these past few days. It *is* much better." She held on to the small table in front of the mirror, closed her eyes for a moment, and headed toward the door without a look back. "Come on, girl," she said, carrying the basket of Ford's laundry.

The dog did not obey her command in the least. "Lex." She slapped a hand on her thigh. Ford let out a soft laugh as the dog took a deep and snorty breath and curled into a ball on the smallest bit of carpet sticking out from under the guest bed. "Fine. Lex, get me if she needs anything. Traitor."

CHAPTER TWENTY-ONE

Salve's Healing Properties

"Damn it." Clammy and cold unpleasantness did not make for sweet dreaming. Ford stirred awake. "Shit." Her gel pack had leaked. Her pajama bottoms were soaked through, leaving a wet spot on the bed. She removed the damp bottoms and hung them on a hook in the bathroom. Taking a hand towel back to bed, she placed it over the wet spot in hopes it would provide a sufficient barrier to keep her dry and warm so she could fall back asleep. After an hour, she was still tossing and turning. She wondered if another application of the magical salve would help soothe her into slumber.

She almost had the lid off when it slipped between her fingers, clattering loudly onto the wooden floor. "Shit." The tin clunked one way and the lid whirled another. "Really?" She found the lid quickly and knelt to find the missing tin, when she heard a gentle knock. "Come in." She grabbed at her side, which had worsened in the night.

"Everything okay in here?" Soto whispered from the door. Lexy was beside her.

"Sorry. Did I wake you?" Ford saw Soto wore boxer briefs and a loose-fitting T-shirt under a zip-up lightweight jacket. "No, no. I was taking Lexy out and figured I'd better check to see what the commotion was all about." She leaned into the doorjamb and squinted. "What are you doing down there?" "Being clumsy. I dropped the salve." She held up the lid as evidence. "I think it rolled that-a-way." She motioned under the bed.

"Do you want help?"

"I'd be forever in your debt." Ford groaned as she stood, acutely cognizant of her T-shirt and bikini briefs, thanks to Soto's lingering gaze. She leaned against the bed and crossed her arms.

"Well then. Come on, Lex, let's help her out." The dog led the way but stopped short. "Come on, girl." But Lexy held her ground. "Fine." Soto crouched next to the bed.

Ford couldn't look away from her wiggling backside in the air as she burrowed under.

"Uh." A muffle from down under. "Lexy, seriously. Help me out. I know we're not officially on the job, but come on. Find it."

The dog begrudgingly came to her aid, disappeared under the bed, returning with the tin in her mouth moments later. "Yea." Lexy offered it over, along with a couple of dust bunny–induced sneezes. Ford didn't try to hide her amusement watching Soto avoid the spray. "Thank you, girl." Soto laughed her standard melodious tune and then gave Lexy a kiss on the head. The dog was not amused and headed out, likely to Soto's room and her own dog bed.

Soto investigated the tin. "Oh, no."

"What is it?"

"It's full of dog slobber."

"That's okay."

"Let me clean this up for you." She pressed a couple of her fingers into the tin to wipe out the slobber. She studied her fingers and the slippery substance coating her fingertips. She rubbed them together.

"You might as well put it to good use." Ford hoisted herself up on the edge of the bed and revealed a scraped kneecap.

"It's a bit slobbery," Soto warned.

"It's okay. I'd hate to see that precious stuff go to waste."

Soto eyed the bruise on the agent's knee. "You poor thing." Ford watched her get to work. "That stuff…" Dark fingers danced and twirled around the peaks and valleys of the muscles on her leg. "…is amazing…"

"I use it on everything," Soto said as she took another dip of the salve. "Anywhere else?"

Ford lifted her T-shirt to under her breasts, excited and embarrassed as the points of her breasts stiffened against the shirt's fabric. She hoped the soft glow of the coming dawn was enough to mask that level of detail. It wasn't. Her masseuse stole a glance.

"Ford." Soto leaned in for a closer look at the bruise. "What the hell? That looks really bad." Shades of reds, purples, and variations thereof colored a large portion of Ford's right side. "Should we take you in?"

"No."

"You could have a broken rib," Soto pleaded. "Seriously, Ford."

"I didn't."

"Okay, well brace yourself," said Soto.

"For what?"

"It might hurt a bit at first," Soto whispered.

"I doubt…" Her body clenched at contact.

"Easy now." Soto was tentative at first, using the very tips of her fingers to touch her. Then inquisitive fingers took over to spread the salve. "You want to go ahead and breathe?" Soto asked. Ford followed orders, taking a long draw of air in through her nose and out through her mouth. "There you go. Why didn't you say something earlier? This must've killed when it happened."

"I have a high pain tolerance," she hissed. Other noises escaped Ford's lips without her permission. The cool eucalyptus did little to temper her heated skin. The feeling made its way down her torso, swirled in her belly, and settled between her legs. Another hiss between her teeth and she bit her bottom lip. She grabbed a fistful of the sheet. "You gonna make it?" Soto asked, lightening her touch. "I'm ticklish," Ford said. But she wasn't. Truth be told, it had been a while since a woman had touched her that way, let alone looked at her that way.

"Do you need me to stop?"

"No," Ford said with too much urgency. She placed her hand on Soto's forearm, stilling her. "Don't stop."

"Maybe lying down and getting comfortable would help?" Ford accepted the suggestion and lay back against the soft down pillow. "Well, now I can't reach you very well."

"Why don't you climb up?" Ford asked and groaned as she scooted over to make room, tapping the space next to her. Soto took the suggestion and climbed atop the elevated four-poster bed. She sat on her knees inches from Ford. She watched Soto struggle to avoid getting the oily substance on the cuffs of her jacket. With one hand coated in salve and the other holding the tin, she was having a hard time. "Here. Let me…"

"Oh…" Soto first held out her left arm and then the right while Ford pulled off the jacket. "Almost," said Soto, as they struggled to free her from her coat. "Much better." Soto used her wrist to shift her hair out of the way. "Is it better for you?" Soto asked. Ford nodded, and Soto's nimble fingers continued their magic, soothing her poor battered body. "We're so different, you and I," Soto mused.

"Very."

Ford observed their many differences: Soto's dark skin and mass of black hair, her full lips that she licked with the very tip of tongue repeatedly, when something needed her utmost attention. And the rise and fall of her chest and the swell of her breasts under the loose-fitting top. "Compared to you, anyone would appear pale and scrawny. You're pretty fucking stacked, Officer Soto." Ford chuckled. "Way more capable than myself in infinite ways," Ford whispered and continued focusing on Soto's fingers at work. "You're fearless and daring and all the things I'm not."

"You're fearless too, Special Agent," Soto said. "Chasing down the unknown, uncertain what you will find, but going after it anyway." Soto smiled. "And too trusting."

"What do you mean?"

"Here you are letting a near stranger touch you."

"You're hardly a stranger. We've met before," Ford said, shifting position as she grew uncomfortable, though not because she was in pain. Soto took Ford's hands into her own and kneaded her scratched and sliced fingers one by one.

"What else will you give me permission to—"

Ford grasped Soto's slippery hand in her own.

"Have you had enough?"

"Not quite."

"What else can I do for you?" Soto asked as she pushed her hair out of her eyes with the back of her other hand and set the tin on the bed.

"Let me thank you." Ford pulled Soto closer and placed a tender kiss upon her lips. Then another and another, letting each new one linger longer than the one before. Tasting her, testing her. "Is this okay?" Ford asked. She placed the tips of her fingers on either side of Soto's face, searching her eyes for her answer.

"Is this how you normally express gratitude, Winifred Ford?" Soto whispered against Ford's lips. She offered her response with kisses of her own, gentle licks, and teasing pecks at first, before she worked her tongue into Ford's accepting mouth.

Ford ran her hands along the lines of Soto's back, causing Soto to arch into her while cursing her appreciation. Ford cupped the back of Soto's neck and sifted through her soft black hair. "You taste of crisp air, absolutely exhilarating. I feel like I can breathe again."

She pulled Soto's small body onto her own. She was hot and wet against her stomach. The scent of her mingled with the lavender was intoxicating. Ford lifted Soto's loose white top, freeing full, heavy breasts, revealing dark and hard nipples, inches from her lips. "Is this okay?" Ford asked.

"You don't have to ask." Soto gasped when she took her voluptuous breasts into her greedy mouth, wildly and without hesitation, slurping and savoring and smacking her lips. Ford was giving her a tongue-lashing she would feel well into tomorrow.

Ford rolled them over, flipping Soto onto her back before crying out in pain at her overexertion both from the injury and the building at her core. She was okay and communicated so by hooking Soto's leg around her own hip, locking her in. Slowly at first she met Soto's center with her own. They shared cries of bliss at contact and found a rhythm that grew in intensity.

"Touch me," Soto said and she struggled about, working off her boxer briefs. "Please." Then a harsh metallic sound reverberated in the room. "Shit! What was that?"

Ford sat up on her knees and looked over the edge of the bed. "I think it was the...the tin."

"Fuck." Soto moaned. "This is a bad idea."

Ford didn't believe Soto's words because her eyes shifted between Ford's swollen lips and the points of her breasts. "Should we stop?" Ford asked while eying Soto's breasts, still within reach and still wet from her kisses.

"You *know* this isn't a good idea." Soto closed her eyes. She placed her hands on Ford's chest, pushing her away with the faintest of effort. "I won't be able to focus on anything if we do this," she whispered as she reached for her T-shirt.

"I won't be able to focus on anything if we don't," Ford said, working her own shirt back down her torso. "What should we do?"

"I don't know, but I know myself and—"

"I know you too," Ford said.

"No you don't, Ford. I'm more complex than words on paper. And so are you..." Soto held her head in her hands. "This case already has a microscope on it. We're supposed to be working together, not..." Soto searched for the words. She closed her eyes and reopened them, looking out the window to the light of the early morning. "It's not a good idea, that you and I... Damn it." Soto's hands were balled against her side.

"Hey. It's okay. Soto. Look at me," Ford said, turning her face so they made eye contact. "We got carried away. That's it." Soto closed her eyes while Ford caressed her neck. "That's all this is." Ford assured. "Okay?"

Soto nodded that she understood. "We'll talk tomorrow." She climbed off the bed and closed the door gently.

Again Ford felt cold and clammy, wet and alone, and in need. The cool feeling of the salve on her skin did nothing to temper the heat of their exchange.

CHAPTER TWENTY-TWO

Father Knows Best

It wasn't the smell of freshly brewed coffee that woke up Ford or the beam of sunlight that shone through linen curtains. It was a particularly lucid dream. She was outside in the employee courtyard at the Bureau back in DC. She was jumping rope—double Dutch, the kind with two ropes. She was high stepping to heaven, kicking her legs faster and faster, tearing it up and throwing her arms every which way.

Colleagues were watching, rooting her on, clapping their hands and swaying all about. "Winifreak! Winifreak!"

She came in second place, but thought she should have won. "I'm doing it in heels!" she protested. Then a bicycle rode past, a dog pedaling it forward. It came dangerously close to her and she naturally leaped out of the way. Ford jolted awake, her hand already on her chest trying to calm tremendous nervousness.

After last night's encounter, she wasn't sure what she should feel or how she should react when she would eventually, in a few short moments, see Soto again. She lay back down and closed her eyes, shifting from one side to the other, stirring up sweet scents that lingered about, commencing desire all over again.

The sound of dog nails clicked on hardwood. "Shit." Was Lexy's master with her? A soft thud on the other side. The dog was guarding her door again. Noticing the hour, she took a quick shower and threw on fresh clothes from her duffel. Black jeans, a silk blouse, her service weapon under her favorite blazer, heels in her hand, and a poker face.

She opened the door, startling Lexy, who got up as fast as a four-legged creature could on slippery hardwood. "Sorry, girl." She was glad to see the pup and felt calmer because of it. "Thank you for coming. I knew you wouldn't leave me to face her all by myself." The dog shook her head, and Ford knew for a fact this dog understood English.

She headed down the hallway, cognizant of the creaks from the old wooden floorboards. She stopped cold when she heard an unfamiliar voice emerge amongst the clattering of dishes and the smell of coffee. A male voice with a thick Spanish accent. It had to be the father, Juan Soto.

She tiptoed back to the top of the stairs, surprised that Lexy stayed with her instead of heading into the kitchen. She smiled when she heard how Soto talked to her father. It was a different voice about an octave higher than Ford was used to, a voice most likely reserved for him.

"Doesn't it make sense? How it's getting around the preserve quickly and undetected?"

"Sort of, *mija*."

Someone poured a cup of coffee and was stirring in sugar or cream. It smelled like a dark roast and it was making Ford's mouth water.

"There would have to be several of them connected somehow under a large part of the preserve and under the water table," he continued. "I'm not sure the reservoir was built like that. Besides, the wells were capped."

"All of them?"

"Supposedly. And what wasn't likely crumbled into nonexistence. Those types of wells back then wouldn't have lasted more than fifty years," he added.

"Except for the one we found," Soto said.

"If it is indeed a well and not a random sinkhole. But you said it was covered with a plank of wood?"

"From what I was able to see. I haven't been on location yet. *Papá* where can I find out more about the reservoir, how it was built and its early years prior to its federal status?"

"The historical society should have the records on the area, its inception, maps, or at least know where to point you."

"Fantastic."

"*Andele, mija.* I need to go meet Grace at the event space for the walk-through. She's still nervous about it," he said.

Ford felt a tinge of guilt at this statement.

"Should she be?"

"No. Everything is in place. I'm looking forward to hosting, aren't you?"

"Yeah. It will be fun."

"How are you getting along with the FBI agent?"

Ford considered making her entrance.

"Better."

"Is she still pushing herself around?"

"Not anymore. I got her under control."

Ford grinned at this.

"Besides, she's…She's not pushy. She just has a unique way of expressing herself. And a way about her that comes across abrasive, but isn't really once you get to know her."

"That's not what I heard," he said.

"In any case, be quiet. She's right upstairs."

"*¿Está bien?*"

"*¡Papá!* It's not like that. She got hurt last night on patrol and ran out of ice at the preserve. Well, she had three pieces of ice, which wasn't much for how banged up she was. I already told you."

"Oh, she's the one who fell down into the hole?"

"Yes. I already told you that too, *Papá.*"

Ford loved the way Soto's breath hitched in places as she tried to explain herself.

"*Cuidado, mija.*"

"*Por qué?*"

"*Por qué* it's a small town and people talk."

"I don't know what the hell they are going to talk about. Besides, no one knows she's here except me, you, and Lexy. And she's not talkin'."

"And her colleagues I imagine?"

"And her colleagues," Soto whispered.

"Just be careful, *mija*."

"Oh my God, *Papá*. It's not like that. She was sleeping in this crappy cot at the preserve."

"That's dedication."

"She is very dedicated."

"And why not go back to a hotel?"

"It was past midnight when it happened. Besides, we're three miles from there and we have six rooms."

"Sure. Sure."

"I'm a professional working on a case with her. It's nothing like that."

"Uh-huh."

At that, Ford took the cue to cease her eavesdropping and make her way down the stairs, putting on her heels on the way. "Good morning," she said as she entered the room, not sure what to expect, but having the upper hand on the conversation. She acknowledged both of the Sotos with a single smile. Both of them froze with their coffee mugs inches from their lips.

"*Papá*, this is Special Agent Winifred Ford."

"So this is what all the fuss was about?" he asked with a grin.

"¡*Papá*!"

Ford laughed along with Soto's father. Thoroughly enjoying watching Soto flounder and fume.

"Good morning, Special Agent Ford. I'm Juan Soto." He had a mustache as thick as his accent, and he had the same small dimple in his chin as Soto did, though he was much taller than her. He was dressed for work on the vineyard—white straw hat, a chambray shirt, blue jeans with leather gloves in his back pocket, and dusty cowboy boots.

"A pleasure, sir. Thank you for your hospitality," Ford said as she shook his hand.

"Okay, *Papá*, I'm going to give her a ride back to the preserve." She reached for keys from a dish on the counter.

"That's not necessary. I called one of my guys," Ford said.

"What? You didn't need to do that."

"You've done enough already, Officer Soto. Really."

"Your clothes are still in the dryer. Sorry I didn't start them until this morning," Soto said, but avoided direct eye contact.

"Totally fine. Thank you again," Ford said and kept her focus on the kitchen counter.

"I'll bring them with me this afternoon." She gave her a thumbs-up. "Coffee? Black?" Ford nodded and Soto handed her a mug of pure joy.

"Thank you."

Juan Soto said settled his hat on his head. "A pleasure to meet you, Special Agent Ford."

"Likewise, sir," Ford said before she retreated through the house and toward the door, then backtracking, remembering she needed to tell Soto one thing. Until...

"*Ey, mija.*"

"What?"

"*Tú.*"

"We're working together, that's it," her voice even higher than before.

"*No fue lo que me pareció.*"

"I'm not sure what you *think* you saw. But it would take a pretty big..." She was flustered. "...a big...thing for me to push aside my professional morals."

"Sorry...to interrupt," Ford said, inciting that guilty look on their faces yet again. "But we have a change in schedule." She tapped the phone held in the palm of her hand. "Marnie is available earlier than expected."

"When?"

"This afternoon."

"Great. I'll meet you in a couple of hours. We'll ride over together."

"*Perfecto. Y much gusto señor. Buena suerte con la recaudación de fondos.*"

"*Gracias.* I hope we raise a lot of money too and that you will join us for the event?"

"I will if I can."

Soto's head bopped back and forth between her father and Ford at their exchange. "Let me walk you out this time." Both Soto and Lexy accompanied Ford to the front door. "What the fuck was that?"

"*Hablo español,*" Ford said quietly. As they walked side by side toward the door, she whispered in her ear, "*perfectamente.* Seven languages to be exact."

"What? Seven? Wait." Soto grabbed Ford's shoulder, arresting her movements. "So you understood..." Soto edged her fingers down the length of Ford's arm finding her fingers.

"*Todo. Tout.* Everything," Ford said, wiggling her eyebrows up and down, but Soto wiped that cocky look right off her face when she snaked her arms inside her blazer and along her stomach, backing her up little by little. "Soto?" Ford asked with her back against the door. "What are you doing?"

"I don't know." And she placed a kiss on Ford's lips.

"Yes, you do," Ford said, dropping her bag, and placing her free hand against Soto's chest, the other holding the hot mug of coffee away from their frenzied bodies. "Not three hours ago *you* were the one who said this—"

"I know what I said," Soto said against Ford's lips, kissing her, coaxing her. "But your mind is *so* sexy and your body, I want it, I want you..."

Ford hadn't the willpower to push her away, especially because Soto's fingers were everywhere, encouraging her, telling her something different than what was communicated earlier.

She pushed her tongue into Soto's hot mouth, inhaling her. "God you taste..." She pulled Soto against her. "Wait, no." She pushed her away. "Are you listening to me?"

Soto's subtle moaning into her lips and gentle grind against her body nearly brought Ford to her knees. *Clank!* She had dropped her mug of coffee!

"*Mija,* are you okay?" It sounded like her father was on his way to investigate.

"Fuck." And finally the crunching of gravel. "My ride." Ford pushed Soto away gently and opened the door, turning to get one last look. She saw Soto's fingertips on either side of her face, shocked at what she had done, for letting it go so far. Ford motioned to the spilled coffee. "Good luck explaining this to your Papa."

CHAPTER TWENTY-THREE

Chicken Dinner Road

Marnie Starr. The girl with the neon green backpack lived on Chicken Dinner Road. Ford didn't believe it until they turned left onto it from Highway 55.

The girl had bloodshot eyes, and a pungent combination of marijuana and cigarettes emanated from her entire being. Ford had wasted enough time with small talk, especially after they had to wait nearly two hours for both of Marnie's parents to arrive home from work.

"Marnie, why didn't you speak up? Why did you let that Larissa bitch steamroll you?" The girl's brows knitted together in unison with Soto's.

"Let's take a step back," Soto interjected. "Marnie, do you have any questions for Special Agent Ford and me before we start?"

"So you're with the FBI, or you both are with the FBI?" She wagged a finger between the two women.

"Special Agent Ford is with the FBI, Paranormal Investigations."

"Rad. So like the X-Flies?"

"Exactly."

"And you?" She wagged her finger toward Soto.

"And I'm with Washington State Fish and Wildlife."

"Washington like DC?"

"No, like Seattle. Like Nirvana, coffee, and rain."

"Oh, my God. Isn't weed, like, totally legal there?"

Soto laughed at her comment. "Yes, it is."

"That's lit."

Ford's ears perked at her choice of words.

"You're so lucky," Marnie gushed.

"She's totes lucky," Ford replied and shrugged her shoulders at her own word choice and the corresponding teasing look Soto gave her.

Marnie's attention went to Lexy. "What about her?"

"You can pet her." Soto unclipped Lexy's leash to the girl's delight. "This is Lexy. She's my partner."

The dog wagged her tail furiously and bobbed her head up and down. She rolled on the ground clearly enjoying the free tummy scratches.

"She's so cute! Do you think she knows she's cute?" Marnie patted the dog's head.

"She knows." Soto folded Lexy's leash in her hands.

"I wish I had a dog." The girl was sitting on the floor practically wrestling with Lexy. She asked Soto numerous dog-related questions that spanned grooming, dog clothes, and toys.

"Look," Ford said. She was close to the end of her rope. "We need to get going here. The sooner you can help us, the sooner you can go back to smoking weed and getting on with your life, got it? Maybe after this your dad can get you a puppy, huh?" Her comment got her Soto's elbow to her ribs and dangerously close to her injury. She winced and gave Soto a stern look and rubbed her side. Soto mouthed "sorry," while trying to hold in her amusement.

Ford leaned toward the girl. "Marnie, I am deeply sorry you have to relive the horrible experience. We're sorry we're here talking to you because that Larissa bitch got in the middle of everything." The girl flipped a package of rolling papers from hand to hand, seemingly uninterested in what Ford had to say. "Believe it or not," Ford continued, "you are one of only a handful of eyewitnesses. Despite what you might think, you are extremely important to us and to this case."

"I am?"

"Important as fuck, and I promise you, after it's said and done, you will feel loads better. You will be the town shero."

This got a smile from her. "I'll do my best to remember everything." She took a big breath. Turning to Soto she said, "Can I still pet her?"

"Of course. For as long as you want." Soto's fierce tracker turned therapy dog put her head in the girl's lap and seemed overjoyed at the attention.

"She's so sweet." Marnie gave Lex another kiss.

"She's a real peach," Ford agreed. "Now let's started. What were you doing at the lake?"

"Hanging out. We legit wanted to see how far away the hole was, you know from the new trail project? I collect rocks and wanted to see if there were any down there. We seriously weren't going to skip Mr. Barnett's class. We got sidetracked from rock collecting and smoking weed. Then we heard the whispering sounds. The boys took off one way and I went the other."

"Why didn't you go together?"

"They took off like the idiots they are. I went to catch up, but I heard a noise coming from another direction so I followed it. Have you been out there, Special Agent Ford?"

"I have."

"Do you like it?"

"It's nice."

"That's like an understatement," she said. Ford smiled at her honesty. "The trees are so green in the summer at the spot we like to hang out at. We call it Oz." She leaned in and gave Lexy her thirtieth kiss.

"Why Oz?" Ford forced herself to ask, attempting a more Soto-esque approach to working with people.

"Because the sun shines through the trees and makes the whole place look like this vivid-ass green, especially after smoking primo chronic."

"You know that possessing marijuana is illegal, right? A federal offense," Ford said.

"Am I in trouble for that?"

Both Marnie and Soto turned abruptly to see Ford's response.

"Of course not. Just be careful. There are some assholes around here. If anyone gives you a hard time, call me." Ford handed over her card.

"Oh my God. Thank you. I will and I'm like legit careful. Oh!" Marnie fished something from her pocket. "For you. A cool rock. I think it's an agate. It can be your lucky rock if you want."

"Fair trade." Ford rolled the stone between her fingers and put it in her pocket. "Shall we get back on track?"

"Okay." Marnie rubbed her eyes.

"I want you to take a moment and think about the answer to my next question before responding." Marnie opened her mouth, and closed it. "What did you feel when you were out there?"

Marnie ran her hands through the fur on Lexy's back and pulled her tail gently to follow through.

"I felt blood. And it wasn't because I walked right through it and didn't notice until I tripped over a fucking branch and got it all over me. I had to throw away all of my clothes. Fucking nasty. I felt it because I had this accident when I was a kid, like eight or something. Me and my mom and my sister went into the Kings Super Thrift, downtown, you know? I wanted to stay in the car and finish reading my book, *Too Much Magic*, even though it was way hot in there. I got a bloody nose and it bled for, no joke, over an hour. I had nothing but my shirt to stop the bleeding after I had used the entire box of Kleenex. It was everywhere, all over my face and on my shirt and shit. I almost passed out by the time they were done shopping. I can still see the looks on their faces to this day. We could smell the blood in the car for days and years after, whenever it got hot in there."

"What else Marnie?"

"My nose started bleeding, right there on the preserve, when I, when I found it and it kept bleeding, as bad as it did that day in the car, and I thought I was going to die. I kept thinking about my friends and my dad, school."

Ford felt bad for the girl, knowing firsthand the emotional memories the whispering evoked.

Marnie turned to Soto and asked, "Officer Daya, do animals think about things like that before they die?"

Soto settled her brown eyes upon her dog and she lowered her head and her voice as she spoke. "I like to think that before an animal passes, they relive every special part of their life. They remember their owners, their toys, laying in a patch of sun, their pals at the park, and running around in crazy circles when their people come home from being away. And they hold onto those memories when they close their eyes for the very last time."

Soto's words nearly moved Ford to tears, even though she had never had a pet before, let alone lost one. She gave Soto a smile and a nod and got one in return. "They're only with us for a short time, aren't they?" Marnie mused.

"They sure are."

"Special Agent Ford?"

"Yes."

Ford broke eye contact with Soto's soft brown eyes and the pouty pink lips she had kissed earlier that morning and had teased relentlessly the night before.

"Do you think the deer thought about Oz and her babies and berries and stuff before she died?"

"I have no doubt," Ford said, noticing the poor kid was working hard to hold back tears of her own.

"What else did you notice, Marnie?" Soto asked. "When did you feel that something was strange?"

Ford didn't think the girl was going to answer.

"Take your time," Soto coaxed.

"Honestly, I felt something weird before we actually heard the strange sounds. When I was looking for rocks inside the pit by the trail opening, Forrest was being stupid and rolled a huge rock down into it. A sound came out of the ground, like when

my dad turns on the irrigation. It kind of like sprays at first."
The girl's voice got softer. "I smelled an old smell, like opening
a room that was closed for too long, kind of like going into
my grandma's basement or something. I thought it was just the
weed, like maybe we accidently scored synthetic weed. I don't
know. It was hot and I was really thirsty."

Her words sent Ford flashbacking to wandering through the
wilderness in Oregon, sick, hearing things and being in jail.

"Then we got bored doing that, so we rolled a joint, and
that's when I heard whispering noises. We all thought it was a
hurt animal which is why…" She trailed off and started sniffling.
Her nose grew red. She wiped it with the sleeve of her flannel
shirt.

"It's okay, Marnie," Ford assured her. She pulled tissues from
her bag and handed them to her.

"When I followed the sound under the trees, that
whispering got louder and echoed everywhere. Like that part
at the beginning of a movie where they show off how rad the
speakers are?" Ford gave Marnie the courtesy of her patience
as the girl rolled herself a smoke and lit it. "I was the one who
found it." She blew at the tip of the cigarette. It burned a red
amber and ash flew everywhere and floated around them. "The
deer's insides were all fucked up. It was a mess of guts and blood
and fur. Its stomach was torn out and teeth were everywhere.
Its eyes. It was still twitching and blinking. It fucking freaked
me out."

"We've all been scared like that, Marnie," Ford said.

"But I thought I was a stronger person than that."

"Marnie, strength doesn't have anything to do with it. Being
scared means you're real, you're alive, and that you feel things,"
Ford said. "And there's nothing wrong with that."

"There isn't?" Marnie took another drag.

"Nothing at all. What else?"

"You're not going to believe me." She exhaled a white cloud
of smoke.

"Try me. X-Files, remember?" Ford's comment got a
chuckle from her.

"It was another deer that killed it."

Ford looked over to see confusion on Soto's face that likely mirrored her own.

"I can't, like, prove it. The only thing I know for sure is there were two deer at one point. One of them was dead and the other deer, or thing that I saw, was fucked up, like deranged or something. It reminded me of that movie *28 Days Later*. Have you seen that movie with those like superfast jolty-ass zombies?" Her pupils dilated as if she were reliving the moment in real time.

She took a long drag of her smoke and blew into the air. "Its head was burrowed inside the stomach of the other one and it was covered in blood. In all honesty, I didn't see very much of it to know for sure that it was another deer because it disappeared into a hole in the ground all contorted and twisted. It was really fucking fast and dark, misty kind of. I remember red eyes and it smelling disgusting and making me dizzy." She took another long drag before she said, "It was a shape-shifter, Special Agent Ford. Because it said things to me, like it knew my name and was talking to me. That's why I don't think it could have been a possessed animal." She started shaking.

"What else?"

"Forrest said I was talking all weird. Like I was saying I was trapped and couldn't see. Then my fucking nose started bleeding. Like I was in that car all over again when I was little." She had tears in her eyes. "I realize my story doesn't sound much different than the shit Larissa was spreading, but it's the truth." Fat tears fell from her cheeks. She put out her cigarette, and the ashtray rattled as she smudged it out. "I knew you wouldn't believe me."

"I believe you, Marnie. I promise I do." Ford had no other choice. The writing was on the wall, written with the blood of mauled wildlife.

"We both believe you," Soto added.

"You do?" She sounded as though a weight had been lifted. "Because Forrest and Kristoff didn't see what I saw. They have no fucking clue, and they're being total dicks about it." She was getting it all out. "Everyone is being a dick about it."

"Fuck them," Ford said.

Marnie laughed and smiled through tears, wiping them from her face. Even Lexy got up and danced about. "So do you think there's a shape-shifter creature living at the lake?"

"Absolutely," Ford said. "I've spent my entire career tracking down the paranormal. This isn't anything I haven't encountered before."

"And I've seen destruction caused at the hands of an introduced species," Soto added. "I've seen habitats ravaged and destruction you wouldn't believe."

"And I've seen things I can't explain to this day or voice without sounding bat-shit crazy," Ford said.

"And I have spent my career trying to help animals live a peaceful life despite man-made horrors, chemical spills, and pollution that can permanently alter their physiologies," Soto said.

Ford thought about countering again, but realized now was not the time to try to get Soto to entertain the idea that they weren't up against anything man-made.

"So, what are you going to do about it?" Marnie asked.

"Try to track it and trap it," Soto replied.

"Is that why Lexy is here? To help you find it or something?" Her ears perked at the sound of her name.

"Sure is, kid," said Soto.

"But won't she freak out too?"

Soto straightened the dog's collar. "Not if her life depended on it."

CHAPTER TWENTY-FOUR

Directionally Challenged

Soto and Ford were parked driver window to driver window. One faced east toward logic and order. The other faced west, toward the seemingly impossible.

"Do you really think it's rabies?" Ford asked. "That was the first thing we tested for and nothing was confirmed."

"I want it tested again."

"For what?"

"A mutation. Marnie clearly said it was a possessed and deranged animal that had its head burrowed into a bloody carcass with—"

"Is that how rabies works? Turns a wild animal into a crazed zombie from *28 Days Later*?"

"No. But the preserve is home to animals that have those tendencies." Soto counted the possibilities on her fingers. "Foxes, coyotes, badgers, mountain lions. If they were introduced to a chemical of some type, it could seriously affect their physiologies. Marnie felt a mist release from the trail pit. Isn't it obvious that this is perhaps a chemical reaction?"

"Nothing is obvious to me in my line of work, Soto. And we won't be able to rule out—"

"Or confirm anything until the pathologist can run the tests from the remains of Norma Jean again and the other mutilated animals. In the meantime, a mutated form of rabies is the only rational explanation I can think of," Soto said with finality.

"God. That word!" Ford gripped her steering wheel.

"What word?" Soto said as she threw her arm in the air and her head back against the seat a little too hard startling Lexy and doing nothing to help a building ache in her neck.

"Rational. Reasonable. Logical. It's so very limiting. It hinders creativity and exploration and narrows possibility. How can you think that way?"

"Because that's how I think." She had never had a more complex conversation with someone where she had to defend her most basic beliefs.

"Well, you need to think differently."

"Why is that all on me? How about instead of debunking every one of my theories, you tell me what you think we're after?" Soto yelled as she loosened the top button of her uniform.

"I can name five explanations off the top of my head," Ford said calmly.

"Such as?"

"The Swamp Ape for starters."

"Come again?"

"A Swamp Ape. How can you not know what a Swamp Ape is?"

"Because I don't encounter them regularly in my line of work." She pinched the bridge of her nose.

"It's a variation of Bigfoot. It's about eight feet tall? Three hundred pounds? Hence the sightings of the massive creature with red eyes. It has a horrifying stench and it's said to roll itself in the blood of animals in an effort to mask itself."

"Are you serious?" She worked overtime to avoid laughing manically at this particular theory. "Because I thought you were there when we learned that Larissa was making shit up."

"I have a case file where I documented an instance if you need to see the proof, Officer Soto," Ford said through clenched teeth.

"Don't bother," she said as she watched a few cars speed by, then slow considerably, when they saw the police lights atop her vehicle. "Oh, my God!"

"What?"

"Of course. A Cephalopod."

"A squid?"

"A *giant* squid." Soto opened her arms to allude to its size.

"Architeuthis? Really?"

"I'm trying to think outside the box. Think about it. We've only recently discovered they can edit their own genes and adapt to any environment. And it validates Marnie's account of the thing morphing before her eyes and disappearing."

"Sure. Okay. So tell me, do you think it's a new giant squid or the same giant squid from nine years ago that has migrated hundreds of miles using an underground network of tunnels that we don't even know exist?"

"What the hell else do you got?" Soto asked as she popped a ginger chew in her mouth taking a bit of paper with her. She spit it out onto the floor of the cab.

"Ogopogo."

"Which is?"

"The Native American Loch Ness, basically. A large sea serpent that can grow to be between forty and fifty feet long. There have been sightings in the Columbia River, which feeds into the Snake and into the Boise River that fills Lake Lowell."

Soto groaned. "Is this another creature that bathes itself in blood?"

"And mauls animals and can traverse land."

"You're not kidding are you?"

"There's Wally, and Willy, the Beast of Busco. I could go on and you rolling your eyes doesn't negate the fact that some things simply can't be placed into a neat little box with a bow on the top."

"I've seen my fair share of unexplained things, and ninety percent of the time it's human involvement."

"And the other ten percent is my field of expertise."

"I don't have the words."

"Sure you do." Ford took off her shades, forcing eye contact. "I can take it." She reached over and tapped Soto's elbow. "Tell me."

"I don't understand how someone with your education and your level of intelligence can believe in this sort of stuff? There is no science to prove any of it. Look, I get it. This is your world. But again I'm not—"

"You're not there yet. Got it. And while you're working your way toward wherever it is you need to be, my intelligence has nothing to do with it. And second, science isn't always the be-all end-all answer. Can you prove God?"

"That's different."

"How so?" she asked, but Soto didn't have a response. "God isn't any different than Ogopogo. Absolutely no different. It's something someone believes in that they can't prove, and they choose to believe regardless of the facts."

"But—"

"What about that thing between you and Lex."

"What do you mean?"

"I've seen you both communicate with a look, a glance, no words or commands exchanged."

She turned to see her dog licking at something in the wind. "We'll go home soon, girl." Lexy snorted and curled herself into a ball.

"Case in point, Soto."

"But what about eyewitness accounts? The memories from their past. Do those creatures have the ability to stir up those types of emotions?"

"Can a cephalopod stir up those types of emotions?" Ford countered. "Can they whisper sweet nothings into your ear? Can a rabid deer talk to people?"

"There's an explanation for that too."

"Such as?"

"It could be a hidden sedimentary basin," Soto offered.

"Under Lake Lowell in Caldwell, Idaho? A pocket of natural gas?" Ford held up her hand to signal she wasn't done. "If it were that, everyone would be dead or close to dead from the poisoning."

"Then trauma. Seeing a mutilated animal can be traumatic especially if you weren't expecting it. I've seen it with injured hunters. It's shock. That's all it is."

"I happen to think that Marnie and Mrs. Bird Watcher reacted to the mist-like substance because it's the creature's defense mechanism," Ford countered.

"But it's stuff from their memories," Soto insisted. "It's not telling them anything. Marnie remembered a traumatic bloody nose, right?" Ford gave her a nod. "Mrs. Richards relived Wilbur's heart attack."

"Yes, but why would they report saying the same things. 'Can't breathe. Trapped.' And why didn't it affect Mr. Richards in the same way?"

"Hell. I don't know, Ford. Maybe it was his ginger tea for all I know. But there is a logical—"

Ford startled her when she slammed her hand on the steering wheel.

"A logical explanation for that too!" Soto shouted. She took a breath and said, "You heard how stubborn Mr. Richards is. It takes a lot to put yourself out there and admit that you're hearing things." Soto pushed it further, adding, "What did you hear when you encountered it all those years ago?"

"I heard and I saw and I said a lot of fucked-up shit," Ford admitted. Her entire body seemed to deflate and her expression darkened.

"What did you hear last night? I saw you in the video the drone captured," Soto said more emphatically this time. "You were talking. What were you saying?" Soto wished she could see Ford's expressive eyes, the ones that told her things that her words did not, but Ford kept her sunglasses on.

"I wish I could remember."

"Do you remember what you felt?"

Her response was to pick up her phone and ignore her.

Soto exited her truck making her way to Ford's passenger door.

"What are you doing?" Ford asked.

"Let me in," Soto said. "Please."

Ford relented and unlocked the doors. Soto took hold of Ford's phone, placing it on the dash with a thud, though Ford quickly found another distraction, a paper clip she immediately began unfolding. "Fine with me if you don't want to talk right this minute. I have all the time in the world, but you have, what, four more days?"

Ford threw the mangled paperclip in the backseat. "Memories and feelings and stuff...of my mom, when I found her."

"Damn."

"I know. It's fucking dark shit and it's not easy to talk about at a moment's notice," Ford said, her teeth gritted as she spoke.

"Will you look at me?" Soto asked. "Please?" Ford turned her way. "Preferably without your sunglasses." Ford followed orders. "Why didn't you say anything last night?"

"I wanted to hear what Marnie said before I revealed that part to you. I wasn't ready."

"You need to trust me."

"I'm trying."

"But?"

"It's almost too much that you look at me the way that you do."

"How do I look at you?" Soto asked. She had to know what impression she had been giving off aside from straight-up lust.

"Like that. Like what you're doing right now," Ford said as she reached out of the open window, palming the air as if trying to catch the right words. "Like I'm not of this planet? Like what I'm saying is so farfetched you can't comprehend. Like last night when—"

"I promise you that is not what I think. You're reading me all wrong. I'm trying to have an open mind. I want to believe, okay.

I'm not there yet and you could extend me the same courtesy by opening your mind to the realm of rational thinking."

"I'll try." Ford gripped the steering wheel with both hands and pretended to bang her head against it several times. "We're not going to solve this sitting around. I can think of a hundred other things we could be doing right now, like tearing up that fucking hole I nearly fell down. I want to know what the hell is down there."

"I know. Me too." Soto pulled her phone out and typed a text message. "We need to bring everyone together—the volunteers, Grace, experts I think can help us. But I need the rest of the afternoon to do that. Is that okay timewise?"

"Yes, that's fine. I got to make some calls."

"As head of intel, you need to take point on the historical society. I texted you the name and number." Ford grabbed her vibrating phone from the dash. "So put on your Little Miss Manners hat because they are elderly volunteers that tend to talk. A lot." Soto wanted to laugh at the look Ford gave her, but she didn't want to make Ford feel bad about lacking patience. "Is it that hard?" Ford lingered a look at her before putting her shades back on. "So we good?"

Soto got out of Ford's rental, bent over and leaned through the driver's side window. She sensed that Ford wanted to talk about the night before, but now was not the time. The case needed her focus. Besides, she wasn't ready to acknowledge it, because for the first time since the start of the investigation, a feeling crept into her mind that traveled through her rational thoughts—knocking them down like a set of strategically arranged dominos and she didn't want to acknowledge that either.

Instead she did what she did the last time she didn't want to talk about it. She leaned in and offered several kisses, leaving Ford flushed. "I promise we will talk."

"Roger that."

"Take photos of whatever maps you can get your hands on. If they won't give them to you, pull the FBI agent card," Soto instructed.

Ford laughed at her comment. "You know, I actually have an FBI agent card."

"I know. So use it."

"Affirmative."

"Let's regroup tomorrow."

"Copy."

The truck rumbled to life. "I love it when you talk all FBI agent–like," she called to Ford over the engine. Ford's face flushed as Soto and Lexy rolled away.

CHAPTER TWENTY-FIVE

There Were Never Such Devoted Sisters

Finally in her car after spending half the day at the historical society, Ford pulled out her phone to call Soto to report her findings. She stared at the newly programmed name and ran her thumb over the glossy screen. She wondered what feelings were holding Soto hostage from talking about what had happened that night.

But the more she analyzed her own feelings, it *was* frightening to acknowledge that for her, it was more than getting carried away. She respected Soto, her abilities, her intuition, her dedication. She cared about her more than she should care for someone she'd only known for two weeks. Was Soto avoiding talking about it to avoid hurting her feelings, so things didn't get weird while they worked the case? The case needed their utmost concentration. Likely, more like hopefully, that's what this was all about for Soto. Then why did she keep kissing her? Ford wanted to know. She needed to know! But Soto needed time, but time was running out! She sighed and pressed dial. She got Soto on the third ring. "Did you know that Caldwell was quite the happening place during Prohibition?"

"Uh-huh," Soto replied. She was sucking on something, likely a ginger chew.

"In fact, during the height of it there were two sisters, Anna Margaret and Mary O'Gara, who made their way here from across the pond in County Cork Ireland. Home of the Blarney Stone, if ye didn't know," she said in her best Irish accent.

Soto laughed.

"So, these sisters settled in Caldwell, Idaho, of all places and opened a hotel right down the road from the historical society. They had a booming business as they catered to the town's timber workers."

"Where is this going?"

"Patience," Ford said. "So these sisters operated an establishment, a restaurant and rooming house that was well-known for bootlegging. As you can imagine, raids were conducted often. One day the authorities stopped by unannounced, as they so often do in stories like this. And the sisters, in their quick thinking, poured their precious liquid into the hotel's several bedpans. They kept a lot of them on hand for just that purpose. And at the last moment, with the authorities at their doorstep, and a handful more bottles to hide, the brilliant sisters hid the rest under their voluminous hoop skirts. They held their heads high, laughing inside I imagine, and watched the authorities as they searched their premises but found nothing at all."

"Fascinating," Soto said in way that didn't convey actual fascination.

"True story. Look it up."

"I will. But, can we back up? How does this relate to anything?"

Ford responded slowly, enunciating each word. "Guess how the sisters got their contraband?"

"I haven't the slightest."

"Waterways!" Ford shouted.

"Wait, what?"

"The historian thinks their goods were transported from Boise via the Boise River to Caldwell and then Lake Lowell."

"Holy shit!"

"And guess how the sisters collected their goods from the river undetected?"

"Wells? Tell me wells!"

"Wells," Ford confirmed.

"I knew it! How? Oh my God, Lexy. Did you hear that?"

Ford waited for Soto to finish celebrating with Lexy, and then said, "There were approximately thirty or so wells that were active in Lake Lowell's early days, prior to it being an actual reservoir. They dried up quickly or crumbled into the ground. They weren't exactly made to last. The ones that did last were capped in the sixties, but not all of them. They couldn't cap the ones they didn't know about."

"How many do they think are still uncapped?"

"About twelve or so, and guess where?"

"Within a certain perimeter of the kill sites."

"God, you're good."

"I am, aren't I?" Soto whispered.

"Very good," Ford responded.

"And tell me you got photos or maps or something we can use to help us plan our next step."

"No," Ford said. She could feel Soto's sigh over the cellular waves. "Not from them. However, we're expecting a digital file from the home office with schematics and work plans from the Army Corps of Engineers that capped the original wells. That should help us out tremendously."

"Good girl," Soto said. Ford squeezed her legs together at the playful name.

"Are you smiling?"

"A big toothy grin," Soto reported. "We both are, aren't we Lex?"

"Wasn't that lucky that I happened to take a tumble down one of them?"

"Pretty fucking lucky."

"And it only took a scraped-to-shit knee and…" Her mind wandered to Soto's soft kisses and tender touch. "…and a few bruised ribs." Ford shifted in her seat thinking about the other parts of that night—in between Soto's legs, grinding into her and making her whimper and licking Soto's soft lips and when she had her in her mouth….

"What are you thinking, Ford?"

"What do you mean?"

"I mean, how are you on time?" Soto said a little too quickly. "Did you make all the calls you needed to?

"Oh," Ford failed to hide a nervous laugh. "I feel okay. I got myself a couple more days in case things go awry. If we can wrap this up in five days, I'll be happy."

"Lex and I will do everything we can to help. Everyone is meeting at seven at the preserve. We'll tell our volunteers that Larissa was full of shit and we're tracking a marine creature or rabid animals who can mess with your mind and may or may not traverse the preserve via an old underground network of long forgotten prohibition wells."

"Easy-peasy," Ford said with a laugh.

"Aside from that, are you feeling better after last night?" Soto asked, her tone boarding on whispering. "Your injuries?"

"Almost back to my old self." Ford absentmindedly rubbed her lips, feeling Soto's kisses on them.

"I'm glad. If you need anything at all …"

Like more salve, she thought.

"Please let me know."

"You'll be the first person I ask."

CHAPTER TWENTY-SIX

Everyone's an Expert

Over fifty people gathered in the preserve's small theater, including volunteer trackers and their dogs, the special agents, Executive Director Jewell, her staff naturalists, as well as other experts Soto had identified. And of course, the center's stuffed birds, fish, mammals, and other taxidermy stood watch, as if to take witness of the plan to trap the terror reigning over their preserve. After the initial shock of learning Larissa's stories were works of fiction, the group wrapped their minds around the pivoting plans based on the new information about the possible rum-running sisters.

"What a find!" Marcus Johnson said. Marcus was a naturalist and history buff who proved to be the investigators' best advocate. "This changes everything." The comment garnered a round of nods. "Wells! That makes total sense."

"Also explains why my dogs keep losing the scent," said Margo Crawly. "When we think we may have something, it disappears into thin air leaving my poor pups wanting to dig up the ground."

"Can we please not forget that the presumed locations are peppered around the ever-delicate sage rehabilitation project? I can't stress enough how carefully planned this needs to be," Grace Jewell added, making sure everyone knew that this investigation was a major pain in her ass.

"I'm sorry," a particularly negative, headstrong old naturalist named Gary Gladd interjected. "I find it hard to believe that these wells have been here all these years and this is the first we've seen or heard of them. Do you know how many restoration projects we've worked on with no indication that they exist? Then out of the blue *she* falls down into one of them?" He motioned to Ford, who nonchalantly sipped a cup of coffee while scrolling through something on her phone.

Soto defended Ford. "We don't know anything with—"

"One hundred percent certainty. Yes. Yes. Got it, Officer Soto," Gary said, sitting down and folding his arms.

Soto ran her hand atop Lexy's fluffy head to remind herself to remain patient with the skeptic. "Look, these plans are old, but my assumption is they're valid. These are all we have to go from. Our big break." She motioned to the center's repurposed theater screen. Heads turned to study the photos, old maps, and schematics outlining a supposed underground network of waterways and tunnels.

"Come on. A prohibition story about two sisters? *Pft!* It sounds extremely far-fetched if you ask me. It could be a random sinkhole for all we know," Gary argued.

"Why wouldn't it be real?" Marcus rebutted. "These old wells have been hiding for over a hundred years. It was only a matter of time before one of them caved in and something crawled out." Many nodded in agreement. "We just broke ground for the trail project around the preserve. Who knows what that unearthed?"

Soto observed Ford suddenly putting her phone in her back pocket and pulling out her lucky stone from Marnie.

One of Soto's more level-headed experts, Ted Day, an urban planner, got up and motioned to a void in the map. "Where does this section lead to?"

"Another thing we don't know," Grady said as he toggled into the location and tried to sharpen it. "This is all we have to go from. Your guess is as good as mine, and we won't know for certain until we can get down there to look around."

"Can we talk about that for a moment?" Ford finally chimed in.

"She speaks!" Jewell's comment drew the crowd's attention to the redhead.

"How do we get down there?" Ford continued, ignoring Jewell's attempt to derail the conversation.

"The safest way to get down there is to follow the liquor," said Ted. He stood and walked to the screen. "Grady, are you able to project a map of the Boise River?" The river appeared on the screens. "And can you bring the schematics of the underground wells back up, but flip it one hundred and eighty degrees? Ah, perfect." He gave Grady a thumbs-up. "So I think that, if you can get a boat on the Boise River, and follow it this way…" His finger followed a twisted path. "… I think it would land you at the mouth of the underground and to the old wells. That's how I would do it."

"How far is that?" Ford asked, joining Ted at the screen.

"Thirty or so miles by boat."

"Who has a boat?" Ford asked the crowd.

"A lot of us do," Ted said. "But we need a specialized boat. I'm thinking a souped-up bay boat would get you down there. Because you see this area here?" He motioned to a tangle on the map. "This is where the Boise River converges with the reservoir. It's shallow and rocky with sandbanks and several dam drops along the way, not to mention low clearances once you get closer."

Then he motioned to the missing information on the map. "Here, I can't tell you what to expect, or if a boat can get you any closer, but, if you give me some time, I may know where we can get a boat that can try."

"Can you look into it for us?" Soto asked.

"I'll do my best," he said. He took his phone out of his pocket and headed out to make the call.

"Thanks," Soto said as he exited.

"Can we go back to what it is we are tracking?" Margo's question brought the group back together. "So, Daya, forgive me if I still don't understand. Are you for certain it is a giant squid?"

"Not one hundred percent, not even fifty percent or ten percent. In fact, our best eyewitness claims she saw something not much different than the fantastical reports that Larissa was spreading in her social media." Murmurs and confusion filtered through the room. "Our eyewitness claims to have seen a large rabid-like animal. So to level-set with everyone again, this continues to be an extremely dangerous endeavor." Louder chatter ensued. "And we don't know for sure what exactly we're tracking, or if it's one creature or multiple creatures, or if they are mammals or something else entirely."

"What do you mean something else entirely?" Gary asked. The room got quieter, poised for the answer. "It sounds made up." The crowd snickered at his remark. "It sounds like we're tracking Bigfoot, and quite frankly, that's a little cuckoo." The snickering grew louder.

Soto had lost control of the speculative crowd. She turned to Ford, her head of intel, who looked elegant and composed and ready for her role.

"You're right," Ford said. "It does sound absolutely crazy to me too. Did you know there are over a dozen names for Bigfoot in North America alone?" Laughs trickled around the room. "So it might really be Bigfoot, or a variation thereof, or some other name you haven't heard about before. Just because something doesn't make sense, doesn't mean that it isn't possible."

She walked through the rows of people and continued her performance. "This creature will, without a doubt, kill off every living thing without hesitation. Whether it be weeks or years, it won't stop unless you make it stop. So whatever you want to call it or not call it, it makes no difference at all." She paused. "Grady pull up the photos." Grimaces and gasps were exchanged through the group as they viewed photos of the most recent mauling. Then he showed one of Norma Jean.

"Do you all like your jobs here? And do you love this preserve? Do you want your children to love it too?" Murmurs grew around the room. "Because whatever is out there is out to kill this preserve, and it's best to keep an open mind if you are able to." Silence ensued. All eyes were upon her for the leadership they needed.

"Here is the plan. Forget the other grid we were establishing, the kill sites, and plot points we worked on. Forget it. We're going to redeploy a new grid based on the locations of the wells. My team…" Grady and company stood at attention, "…will locate them, and Officer Soto's team will clear them for capping with the exception of one or two. And that is where we will set the traps. Officer Soto has work crews coming first thing tomorrow to help with the heavy lifting. For those of you who do not want to help, or can't help, we ask that you be patient, please, until we can complete this part of the plan."

There was a collective sigh in the room. "Look, I know you have paying jobs, but we are…" She clenched a fist and pumped it into the air. "…so close to wrapping this thing up. If you want to lend a hand, we won't turn it down, but if you would rather get rest and rest up your dogs for the next part of our plan, that's fine too. Totally get it. Once we get a souped-up bay boat, we'll head below, check things out, and reconvene for the next stage."

"Why can't we simply cap all the wells and say sayonara?" said Gary.

"Do you really want this thing to show up some other place? It seems to like reservoirs and the next closest reservoir is in Boise. Surely as a naturalist, a steward of the environment, you understand why we want to trap it instead of making it somebody else's problem." Sounds of agreement trickled around the room. "So let's work together to flush it out and let's see what the fuck we catch." More nods of agreement and overall chatter filled the room. Heads turned as Ted Day returned.

"Tell me you got a boat," Ford said.

"We do."

"Thank goodness," Ford said, muttering a quick thank-you to him under her breath.

"But we can't get it until day after tomorrow at the very earliest."

"Why the hell not?"

"It's coming from Oregon."

"Ore—"

"We have plenty to do between now and then," Soto chimed in before Ford lost her temper and the crowd. "There are between twelve and fifteen wells that we need to locate, fill, and cap. Ford, as soon as you think you have pinpointed the exact locations, circle back with me. My team, let's convene at the vineyard to work through our part. But before we split up, are there any questions?"

Several hands went into the air.

CHAPTER TWENTY-SEVEN

T Minus Four Days

For Soto the next two days went by in a blur, and not in a 'time flies when we're having fun' sort of way. The time was spent conducting heavy manual labor during the day followed by night patrols.

"Grady, come in," Soto radioed to home base.

"Go ahead."

"We need medical at Gott's Point."

"Copy. Is everyone okay?"

"We got a couple of volunteers who aren't feeling well. Everyone is mostly fine. These facemasks we got aren't doing shit."

Reports of dizziness and confusion increased throughout the night especially as Soto's team continued to make alterations to the creature's presumed entrances and exits.

"And you?" Ford asked.

"I'm okay. Haven't been affected. Had a close run-in with something though, holy shit," Soto radioed, still breathless from the encounter.

"What kind of something? Did you lose radio communications?"

"Um, I don't think so. I don't know. I can't confirm. People started feeling sick, and I think my mind's playing tricks on me, but I'm fine, we're fine, just, can you send medical?"

"Copy. Aside from that, what else do you need us to deploy?" Grady asked.

"That's it. We're going to keep at it for another hour or so and then head back."

"How are the pups?"

"We can hear their little yodeling hearts all the way out here," Ford added. "They don't sound happy."

"They're not. They're going nuts. Sick of chasing imaginary shit."

"Good news," Ford radioed. "The pathologist didn't find any traces of rabies or mutations in any of the remains."

"And on the flip side of that, I'm pretty sure we're not chasing a Cephalopod," Soto said.

Shared laugher circulated through the radiowaves.

"See you in an hour," Grady said.

"Copy," said Soto.

"No one will notice that you're gone for a couple of hours," Ford said as she guided Soto by the shoulders from behind, directing her through the zoo of volunteers in the center-turned-madhouse toward the ultimate destination—the cot in Grace's office. "And if they do, I'll tell them that you've been conducting heavy manual labor and led a patrol last night, so fuck-you-very-much, she's resting for a couple hours."

Soto summoned a weak laugh and a yawn overtook her. "But, there are plenty of other things I could be doing while we wait."

Halfway through capping they realized some wells were deeper than they first thought. A scramble to source more materials, specifically oversized drain rock, earned some of them a few hours off while they waited for the delivery so they could finish the job.

"You're right. There *are* plenty of other things you *could* be doing." Ford's elevated voice barely carried over the chatter and commotion that hummed around them. "Take a cue from your people." She pointed to team members sleeping in any spot available. "Or, take a cue from your dog. Lexy's already curled in her dog bed."

"Poor baby. She had a hard night last night," Soto lamented as she sat down on the cot. She rubbed her eyes a little too hard.

"*You* had a hard night last night too," Ford said. She sat opposite Soto in Grace's office chair. "And you're going to have a hard day, a dangerous day, if you don't sleep for a couple of hours."

Soto unbuttoned her uniform top and threw the balled fabric in the corner and worked her undershirt out of her pants. Next, she unlaced her boots and kicked them off, the right one giving her trouble. "Damn it." Soto shook it the rest of the way off. It nearly took her sock with it. "Fuck." She glanced up. "What about you?"

"What *about* me?" Ford's asked while watching the whole thing with great concern.

"Have you slept?"

"I haven't been shoveling rock or walking night patrols." Soto gave a frown. "I'm fine."

"I can't get those images out of my head…" She pulled at a loose thread on her sock. "The noise that it made. How it moved, all erratically and…"

"And what?"

"I *really* want to catch a glimpse, anything, something. We still don't know if we're chasing one deranged creature or more than one." She turned every which way. "Oh my goodness, that reminds me! I need to see the north quadrant intel." She stood up suddenly, stumbling over her recently discarded boots, flailing backward over the small cot. Ford grabbed her around the waist, steadied her in the nick of time and pulled her close.

"Rest," Ford said, and lowered Soto to the cot, moving her boots out of the way. "I am moments away from using enforcement tactics. I'll wake you before ten." Ford tapped her nail against the face of her watch. "That's three hours, more than three hours, from right now. Use them wisely."

"I'm really sorry if this puts us behind," Soto said, rubbing her temples. "I don't know where we went wrong miscalculating the amount of—"

"We're right on track," Ford said. "Now what do I need to do to put you to bed? Jesus."

"I don't have a good feeling," Soto groaned.

"What part?"

"Nothing." Soto rubbed her lips. "Never mind. *Two* hours, then wake me up."

"I will," Ford said as she exited the room, the door latching closed behind her.

Soto lay down and folded her arms behind her head to stare at the ceiling. "Yuk," she muttered, catching a whiff of her armpits. The fabric under her arms was damp from sweat. She turned on her side and curled into a ball. She dangled her hand over the edge, placing it upon Lexy's soft coat. She could still hear the odd sounds, the unintelligible whispering. She closed her eyes and her mind flooded with figments of the deranged creature, figments of what she *thought* she had seen: shimmering eyes and erratic energy that seemed similar to a bat in flight darting to and fro across the horizon. What was the thing?

Her eyes popped back open. And what was this *thing* she and Ford were doing? She shouldn't have kissed her to avoid talking, to leave her wondering where this was headed. "Coward," she whispered.

She was more frightened of Ford than she was of the creature—another wild force that she wanted to understand. Her eyes were like the horizon before an electrical storm, hazy and unpredictable, green that turned greener when she was content, and the color of steel when she was struggling—and every shade in between when she looked at Soto, or touched her or kissed her.

She felt Ford's kisses deep within, at the very center of a place unknown. She imagined Ford's hands, her slender fingers, soothing her between her legs, eliciting both pleasure and pain.

The memory impressed upon her mind as if she had stared into the sun and looked away, the image repeating its appearance with every blink. Every time she drifted to that place, her breathing became laborious, an unnatural chore. A buzzing close by, an incoming text. She read the message: *Shut your mind off, go to sleep.*

"Officer Daya." The chirping of the CB radio slowly brought her to reality. "Officer Daya. West Entrance. Do you copy?"

"Yep," she said to no one in particular, though her stirring woke her dog. They studied each other at the chirping sound again.

"Stand by," someone said.

"Soto," came a voice inside the room. She felt a nudge to her shoulder. Ford was standing over her, shaking her awake. "It's West Entrance."

Soto awoke, wondering if she had ever fallen asleep. She took notice of Grace's wall clock. "It's ten thirty! Why did you let me sleep so long?" She rummaged around for her phone and found it cutting into her hip. "Damn. I missed like fifty thousand texts. Some of them are from you."

"They are notes for later," Ford said, her eyes closed as she leaned against the wall. "I figured you could use the extra rest. If it's any help, you didn't miss anything."

"Shit. Where's the…" Soto pushed around the covers in search of the radio. "Oh." She realized Ford was holding it out to her. She rubbed her eyes. "Soto here," she radioed and watched the agent swagger out of the office, nearly running into someone with a large coffee order.

"The materials have arrived," said the voice on the radio.

"Fantastic," Soto said as she shook away the grogginess. "Copy."

"Someone from Canyon County water quality is asking about papers that need signing. Also said there's a problem with one of the wells we worked on yesterday."

"Damn it," she said. "Give me twenty minutes." She got on her feet and kissed Lexy, who quickly went back to sleep.

"Copy."

"Fuck me." Soto gazed into the mirror of the small bathroom, aghast at what she saw—purple circles under her eyes, her hair a spider's nest. She ran her hands over her cheeks and down her neck. She stretched her body. Creaking and popping sounds confirmed she was back into alignment. With her boots laced, her hair tamed into a braid, her trusty work gloves in her back pocket, and her handkerchief around her neck, she was ready.

"Coffee?" Ford handed her a tall white paper cup. "A shit-ton of cream and sugar?"

"Thank you," Soto said before taking a needed sip. She wished she could sit and enjoy it, rather than taking it out into the field. "And thank you for forcing me to sleep. I feel a ton better."

"I knew you would."

"What about you?"

"I'm good," Ford's response sounded a little too peppy.

"You need to get some rest too, okay?" Soto said, and then turning to the team, "all of you." They murmured without looking up that they would, but she doubted they had even heard her.

It was after three in the afternoon by Soto's account when the capping project was completed. The only thing left to do was wait on the boat. The idea of heading back to the cool of the preserve to catch up on paperwork, and then home for a much-needed shower and a big fat sandwich, made her feel like she could breathe a little bit easier—until she walked into the preserve and the eye of a brewing category-five shit show.

Ford was aflame and it wasn't because her wavy red hair was a tangled mess of worry. Shades of purple underneath her eyes told Soto she hadn't taken her earlier advice to catch up on rest. Photos, papers, and folders were all over the floor. Random electronics were scattered about, and Grady was cleaning up something that had spilled. The looks the volunteers shared with her as she walked in, said that this had been going on for a while.

"How many?" Ford was juggling talking with someone on the phone and demanding information from her lead tech. "Grady!"

"I already said five went missing last night and two the night before, so you do the math," he barked as he plopped a wad of sopping paper towels into the sink of the kitchenette. He rinsed his hands and sat down hard and heavy on the chair at the table.

"Can we have seven? Actually we need ten. Twelve! The way things are fucking going around here it wouldn't hurt to have backup," Ford shouted into the phone. "We'll be there within the hour." She ended the call. "Oh my fucking God, Grady!"

"Why is this all on me? Why aren't you reaming out enforcement, huh?"

"Because you are the head of tech and technical equipment is going missing with no visual evidence whatsoever!"

"We're managing as best we can, Win," he said, his voice getting louder.

"Five *more* missing cameras would beg to differ," Ford countered. Soto watched as she ripped a piece of fingernail with her teeth and mouthed a string of expletives. "God damn it," Ford said, finding a pile of photos before pushing the lot of them to the floor in one angry swoop.

She lifted a cup to her lips, took a swig, spitting it back out with a grimace that said stale coffee. "How the fuck are people managing to breach the investigative perimeter? For fuck's sake," She got in his face. "Button this shit up now. Like today. We can't head into the caves with our equipment going missing, damn it!" Ford took a breath and placed her hands on her hips. "So are you going to Meridian to pick up the cameras," she asked, "or is that something I need to do along with everything else?"

"Oh, really? You think *you're* doing everything?" Grady laughed. "You're absurd sometimes you know—"

"Can I help?" Soto offered, seeing that Grady could use some assistance in dousing this flame.

"Yeah, you want a job as head of tech? You have to report to that." He eyed Ford.

"How many more cameras this time?" Soto asked.

"Five," he said.

"That's five in addition to the two the night before," Ford added.

"Seven?" Soto knew it was a stupid thing to say even before she said it.

"Um, yeah. Five and two would make seven, Officer Soto. Damn it!" Ford said. She threw her prized pen across the room hitting the pelt display with a thud.

"What the hell, really? You're throwing shit now?" Grady said. "She's trying to help."

"This is unacceptable, Grady. Your work on this case is unacceptable." Ford rummaged around a desk in an attempt to find another pen to abuse.

"Unacceptable, really?" he said as he stood up to face her. "I don't think I'm the one that's being unacceptable. You know what? I'm not going to sit here and…" He shoved off too fast, toppling the chair over and increasing the already tense atmosphere.

"All you are doing is sitting here, so maybe try to *do* something so people stop stealing our equipment, unless you don't care that people are stealing shit and sabotaging our investigation. And if that's the case, you can be the one to go underground. Is that what it is? Do you want to boot up and go play ghost whisperer? Maybe you would be more effective in that role. What do you think? You want to go down there?" Ford's voice trembled.

"No one is being effective right now," he said as he bent to right the fallen chair. "Fuck it. Either I'm done or you are."

"What the fuck is that supposed to mean?"

"I think it's pretty self-explanatory. Isn't it, Officer Soto? You want to help us out, back me up?"

She wasn't going to take sides, and thankfully she didn't have to as Grady continued. "This conversation is over until you grow the fuck up and stop acting like that."

"Like how?" Ford asked, stepping into his personal space.

"Like that?" He inched closer.

"Like what?" Soto saw they were breathing the same air now. "Like you! Like this. You're out of control." Ford closed her eyes at the comment. He warned, "This is the last case I'm working on with you, period. I get why your last partner, your only partner—"

"Enough, Grady!" Ford yelled.

"Enough is right. Good luck solving this case without me," he said, folding his arms in front of him.

"Let me help you pack," Ford offered. She grabbed a paper bag and haphazardly threw in random cables and file folders. The bag started to tear.

"Stop, Ford," Soto said as she took the bag. "Let's all of us take a deep breath. Seriously." She demonstrated, though the only one who followed orders was Grady. He sat back down and slumped into his chair.

"Goddamn it," Ford retorted. She rubbed her forehead and slapped her hands on either side of her face. "God help me if one of you fuckers," she pointed around the room, "is stealing cameras. God so fucking help me—"

"You need to back off, Ford," Soto said as she held up her hands and moved in front of Ford to block an assault on the volunteers.

"I need to do the opposite of backing off, Officer Soto," Ford said as she pushed past Soto, nearly knocking her to the ground as she headed toward the exit.

Soto's shocked expression jarred Ford out of her agitated state. She opened her mouth to say something, but instead, she made her way to the front door of the preserve, pushing it harder than necessary, and storming out of the building.

"Ford. Ford!" Soto called.

The center eerily calmed after the commotion. Soto joined Grady at the table. "Does she always handle stress this well?"

"She's out of control," he said, pulling out his phone. "I'm calling the home office. She's done. This is not good."

"Are you serious?"

The veins in his neck reinforced that he was one thousand percent serious. "I've seen her outbursts before, but this is—"

"Hold up," Soto said as she placed her hand over his fingers. "What happened? I was gone for, like, four hours. She was fine when I left, sleep deprived, but fine."

"I don't know." He shook his head. "She was looking at intel." He motioned to the scattered photos on the floor. "Then we found out about the missing equipment and boom."

Soto got up and collected the photos, righting them in her hands while she walked back to the table. She shuffled through the stack until one in particular caught her attention. It was from the night of Ford's close encounter with the creature, the night she almost fell down into what they recently learned was a seventy-foot drop.

"She's scared, Grady."

"What?" he laughed. "No. That woman doesn't get scared. She's a hard-ass."

"This, what you are seeing, what everyone is seeing, is her scared." Soto ran her finger along the edge of the photo. "To see this image of yourself and realize how close you came to... then knowing you have to go down there..." Soto tapped the edge of the photo on the table and slid it over.

"Shit." He inspected the image and scratched his beard. "But you're going with her, right? Aren't you freaked too? I don't see you reacting like that."

"I handle it differently."

"Better."

"Different."

"Her poor coping skills are no excuse," he said. "And shouldn't be everyone's problem."

"I know," Soto agreed. "Let me try to talk to her."

"And do what?"

That was a good question. "I don't know. Try to assure her that it'll be okay even if more cameras go missing."

"Please don't say that." He took off his beanie and scratched the sides of his head. "You can try, but this is Winifred Ford at her finest, Soto. This is how she is."

Soto didn't believe him despite the swelling ache in the middle of her chest, confusing her perception of the woman with drastically different sides—fire starter and bully, yet insightful and gentle.

"Why even try?" he asked. "She's got like two, three more days here. Why is it *so* important that she stay on the case? Between tech and tracking—"

"Because, Grady, we're too close. I need her...her expertise. I need you too. The preserve, my community needs this investigation to continue. We need help, both of you to help us see this to the very end. Please stay?"

Lexy joined in the pleading by nudging her head softly into his leg. Grady turned his attention to her and run his hands through her fur. "Of course I will."

Soto wanted to think it was her words that swayed him, but she knew her dog's magical effect on others. He gave Lexy a scratch behind the ear and leaned back into his chair staring at the ceiling. "Well?"

"Well, what?"

"Are you going to talk to her now or later?"

"I'm going now." She stood. "But, what was that thing you said about her partner?"

"You need to ask her about that. But not now. Just get her back on track."

"Of course. I understand."

"I got our boss's number on speed dial," he warned.

She took that as her cue and got moving. She took a breath that released a couple of vertebrates in her back and slow-stepped toward the door on her way to catch a wild animal—Ford. She exited alone. Her dog stayed behind, preferring free ear scratches from Grady.

She headed toward the bird observation deck where she figured Ford had fled. As she walked, she inhaled the warm summer air, letting the scents ground her. "Ford," Soto said as she approached. "Are you okay? I'm sorry about the cameras."

"Sorry won't make them magically reappear," she replied, leaning on the railing and tossing small pebbles one by one into the water below.

"I'm sorry it's making this more complicated is what I meant." If Soto had learned one thing about wild animals, a gentle approach made all the difference.

"You don't know what complicated is," Ford spat back.

"Oh, I do. Grady nearly called your boss to have you removed."

"I don't fucking care. In fact..." Ford turned to face her and pulled out her phone. "It's probably a good idea I step out now. Everything I can advise on is done. The rest is tracking and trapping, which I trust you can manage with competence."

Soto heard the phone beeping. "Please put it away." She placed both hands over Ford's to stop her. Ford was trembling when she touched her and avoided eye contact. "You need to stay."

"Since when do you dictate what I do?"

"I need you here, we're too close to—"

"Close to what, Soto? Fucking or getting to the bottom of the case?"

Soto closed her eyes and opened her mouth with nothing to say.

Ford turned to face the water. She continued to fidget with her phone, making Soto nervous. "I've been giving you mixed signals."

"A little bit."

"Did it ever occur to you that I might be scared?" Soto inched closer to her.

"Scared of what?"

"To say, to acknowledge...how I feel...about you. About what is happening between us," Soto finally admitted. "It scares me."

"Thanks for telling me what you're scared of, Officer Soto. I, on the other, hand don't have an excuse. This is me, how I am. Simple fact." Ford finally placed her phone in her pocket.

"I don't believe you," Soto said, wishing Ford would look at her so she could see what other conflicts were running through her mind. She moved closer, gently placing her hand on the redhead's shoulder.

"I'm a bitch, plain and simple. It's the work I do, and it's how I choose to handle things."

"I've worked with you almost two weeks. You have an array of emotions. I've seen how you interacted with Marnie, the volunteers, with me," Soto whispered that last part. "You don't need to freak out when things go sideways."

"Whatever." Ford said, her voice faint. She wiped tears from her eyes. "Leave me alone."

"No. And you can't *whatever* your way out of this."

"It's all I got."

"No. It's not."

Ford didn't respond with words. She sniffled and wiped more tears from her face. It hurt Soto to see her falling apart. She already knew from experience that she could soothe her by simply touching her, that the wild creature could be subdued temporarily when she was being angry, bitchy, and rude. But would her touch hold the same power when Ford was scared and exhausted? Would her kisses wield that same power then? Soto had to stand on her tiptoes to reach her. "Don't be scared." She brushed Ford's hair from her neck and ran her fingers on the soft skin. Ford let out a long sigh and her shoulders dropped.

"You should be scared. Oregon was…Anything could be down there," Ford whispered. Soto felt the tension try to snake its way back into Ford.

"But, I'm not," she said into Ford's ear. She placed a couple of light kisses on her neck and Ford started breathing evenly again. She held her head back to offer Soto more space for kisses.

"Why?" she moaned.

"Because…"

Soto caressed Ford's chest, feeling her heartbeat in her hand as she brought her down off the metaphorical ledge. Ford placed her arm over hers. "I trust you." Soto moved her other hand lower. Ford squirmed when Soto's fingers were nearly inside her jeans. A sudden jolt from Ford. Lexy had arrived on the scene and was licking Ford's fingertips. The women took a collective deep breath and backed off.

"I'm sorry," Ford offered as she faced Soto and waved locks of red from her eyes. "I feel crazy and out of control. I keep hearing the same song loop in my head over and over, and I don't know how to stop myself when I go down that path."

"I know," Soto whispered as Ford got on her knees to give the pup a solid rub behind the ears and a kiss on her head.

"What the fuck did I do in there?" Ford asked. More tears ran down her cheeks and she nudged her head against Lex's.

"I don't have a clue. Did you get *any* sleep when I was out?"

A sheepish look crept across Ford's face. "No." She looked at her watch. "I've been up for, I don't know, fourteen hours."

"Time to rest. But not on that shitty cot of yours."

"My guys need me." Ford made a motion toward the building at the top of the hill.

"Um, no they don't." A good laugh from the special agent was a welcomed relief. "I have a better idea."

"What do you have in mind?"

"Food, showers, and a nap. Then let's talk more, okay? But first, you need to apologize to Grady and our volunteers."

Ford agreed.

CHAPTER TWENTY-EIGHT

Yellow Warblers

Minimal arm-twisting was all it took for Ford to accept an invitation to spend another night at the vineyard. Good idea or not, Ford needed peace and quiet as did the volunteers and the special agents. Soto tapped her knuckles against the door and poked her head into the guest room. "I'm headed out." Ford was focused on her laptop. "You want to come?"

"Depends." Ford looked up from staring into the screen and peered over her glasses to look at her. "Where?"

"To the Richards'." Lexy sniffed into the air.

"No, thanks." She pushed her glasses back up.

"Okay, see you later."

"Wait. Why are you going to talk to the Richards?"

"To check out the nesting birds," Soto said.

"Why?" Ford scratched her head with the tip of her pen.

"They'll ask me about them next time I see them. Want to join?"

"It might be nice to stretch my legs. But I don't actually want to talk *to* them." Off came Ford's glasses. She placed them on the desk and picked up her phone.

"Me neither. I'm only interested in the birds. Oh, and I'll probably get some food on the way back."

"You *really* should have led with that idea."

Ford clicked off her phone and shoved it in her back pocket. She patted her stomach as the three of them filed out of the house. They enjoyed a comfortable silence during the drive through the back roads. There wasn't much more to say that the smell of fresh mint, dusty roads, and intermittent sprinkler spray casting prismatic gems in the air didn't already.

"Whoa, Nelly."

Lexy jumped out the moment Soto opened the cab door. With a blanket in hand, they set off. They pushed through a creaky gate at the end of a path that ran adjacent to the Richards' property line. A tall wooden fence, warped and lined with tufts of grass stood between the trio and the elderly couple. Soto hushed with a finger against her lips. She crouched and lightened her step, gravel crunching underfoot. "Don't let them hear you."

"Good call." Ford followed her lead.

They navigated through knee-high green and yellow flowers, toward a canopy of syringa, willows, and poplar that were missing leaves at their tops.

"Goodness, they're loud," Ford said and pointed to a family of crows cawing, cackling, and causing commotion as they floated overhead. "Why are they so crazy?" she asked as one threatened to dive-bomb.

"There's probably a nest nearby. Let them know we're simply passing through and we mean no harm," Soto instructed.

"Hey, crows? We're just a couple of ladies and a dog. Nothing to see here." Ford laughed at her declaration. "How was that?"

Soto giggled her approval. With the sounds of the concerned squawking crows behind them, another family of birds sang and whistled a different kind of tune—high-pitched songs and delightful melodies.

"What do you suppose they're saying?"

"Probably exchanging shopping lists or talking about a good book." Soto laughed. "Right through here."

"Look at all of them." Ford held her hands out in front of her. "All shapes and sizes and colors." Winged beings darted in and out and through the dancing vines of their massive tree homes. "I thought birds went to sleep early? That whole early bird gets the worm thing."

"Actually birds get worms all day long until dusk," Soto said. Ford had stopped walking and twirled her shades between her fingers, wearing a look of wonder. Soto was stooped in wonderment of her own, how the uptight redhead transformed whenever she was outdoors in nature. "This way."

They continued their trek off the pebbled walking path to a plateau that overlooked farmland dotted with neatly cut alfalfa bales. Orchards with gnarled, warped, and crooked tree branches rounded out the landscape. "Look. That's one of my favorite things. Those whirlwinds in the distance."

"They look like dancing banshees holding their skirts in their hands as they twist and twirl, and kick up dust," Ford said.

"Couldn't have described it better myself," Soto said, a smile spreading across her face. She gave the blanket a good shake before spreading it over the native grasses and wildflowers. At last, Soto kicked off her tennis shoes, sat down, and leaned back onto her elbows. "God that feels good." She wiggled her toes in a patch of sun. "Have a seat, stay a while." Soto patted the space next to her. Lexy plopped herself down and sported a grin while panting, her tongue out to the side. "Not you." The pup didn't care for the gentle nudge Soto gave her with her toes. "Scoot." Lexy did but only an inch. "Give her some room, little lady." The dog snorted and finally got up.

"Thanks for sharing, girl," Ford said, giving Lexy a good scratch behind the ears before the pup pounced away through the brush and disappeared down the trail. "Will she be okay?" Ford stepped out of her shoes and sat down.

"Totally."

Ford motioned toward the general direction of rows of trained green vines lining the hillside. "Is that the vineyard?"

"That's it. See that area over there?" She pointed to a patch adjacent to an orchard with glittering foil bird tape gusting in the wind. "When I was little, I helped plant that section with my mom and my dad a couple of winters before she died. It produces the best of our wines."

"I'd love to taste it." Ford licked her lips.

"I'll send you home with a magnum of our finest."

"A magnum! Do I look like a lush to you?"

"At times." She smiled and settled back onto her elbows.

Ford tossed her sunglasses in the space between them and squinted into the distance. "Where are these infamous yellow warblers?"

"Right through there." Soto pointed through an opening to small yellow birds darting in and out. "Do you see them?" she asked, noticing Ford looking everywhere but. "Come over this way more." Soto patted the area next to her and Ford closed in.

"I see them!"

"Are you sure?"

"They are kind of hard to miss, being bright yellow and all."

"Just checking." She lay back and enjoyed the warm breeze. Her hair blew in her face tickling her nose at times. She traced a southbound flight high in the sky. "I wonder where they're going?"

"Oh my God. Look!"

"What!" Soto said. She worked herself up, expecting to see a hint of the creature they were tracking, or something else horrible enough to warrant Ford's expressive reaction.

"There." Ford inched her way closer to Soto and said, "yonder," and pointed in the general direction. "Those little babies with the little curlicue-looking things on their heads. Are they hurt? Why are they dragging their wings like that? All of them. Look."

"Oh, my goodness," replied Soto with a hand to her heart. "Those are quail. They pretend to be injured when they think a predator is close by, which in this case, is probably Lex. And when she gets close," she whispered into her ear, "they will take off into the air." She demonstrated by gliding her arm in the air across the horizon, the action startling Ford. "And then scare the shit out of her." She laughed. "It's quite cute how those little bitty birds get the best of her every single time."

"Will she hurt them?"

"Oh, God no. Lixi is so gentle." Soto lay back down, this time on her side facing Ford. She propped her head up with her arm.

"Lixi?" Ford said. "I've noticed you have an array of special names for her, but Lixi? What's that all about?"

"Early in our time together, we were called to a scene where a bear had been killed by poachers. And what was worse was that she was a new momma. She had cubs hidden somewhere, but no one could find them. It had already been a couple of days by the time we were pulled in to help. We show up and after fifteen minutes, guess who finds the den?"

"Lex?" Ford said.

"You got it. She signaled us over and we found her licking the orphan babies to pieces. Poor little things were so hungry. They inhaled several bottles."

"And that's why you call her Lixi? Because she licks so much?" Ford asked. Soto nodded. "That's the sweetest story."

"I have..." Soto hesitated, aware of the heat growing between them, their legs moments away from intertwining. "I have more stories." And there it was, contact. It lit Soto from within and spread throughout her body like a flame.

"I'm sure you do, Moose Wrangler," Ford said. The sun illuminated her auburn hair, made it shimmer like wildfire as it floated on the wind feeding Soto's flame.

She had never experienced that feeling of watching one's self from above until now. She reached toward Ford and twirled her soft and fiery strands of hair around the tip of one of her fingers. "So, the other night..."

"The other night," Ford repeated as she fidgeted with a lavender sprig she must have picked along the way.

"I'm not sorry about it."

"You're not?" Ford asked, looking up from the lavender.

Soto studied Ford's stormy gray and green eyes as they met her own. "Not in the slightest." Soto closed her eyes and relived scenes from that night. Ford pretending she was ticklish as she spread the oily salve all over her body. Ford between her legs, pushing into her. "I liked it. Too much." She watched Ford twirl the small purple flower between her fingers.

"Me too," Ford whispered.

"You were putty in my hands." Soto smiled and swiped the lavender sprig from Ford's fingers. She brushed the flower tip against Ford's wet pink lips. She leaned in and stole a lavender-tasting kiss.

"Putty?" Ford laughed. Her elation caused the warblers to pause momentarily. She grabbed a hold of Soto's T-shirt, preventing her from pulling away. She licked Soto's lips in response. Soto let Ford taste her desire, and the warblers resumed their chattering. "Are you quite sure you had *me* in the palm of your hand, Dayanara?"

"I love the way you say my name," Soto said. "I want to lick each syllable as it rolls off your tongue with the same—"

"*El mismo fervor que el azote de lengua que le di a tus pechos?*" Ford whispered into her lips.

"With that exact fervor." Soto thought back to the memory Ford voiced in Spanish. Of Ford at her breasts, sucking her, as she held Ford close with her fingers tangled in locks of red hair.

"What did you like best, Daya? Did you like it when I kissed you?" Ford asked the words against Soto's lips, the vibration tickling them and making her entire body hum.

"I..." Soto felt slippery as she shifted her legs.

"I'll assume your answer is yes."

"What proof do you have?"

"You felt hot and wet against me when you climbed your little body onto mine." Ford inched closer. "You smelled like the kiss of the early sun." She reached through Soto's locks of hair and caressed the back of her neck.

Soto groaned and grew breathless when she felt Ford nibbling at her neck. "What other observations did you have from that night, Special Agent Ford?"

"I only have questions now."

"Ask me."

Ford ran her finger across Soto's chest and over her breast. "Did you like it when I kissed you here?" Ford's touch caused Soto's nipples to tighten instantly. Her hand continued her trek lower. "Would you like it if I kissed you here?" A gentle caress of her center gave way to a grunt. "Or, if I were to spread you open with my tongue and taste what you're all about. Would you like that?" She moaned and pressed herself gently into the palm of Ford's hand. She bit her lip and closed her eyes and pressed harder before Ford assaulted her wet lips with her own. "Do you have answers to my questions, Daya?"

"Yes," Soto hissed. "Yes." She further confirmed by deepening her kisses. She hoped they would tell Ford fact from fiction.

"Why did you leave me wanting you?" Ford whispered in her ear. She grabbed Soto from behind and pulled her tightly against her hip, settling one of her legs snuggly between Soto's. "You nearly gave me a heart attack, young lady. Why would you do that to me?"

"I don't know," Soto managed between kisses. She felt Ford's fingers at her waist, unbuttoning her jeans and then unzipping them, promising eventual combustion.

"Sure you do." Ford worked a finger under the waistband of Soto's boxer briefs. She ran her finger underneath, her nail tickling Soto's stomach her kisses expressing her finger's intent.

"The case. My reputation..." Soto said between their rapacious kisses. "It's all on the line."

"That's a tired excuse."

"It's a logical, believable—"

"But it's not the truth." Ford pulled back and looked into her dazed eyes.

"I didn't trust myself."

Soto knew at first taste she would need more. Satiated and content, weren't words that came to mind when she thought of Winifred Ford.

"To do what?" Ford asked, saving Soto from her internal ramblings.

"Lose my fucking mind," Soto admitted.

"You owe me," Ford said between kisses.

Soto laughed at her demand, the noise sending the birds from their perch in the trees. "Then I should settle up." She pushed Ford onto her back gently but with authority, and continued her tender kisses while popping open the buttons of Ford's silk blouse. Soto tickled her fingertips along Ford's milky white skin. "You poor thing," Soto said, caressing the area around Ford's healing bruise. Then she settled her gaze upon Ford's cleavage and her front-clasped black lace bra. "My lucky day. You're making this too easy for me." Soto unhooked a silver clasp to free willing breasts. She grazed her knuckles over tender nipples that responded instantly to her beckoning. She took them into her mouth licking and pinching them into a frenzy until they were as pink as spring cherry blossoms and Ford was clawing at her.

"Let me kiss you," Ford demanded, her fingers tangled in Soto's hair as it lay upon her chest.

"No," Soto voiced into her green and gray eyes. She was subduing her charge.

"Please?" Ford pleaded. "Pretty, please?" She moaned.

"Manners won't help you this time." She climbed on top of Ford and ground herself into her getting exactly what she bargained for: a wild creature to tame. This singular task would be a testament to her own patience. Was she able to prevent *herself* from losing control? Would *she* turn into a wild animal in need of a firm and steady hand? Would she lose her mind somewhere along the way? Her questioning slowed her course significantly. Thinking about what she was doing, however it had the opposite effect on Ford; it pushed her toward hysteria and she nearly overpowered her, but she maintained the upper hand.

"Let me kiss you now for fuck's sake," Ford cried. She dug her fingers into Soto's thighs but Soto stopped her from feeding her own desire. "I'll rip you apart," Ford threatened.

"No you won't." Soto held Ford's arms in place. "I'm going to teach you patience, Winifred Ford. Of all the virtues, it's the one you lack." Soto teased her and traced shapes onto Ford's stomach, spelling names of animals with her tongue, making her guess correctly to earn a kiss upon her lips or upon her breasts. But Ford was a fast learner, so Soto abandoned the game. A frustrated whimper, then pleading and cursing came from Ford's lips especially when she knelt between Ford's legs, unbuckled her belt and unzipped her jeans.

"Touch me," Ford demanded.

"Patience," Soto said as she opened Ford's legs and nearly lost dominance again when Ford reached under Soto's shirt and caressed her breasts. "No!" Soto ordered. She froze. "Good girl," Soto said and smiled at her subdued charge.

"You're going to kill me."

"You'll be fine," Soto assured. "You're ready when I say you are," Soto said into Ford's lips. She climbed back on top of the redhead, pressing with her entire body, moments away from feeling her hot heat on the tips of her fingers.

"Wa-wa-wait." Ford sounded confused. "W-what is that?" she yelled, squirming.

"What's wrong?" Soto asked. Then she felt a sensation coming from her jeans. It was her phone vibrating in her pocket and against Ford's swollen core. "Fuck." She squirmed about, reaching into her pocket to retrieve the vibrating unit, but instead, she dropped it onto Ford's stomach. Ford bucked in response "Sorry." Soto's fumbling had accidently accepted the call. "Damn it," she whispered.

"Daya…" Ford said behind clenched teeth.

"Officer Soto? Hello? Is that you? It's Mike Martin. The Boat Guy."

"Shit. I'm coming…" Ford said.

Soto's eyes widened and she placed a hand over Ford's mouth while she juggled talking on the phone while riding a wild filly that bucked underneath her.

"Soto here. Mike? Oh, really? Are you okay?" Soto asked as she mouthed sorry to Ford. She climbed off and adjusted herself, releasing the tight pressure of her jeans. "Where are you? La Grande?" She turned to Ford. Her cheeks were a bright shade of pink and her chest was heaving. "No, you stay put. I'll come to you. Can you send me a photo of the tire? Perfect. Thanks a

million. I'm on my way. No. No. It's okay. Thank you so much."
She hung up and met Ford's hazy gaze. "Are we even?"

Soto laughed watching Ford put herself back together,
button by button and curse by curse.

"Hardly."

CHAPTER TWENTY-NINE

Dog & Dad

Ford had hoped that she and Soto could spend the night doing more...*talking*. A lot more talking and in more depth than they were able to get out on the preserve, nestled on the soft blanket, hidden in the tall grasses with the birds singing overhead and the sun warming their skin. She didn't try to hide her disappointment. "It's his own damn fault for not having a spare tire. I mean who doesn't travel with a spare fucking tire?"

"Apparently not Mike."

"Isn't there someone you know closer to him?"

"I wish there was." Soto's pursed lips told Ford she was disappointed too.

And on top of everything, Soto wanted her to watch Lexy while she left on the four-hour drive. She was freaked. She'd never watched a dog! "Why can't Lex go with you to meet the boat guy?" Ford moved an upturned palm between Lexy and Soto.

"Between the three of us, she's the one that needs to be the most rested for tomorrow," Soto said, stifling a yawn.

"She seems fine to me."

The dog sat down and yawned.

Soto laughed "Case in point."

"How *do* you guys do that?" Ford wondered out loud. Lexy alternated looks between the two women.

"We have a special connection, don't we girl. Yes, we do," Soto said while she bent over and took her dog's head in her hands. "So, can you watch her?" Soto stood back up.

"I don't understand why Mike can't call Triple A and you stay here?" Ford asked, reaching across the counter toward Soto with both hands. "How about right here?" Ford tapped her hand on the granite countertop.

Soto closed her eyes. "Ford," she groaned. Her knuckles white-tipped from gripping the counter. "Can we focus, please?"

"I'm sorry." Ford slid away from Soto, the sound of her fingers squeaking against the granite countertop. Lexy's ears perked at the high-pitched sound. "Yes. Of course I will watch her."

"Thank you!"

"But, I've never watched one of those before." She looked to the dog as if seeing her for the first time.

"You mean a dog?"

She nodded.

"It'll be easy, I promise. Feed her what is in this bowl." Soto stopped Ford from rattling the kibble around, and warned, "Don't do that unless you're ready to feed her." Ford backed away from the bowl slowly. "Feed her thirty minutes after I leave, then take her out after she eats, and then again before you go to bed."

"I'll do my best." Ford started chewing the inside of her cheek.

"You'll be fine," Soto said. "Do you have any questions before I get on the road?"

"Do I need to know any of those special commands?"

"No, you will not." Soto laughed.

"What if she needs to go outside?"

"She will let you know."

"How?"

"She will say, Special Agent Ford, can you please—"

"Stop!" Ford laughed.

"You will be fine." Soto grabbed her keys from the dish on the counter. "My dad will be home later if you need anything," Soto confirmed.

"'Cause that went well last time," Ford said.

"What are you talking about?"

"He totally knows."

"No, he doesn't. Wait. How do you…Why would you say that?"

"Nothing," Ford said. She felt her cheeks burning. "I got a better idea. Why don't we both go with you and keep you awake? Split the driving?"

"You need to sleep, both of you," Soto ordered. "Seriously, I'm in much better shape than you are. I slept this morning and this afternoon, remember? So please, get rest. All you have to worry about is coordinating last-minute details with Grady. I'll be back first thing in the morning."

"Copy." Ford sighed and ran her hand through her hair.

Soto got to her knees and kissed her dog on the head. "Watch her too, okay girl? Take care of her for us. She's going to feed you your cwunch cwunch tonight, okay?" She took a hold of Ford's outstretched hand and stood up. "Enjoy the bed."

"Roger that," Ford said as she and Lexy walked Soto to the front door. She turned on the porch light and admired the view of Soto's back side in her polyester uniform as she bounced down the stairs toward her truck to source a specialty trailer tire before heading out on the four-hour drive to La Grande, Oregon, to pick up Mike, the boat guy.

"And don't let her boss you around!" Soto yelled before climbing into her truck.

Ford gave her two thumbs-up and watched her drive away. "Well, girl," Ford said as they headed into the house, where she and Lexy sat and stared at each other until her phone alarm startled both of them. "Time to eat."

The dog confirmed the good idea by heading toward the kitchen. "Here you go." She rattled the bowl. "Oh, I see how it is." Lexy started dancing around her. She put the bowl down and sat on a stool. With her chin in her hand, she sighed deeply and watched Lexy swallow her dinner. "So." The dog acknowledged her and promptly went back to acknowledging her bowl.

Over the course of the next hour, she called Grady three different times and texted him triple that amount. There was nothing to do. "Why don't you sleep in your comfy little dog bed in your master's room, huh?" Lexy was lying at the foot of the guest room bed. "Should we go get it?" Lexy got up and led the way. "You *do* speak English, don't you smarty-pants?" Lexy snorted. *"Hé fifille parles-tu le français? Viens, on va aller chercher ton couffin?"* Ford asked her the same question but in French. To her amazement, the dog stopped, turned her way and gave a gentle gruff, blinked her eyes and proceeded to the route. She smiled at the thought that the dog was multilingual.

Ford pushed open the door to Soto's room and flipped on the light illuminating Soto's world: uniforms, muddied boots, and an unopened pack of boxer briefs. And on her nightstand: handwritten notes, a glass of water, pain reliever, a tin of that magical salve, ginger chew wrappers, and a bag of dog treats. Ford picked them up. Lexy danced around her. "You want one?" Ford opened the bag and gave it a sniff. "Not bad. Here you go." Lexy gobbled it up. "How about two? You won't say anything, will you?" Ford gave her another and another yet, before zipping the package closed and setting it back on the nightstand. And with the dog bed in hand, she started to head out, but not before taking notice of Soto's bookshelf. *Frankenstein, Little Women, Brother, Eagle, Sister, Sky.* She saw knickknacks from Soto's childhood, board games, class photos, science club awards. She picked up a framed photo of Soto and her mother, and then a knock on the doorframe startled both Ford and Lexy.

"Hello?" It was Mr. Soto. Lexy bolted toward him, giving him kisses and licks as he gave her a good rub down. "Hello, Lexy. Special Agent Ford."

"Hello, sir." She felt red snake its way up her neck. "Just getting Lexy's bed. I think she wants to stay with me in the guest room. I don't know for sure. At least that's what it seems like. She's been with me all night. Dogs, they're so funny. I was just getting her bed." She held it out as evidence. "I'm staying in the guest room. Not here."

"*Está bien*, Agent Ford. And please call me Juan. Daya said you were here." After an awkward shift of Ford juggling the photo and the dog bed, they finally shook hands. "Are you okay? Do you need anything?"

"I'm perfectly fine. Thank you again for your hospitality." She looked at the framed photo in her hand. "I was heading back to my room. This photo caught my attention."

"That is one of my very favorites of the two of them."

"I can see why." She continued to study the photo.

"She was six when that was taken. Life was different for us back then."

"I imagine it was challenging to raise her on your own."

"I had help. Thank goodness for Daya's sake that Isabelle and her wife Ginny were in our lives. I believe you met Isa?" he said. Ford indicated she had. "They taught her how to grow into a woman and all those other woman-type things that I didn't know how to do for her." He smiled and the lines on the sides of his kind eyes creased when he did so.

"I know she learned a fair bit from you too, sir, that shaped her into the woman she is today. She is a beautiful woman inside and out." Ford set the photo back in its spot. "And so was her mother."

"Daya got all her looks from Adela—her mess of black hair, year-round tan. She didn't get a bit of her *papá's* height though, *verdad?*"

"*No, señor.* She did not take after you in that regard." They laughed together.

"*Y tu mama*, Agent Ford?"

"My mom?"

"Daya told me that you lost your mother at a young age as well."

"She did?" Ford said, blushing and realizing she was hugging Lexy's bed in a death grip. "My mom and I couldn't be more opposite—black hair, blue eyes. She said I took after my father, but I didn't know him."

"*Lo siento*, Agent Ford."

"Thank you, Juan. And please call me Winifred."

"*Está bien*, Winifred. So, tomorrow is the big day no?"

"Almost to the finish line. All that is left is mapping the underground. If all goes well tomorrow, the rest is tracking and trapping."

"Then I hear you are off to the islands?"

"Yes, sir. On a three-month leave. Saint Martin. I'm looking forward to it." Her voice strained trying to sound peppy. "I couldn't move the date easily, so it's put me in a bit of a time crunch. But I have team members staying on until the end, however long that is."

"I am sure your time off is very well deserved. I'm about to make a sandwich. *¿Tienes hambre?*"

"No. Thank you. Officer Soto and I had dinner a little earlier."

"Thank you for everything you've done for us."

"I am glad I could help."

"*Así buenas noches, hija,*" he said as they walked out. "Don't let Lex boss you around tonight," he added as he headed down the hallway.

"I won't."

Ford laughed and made her way out of the room and back to her own. She peered out the massive stained-glass window and ran her fingertips over the soft dark polished wood of the ledge. The next part of the journey included navigating a specialized boat through shallow and rocky water, hidden sandbanks, and islands, toward an unknown underground world where sisters transported illegal liquor over one hundred years ago. She would heed Soto's advice and get some sleep.

CHAPTER THIRTY

The Mooring After

Lexy's gently whining brought Ford to the four o'clock hour. She assumed the dog needed to go out. Again. Soto had clearly stated she would only need to go out a couple of times. Every time Ford rolled over, she saw Lexy staring at her, seemingly needing to go out again. But at least the dog was courteous and used what Ford would refer to as an inside bark.

"Okay, let's go bossy boots."

Ford decided she might as well get up. It was nearly dawn. She slipped into a pair of jeans and a blouse and grabbed a throw to wrap over her shoulders. They headed to the front door, and then Lexy took off toward one of the farm cats and around a corner. "I knew it!" Ford yelled. It was still dark out and mostly quiet. There were a few of the vineyard's workers riding John Deere four-wheelers in the distance, stirring up dust against a pink horizon. One solitary bird started chirping. He sounded rusty. She wondered what he was saying. Probably *feed me coffee*. That's what she wanted. After a few big yawns and spine-lengthening stretches, Ford had successfully shaken away the need to go back to sleep. Then the crunching of gravel in the distance. Lexy raced around the corner and started dancing—a fitting action as she set eyes upon Soto's big white truck. Another truck followed in its wake with a slender dart-like boat in tow. The driver jumped out.

"Good morning," he said after a big stretch.

"Good morning," Ford replied.

"Mike Martin," said the boat's captain who gave Ford the kind of handshake that shook her entire body. "And this here is the *One-Two*." The name of the boat was also written on the side of it with an image of a pair of red boxing gloves. "Research vessel at your service," spoken with a cheer inconsistent with the early hour.

"Special Agent Winifred Ford. Thank you for your help Mr. Martin and sorry for the trouble you had."

"Please call me Mike, and I'm glad to help after what I have heard so far." His response sounds suspicious.

"What exactly have you heard?" Ford readjusted her throw.

"Sounds like the find of the century, prohibition wells where a rabid creature may be hiding. I didn't want to turn down this job." He pulled up his jeans by the waist. "You don't hear about cases like this every day."

"Oh." Ford exhaled. "Of course. I'm eager to get down there and look around. Looks like she can do the job." Ford gave the *One-Two* a pat on the bow.

"If anything can get you in there, it's her," he added.

"Special Agent Ford," said a very tired-looking Soto as she rolled out of the truck and had to close the door twice before it latched.

"Good morning, Officer Soto," said Ford as she ran her eyes up and down her body more than once.

"Hi, Lex. Did you have fun with Special Agent Ford?" Soto and her dog were nearly making out. "Yes, you are such a good girl. Yes, you are. Oh, my goodness." Ford smiled at seeing the two maul each other. Soto broke up her love fest long enough to say, "Thanks for taking care of her, Ford."

"I was glad for the company. Saved me from overthinking every little detail."

"Good. And did she boss you around?"

"Naa."

"And how are you feeling?"

"Rested."

"Perfecto," Soto said.

The four of them made their way up to the house. Between Ford and Mr. Soto, breakfast came together easily. What wasn't so simple was convincing Soto she should catch up on sleep instead of going with Ford back to the preserve.

"I'll deliver the briefing and get the operation on its feet," Ford repeated for the third time. "Everything is in place." Soto raised a finger as if in protest, but was cut off. "No. You don't need to be there."

"Maybe I just need more coffee," Soto said with her eyes closed. "I want to come."

"Well, you can't. Federal project, federal orders."

"Federal pain in my ass."

"I'll add you to my list if you don't heed to my advice," Ford said as Lexy helped her corral the zombie-like woman up the stairs and to her room. "Trust me, I got this."

"I know you do. But why are you in such a hurry to get over there? It's hella early still."

"I'm picking up breakfast from Ginny's."

"But we just ate."

"It's for the team, the volunteers. I kind of owe it to them after yesterday." Ford looked at her nails. "And the day before and the day before that," she said, watching a smile spread across Soto's face.

"That's nice of you, almost sweet."

"I can be sweet when I want to." Ford eyed the bag of dog treats on Soto's nightstand.

"How many did you give her?"

"You'll have to ask Lexy." Ford laughed at her response and watched Soto haphazardly work off her clothing, throwing socks, pants, and other layers about the room. Then, clad in only a white tank and her boxer briefs, she fell onto her bed, her hair covering her soft down pillow. Her eyes closed as soon as she was down. Ford turned to leave when she heard, "Do you want to sleep a couple of hours with me?"

"Um."

Ford ignored her internal warning not to turn around and look at the sight before her. Soto threw open the covers and patted she space next to her. She watched Soto slip her hand underneath her tank, stroking her stomach.

"No..."

"Come on," Soto said with lidded eyes. "We'll just sleep."

"I don't think we would just sleep, do you?" Ford said as she walked toward her. "Because the first thing that I would do is slip off that little white tank top. And then I would *have* to..." Ford bit her bottom lip. "I'm imaging the sounds you're making when I take you into my hands and tease you..." She eyed Soto's breasts. "There." Soto gasped and closed her eyes, squirming about. "I can almost feel the soft skin between your legs on either side of my..." Ford ran her fingers down her own cheeks. "When I settle in between on my way to confirm the taste of you." Soto swore behind clenched teeth, squeezed her legs together and tossed about.

"You tease." Soto pulled the covers up.

Ford laughed. "I'm the tease? I think not, especially after that little bird-watching lesson yesterday."

Soto's eyes popped open. "It's not like I left you hanging!"

"Thanks to your unusually aggressive vibrating phone. What model is that?" Ford reached for Soto's phone from the nightstand but wasn't fast enough. Soto grabbed it first. Ford went for it again but Soto shifted it to her other hand and held it out of reach. "Sneaky." Ford tried again with no luck as it disappeared under the covers somewhere. "Oh, you're good."

"I might need it *now*," Soto said into Ford's lips before she placed a kiss upon them and then another and another yet.

"I need it now," Ford said. The taste of her, like the answer to a riddle, the most complex of cases, solved in an instant. "You'll be the death of me." Ford gathered every last bit of her willpower and pulled away. "Sleep. I need to finish getting ready." She smoothed the covers over Soto. "We finally have what we need to get to the bottom of what is out there." Ford focused on Soto's deep chestnut eyes, pools of compassion. "What time do you think you and Mike will be ready?" Ford looked at her watch noting the six o'clock hour.

Soto resurfaced her phone. "No later than noon. I'm setting an alarm," she said and placed the device back on the nightstand. "Are you ready to chase down whatever the fuck it is down there?"

"Affirmative." Ford said, with a kiss that confirmed it.

CHAPTER THIRTY-ONE

T Minus Today

Radios were charged, cameras paired, and tracking devices synced to home base. At one o'clock, Soto, Lexy, Ford, and Mike sailed down the Boise River in the *One-Two*. With a police escort for the majority of the trip, ordering the hordes of people floating on inflatable rafts to let them pass, they were making good time. "At this rate, I'm guessing we'll reach our destination before three," Ford radioed to Grady.

"Perfect." Grady replied. "A clean, quick in-and-out mission."

All they had to do was communicate the unknown areas of the map, mount the cameras, and report on the stability of the underground. Then back to the preserve to prep for part two—flushing the thing out with more officers, more dogs, more traps and minus Ford.

"If all goes as planned, this gives you time to do a proper hand off and make your flight first thing tomorrow."

"Are you so desperate to get rid of me?" she asked. Grady's response, maniacal laughter. "God. That guy..." Ford said and tossed the radio on the seat next to her.

"…is a great partner," Soto said after giving Lexy a kiss on the head.

"I like her better." She motioned to Lex and smiled. Soto held her dog's head in her hands, adjusting her collar, as if they were on a leisurely cruise without a care in the world.

It was a beautiful journey, a story through time. They left cityscapes behind for denser groupings of cottonwood trees and the reds and oranges of ancient rocks and sage brush–covered canyon walls. Finally, there was only the simple sounds of water slapping against the hull and Mike coaxing the *One-Two* through the rough spots. "Come on, you can do it," he said as they traversed through channels that shook the boat entirely. "Easy does it."

"What was that?" Ford's voice shuttered. She white-knuckled the railing on the boat. Even Lexy almost lost her footing at that particular bumpy passage. Soto secured the dog in between her legs. Ford found Soto's gaze and it told her everything would be okay.

"It's getting a *little* unpredictable. Nothing to worry about," Mike assured them with a wide smile. He was clearly enjoying the bumpy ride. "And that's why I call her the *One-Two*." He revved the engine and sliced through sandbank after sandbank.

"I'd say she's doing a knockout job," said Soto.

Ford smiled at the joke and found another of her reassuring looks as they continued forward at a snail's pace through the narrow straights and shallow waterways. What seemed like a hard stop into a canyon wall was another turn deeper through jagged mountain stone. A particularly low clearance told them it was the end.

"This is as far as I can get without damaging her," Mike said. "Note our coordinates," he radioed to Grady before cutting the engine and setting anchor.

"Copy and noted, Captain," Grady replied. "Intel and tracking, confirm when you're on dry land, heading northbound and we'll go from there."

"Copy," Ford acknowledged.

"Thank you, Mike. We couldn't have come this far without you." Soto said. "It's much closer than we hoped."

"Good luck down there," he said. "See you in a few."

Soto and Ford ditched their life vests and swapped their footwear for knee-high rubber boots. Soto went in first with her backpack and dart rifle strapped to her. Ford lowered the bag of gear to her and then accepted Soto's outstretched arms for support, inching into the rushing water, careful to stay dry. Then came a splash next to her—Lexy jumped from the bow, started paddling, and the trio began their trek: a half mile of wading through sandbars and swirls of water down moderate embankments following culverts of transparent water.

"This is quite the journey the sisters went through," Ford huffed as she worked to keep pace with Soto and Lexy. Though glad for her rubber boots that kept most of her legs dry, it took extra effort to slog the bulky things through the river. "Imagine wearing those huge, frilly hoop skirts and *Little House on the Prairie* shoes trudging through this shit."

"Not to mention no tech whatsoever."

"I can't imagine," Ford said, gripping the handle of their bag of gear, careful to keep it from getting wet. "And all for a little bit of alcohol," she added.

"You would be surprised what people will do for a drink."

"I bet you have a story or two to tell growing up in a vineyard, huh?"

"Yes, but most of them involve me stealing bottles before meeting friends at the lake and getting in trouble." Soto laughed. "That was before I knew about this little thing called inventory. Grounded for weeks!" Soto turned her way and laughed again. "Then I wised up and started filling my bottles straight from the barrel."

"You bad girl," Ford said as she caught up out of breath, glad for the break. "God, this is work." Each step she took was a complete workout as the sandy riverbed suctioned her in each time she lifted her foot.

"I bet you two dollars the sisters had a couple of men under their command to do the heavy lifting."

"They sound smart."

Finally they made it to solid ground. Ford climbed on to dry land, thankful for the shade of the rocky walls and the protection of a long-sleeved, loose-fitting button-up and hat that shielded her fair skin from the abusive sun. She tossed the bag of equipment onto the ground and rubbed out her cramped hands.

"Want to trade bag duty?" Soto offered.

"I got it." Ford hefted the bag onto her other shoulder.

"It's probably another quarter mile."

"I'm good. Let's move." And on they went, forming their own path through canyon walls through chips of stone, rock hurdles, and brush.

"You guys should be close," Grady radioed. "Your tracking devices say you're only about a klick away from the entrance. Northbound, Lexy's closer than you two. Quit lollygagging."

"Copy," Ford radioed.

"Lexy!" Soto yelled, and followed up with a whistle. "Hold there." They heard Lex's barking in the distance. "That way." Soto motioned and they headed onward.

"I think this is it," Soto said. "Grady," she radioed. "Do you see our coordinates?"

"I sure do."

"Fucking fantastic," Ford exclaimed and dropped the bag.

"According to the map, the mouth of the cave is dead ahead."

"Dead ahead?" Soto asked and trekked onward. "Where?" Ford followed close behind toward the supposed entrance, then losing sight of her as she rounded the bend. "Jesus and Joseph."

"What is it?" Ford asked, catching up.

"Look." Soto motioned to a narrow cut in the wall.

"Is that it?"

"Have you found the mouth?" Grady asked.

"It's not a very big mouth," Soto said. "It's scarcely wide enough for two women and a dog to get through walking side by side while getting scratched thoroughly."

"I'll save ice for you when you get back." He laughed at his response.

"Such a thoughtful chap," Ford replied. "We're headed in. Will radio from the other side."

"Copy."

Lexy led the way, easily squeezing through the opening. A few muffled barks a short while later filtered their way out and signaled her success.

"After you," Soto offered.

"Please, by all means." Ford motioned toward the opening, as if presenting the entrance to a glorious castle. "Ladies first."

"Clearly that's me." Soto smiled and started inching her way through.

"Hold up," Ford said while rummaging two helmets out of their gear bag. She placed one on Soto, activated the flashlight that was mounted on top and secured the strap under her chin. Soto returned the favor.

"See you in there."

"Wait," Ford said, reaching out for her.

"You okay?" Soto asked, furrowing her brows.

Ford took Soto's hand. She looked over her shoulder and back to Soto, pretending that Soto was the one who had more to wrestle with, that it was Soto struggling with the reality that the whispering wasn't easily explained in rational terms. "I wonder if we're prepared."

"We're prepared, Ford. As best as we can be. We got a solid plan. We got the best dog in the world waiting in there for us. We have Grady on the other side, and the *One-Two* isn't far away." Soto kissed her hands and held them against her cheeks, "and we're in this together. That's the most important thing." Ford gave her a nod that said she was confident, but inside she felt far from it, and it wasn't because she didn't trust her or didn't trust her team. She felt closer to finding the truth than she had been in her entire career, but she wasn't sure she was ready to know the answers. "See you inside."

Soto leaned in and kissed her, giving her courage, before sliding through the tight opening at a sideways angle with her weapon in one hand and her pack in the other, as if boarding a narrow-bodied airplane.

"I hope you aren't claustrophobic," Soto said before she disappeared.

CHAPTER THIRTY-TWO

Dead Ahead

"Are you coming?" Soto sounded deep within.

"Right behind you!" Ford yelled. She placed her fingers upon the rough rock, working herself through the narrow channel, leaving the brilliant blue outdoors for the musty, dark, and cool unknown. Rocks and debris fell, loosened by their burrowing. "Glad we put the helmets on now!"

"There you are." Soto pulled the bag of gear through the narrow corridor.

"Wow," Ford remarked after her eyes adjusted.

Minimal light filtered through narrow cuts above, faint and muted as it traversed around corners, casting a smoky glow on mostly white porous and weeping walls. "It's huge down here. And surprisingly muggy."

She joined Soto on the ground to swap clunky rubber boots for lightweight hiking boots. Getting wet was unavoidable. The cave floor was made up of channel ways of water, splintered streams like cracks in a windshield. "Grady. How do we look?"

"Looking good. All three of you coming in clear."

"I'm giving Lex a head start," Soto radioed. The dog hopped around a corner into the dark.

"I see her."

"Activating the helmet cams," Ford added.

"Copy. They're calibrating," he responded. "I'll let you know when I see your feeds. Mount a camera, I want to see that entrance."

"Copy and standby." She surveyed the area for the best location. She touched the rock walls of the cave. "What kind of material is this?"

"Sandstone mostly and shale," Soto said as she ran her hand along the surface. "With quartz and agate deposits."

Ford broke off a sizeable chunk that crumbled in her hand as she prepared to anchor a camera.

"Needless to say, we'll have to watch our footing."

"Agreed," Ford said. "Grady, I got camera EMC77 mounted and activated."

"Copy. I got it. Nice shot. It's coming in clear."

"You getting our helmet feeds yet?"

"Still working on it. This isn't that unusual…taking longer than it should, though."

"I'd prefer that we have visual confirmation." Ford hefted the bag over her shoulder. "But we should get moving and do what we can."

"Take it slow," he replied.

Lexy's barking reverberated down a corridor, providing her location. They hurried toward her until a wall of eye-watering stench slowed them considerably.

"What the fuck is that?" Ford held her arm over her face to smother the smell.

"Definitely something dead." Soto placed her own arm over her nose and mouth. Lexy came barreling around a corner and let loose a string of barks, and then took off presumably toward the offensive scene. "Right behind you, girl." The light from their headlamps bounced as they trotted after her. Soto stopped short. "Oh, that's bad. Not a dead animal." Dried blackened blood, hooves, and fur. The area was thick with flies and other buzzing insects. "Many dead animals." Soto coughed into her arm.

"Look at the blood spatter," Ford said, fighting through overwhelming nausea. "Grady," she radioed. "Mark our location as an attack scene, nest...of some sort."

"Copy and get a camera up. The helmet cams aren't transmitting. Damn it! I've lost your locations."

"Repeat?"

"I've lost your locations."

"These fucking trackers are made for deep underground exploration. How could that happen?" Ford dropped her bag and ripped the tracker off her shirt. She knew it didn't make sense, and she wasn't surprised, nothing else made sense either. "Shit." She turned it over in her hands and reaffixed it.

"I'm trying something else. Damn. I've lost the entrance cam too. Give me a sec to sort this out," he radioed.

"What the bloody hell?" Ford whispered. She removed her helmet to inspect the connections there. "Anything now?"

"Negative," he said. "Give me another sec, Win. Stand by."

"Copy. Soto, where are you?" Ford's question echoed around the confined quarters.

"I'm here." Soto appeared from around the corner.

"Stay close. Grady lost our trackers. We're off the map for a moment. All of us."

"I know. I heard."

"Let's hold..." Ford steadied herself against the wall of the cave. "I don't feel..."

"You okay?"

Ford tried for the words, only managing to shake her head that she wasn't. "I'm going to be sick."

"Tell me about it. It's pretty fucking rank."

"No. It's not that..." Ford groaned. "It's close," she whispered.

"What is close?"

"*It's* close. The radios, are out...that means..."

"Lexy!" Soto whistled and her dog arrived in the next beat. "Hold here, Lex."

"Soto, where are you?" Ford asked, waving an arm in front of her, the other one bracing herself against the wall. Soto caught her.

"Ford. Hey. I'm right here."

"I can't see…"

"What do you mean you can't see?"

Ford felt Soto's hand on her chest. She placed hers on top.

"I'm right in front of you," she whispered.

Soto appeared unrecognizable, her compassionate eyes distorted, black and hollow. She began to fade away along with Ford's vision.

"Don't go!" Ford swam through a cloud of anxiety and despair. She tightened her hold on Soto. "Daya!"

"Win. Focus," Soto said as she felt *it*, behind her. The whispering along with an accompanied feeling of dread morphed with sobbing that inched closer and grew louder. She backed them up against the wall. "What is happening!"

"They're here…"

"They who?" Soto couldn't hold her flashlight steady enough to see anything. "Ford! Who?" Her voice lost within the agonized wailing of a thousand cries. What had been faint muttered whispers on the preserve were resounding and undeniable screams in the depths of the wells. Hidden within the wailing were words without meaning. Distant, yet suffocating. Everywhere and nowhere. Someone, something was trying to communicate. Terror bloomed within Soto, crept inside her and crawled around like a disturbed nest of ants. She would never be able to brush them away. "What's happening to you Ford?"

"I don't know," Ford groaned. Her body went limp. She slid against the stone toward the ground.

"Whoa…" Soto held on to her. "I got you." She crouched with Ford. "Talk to me. Win?"

"They are working…" Ford managed. Her voice sounded distant and unfamiliar. "They are scared."

"Who is scared?" She looked over her shoulder. "Don't be scared. Concentrate on Lex." Soto found Ford's hand and placed it on Lexy. "Hold on to her. We don't need to be afraid unless she is and she's fine, aren't you?"

Lexy barked several times.

"Dead bodies. Forgotten..."

"Shit, Ford. Come on, focus." But it was no use. Ford seemed lost in another world.

"They can't breathe." Ford sounded winded for absolutely no reason.

"What's happening? Come on. Take a deep...Breathe. Ford."

"Trapped."

"Damn it!" Soto said, looking around for the best course of action. "We need to get out of here."

"No!" Ford demanded between a fit of coughing. "Get a camera up. We're down here. Let's do the fucking job."

"You're not in any fucking position to make that call!"

"It's cold..." Ford whispered. Soto felt Ford trembling, start to shake violently as if she had been wandering in a winter storm. "Oh God!"

"Ford, please..." Then total darkness. Their helmet lamps flickered out. Their handhelds, useless. "Stay close." A garbled message came through the radios. "Grady? Grady!" she radioed. Nothing, but static.

Soto held Ford in her arms along with Lexy, relying on the dog to tell her what was happening. Reading her movements, relying on Lexy's senses that told her there was danger. Soto felt the sensation in her fingertips before she heard it. A growl that originated deep within Lexy's lungs, making its way through her body, she let loose a string of soul-shattering barks. Warnings. Teeth gnashing. Threats. Fangs bared. "Ford, listen," Soto whispered. She felt movement brush past. A calculated effort that snarled and hissed... "Something is in here with us."

"We can't get out..." Ford moaned. "We can't get out!" she cried.

"Ford, stop. Be quiet. Please. We're going to be fine. But we need Lexy's help. We need to let her go, and I'm going to let you go too. Create a diversion. Maybe, I can get a shot. We got to get out..."

"No one will know…"

"Oh my God, Ford… Stop, please…stop." Soto had to stay calm. She couldn't lose her mind while Ford was lost in another world. It was up to her and Lexy to fend off the disembodied cries and the fury of the additional breathing, living, whatever the hell thing that was in there with them. "Lex, get ready girl. Letting go now. Ford let go of her. Trust us. Lex, find it and hold it!"

The dog took off and out of sight, sending whatever it was, scrambling up the side of the wall, leaving chunks of rock and debris raining down. "Now! Ford. Up. Come on. We got to get you out!" Soto pulled at Ford's arms. "Get up! Win, please. Please."

"Help us…remember us…"

"Stop." Soto cried, tears streaming down her cheeks. She tried again, counting on adrenaline to help get Ford onto her feet, but Ford was a puppet without strings. "Come on, Win. Please. Come back!" she screamed.

"Soto!" said Ford as their helmet cams flickered to life.

"Win?"

"Up! Look up!"

Cowering in a corner, two glowing eyes, staring down at them. "Don't move," Soto said. "Don't any of us fucking move," she repeated, keeping her tone calm and collected. "I have a visual. Lexy. Hold it." The dog growled a deep guttural response that traveled throughout Soto's body via her spinal fluid connecting with every single nerve. "Easy." She got onto her knees and worked the rifle off her shoulder.

"What is it?" Ford whispered.

"A deranged mountain lion. It looks fucking rabid. Lexy, on your mark." Then telltale sounds that something was wrong. "Come on, you fucker," Soto whispered. "Fuck," she whimpered and tried again. "It's jammed." She was presently living a cop's recurring nightmare—looking point-blank at mortal danger, breathing its air, feeling cold, hard steel against her temple. "Ford. Your weapon. Give it to me."

"I still can't move."

Soto reached for Ford's weapon, the one strapped on her leg. But she was shaking too much, afraid she would shoot Ford in the leg trying to get it. "I can't…" Instead Soto slipped her knife from her own boot holster, her grip so tight she was losing feeling in her hands. "I can't…" she repeated, but her words got lost inside a more powerful competing sound—a deafening commotion of stone grating on stone, chipping, sliding, falling rock, something destructive combusting in the distance.

"Daya!" Ford yelled. "Listen to me. Get a camera going to home base. Grady needs to—"

"There's a rabid cat trapped in here with us. My priority is our safety and my rifle isn't working and I can't…" Soto couldn't bring herself to admit that she was petrified by fear. "I can't…" She held back the intense need to sob for fear of entering a place she couldn't return.

"It's gone."

"I can't risk it." Soto rubbed her eyes free of the settling dust, trying to focus through the cloud of matter and madness.

"I can feel it. It's gone. The rocks, the noise, scared it off."

"Damn fucking rifle!" Soto's frustration echoed inside the cavern. She pressed herself against the wall and banged her helmet against the stone.

"Good news, ladies. I'm picking up your trackers again." Grady's voice was a welcomed sound. "Have you got that second camera mounted at the kill sight? If so, I can't see it."

"Grady!" Soto radioed. She scrambled to her feet. "Oh my God, Grady!"

"I'm here. What's going on?"

"Our helmets…did you see any of what just happened?"

"They're still calibrating. I've tried cross—"

"Grady, stop." Soto rummaged through their equipment bag pulling out a camera pack.

"What's wrong?"

"Help me get a camera going." She turned the device over in her hands. "How do I get one of these working? Fuck, I should have paid better attention. Grady, you there?"

"I'm here. Where's Ford?"

"She's fine. Tell me how."

"Hey, okay. I got you." Grady talked her through it.

"I think we're online," Soto said when she heard beeping noises. "Red light!"

"Success! Whoa," he said. "What's wrong with Winnie?"

"I'm fucking fine," she said. "Get that camera off me."

"It's *rank* down here," Soto said and adjusted the angle of the camera toward the carnage.

"Holy shit! Is that what I think it is?"

"If you see a shit ton of carcasses, then yes."

"It looks like a slaughterhouse. It's also smoky. Is something covering the lens? Damn it," he radioed. "The camera quit transmitting. Something is interfering with them," he said. "And now I've lost your trackers again. Jesus what is going on down there? You to need to retreat. Abort. Make your way to the *One-Two*. We need to rethink this. Now," he ordered. "Time for Plan B."

"We can't," Soto responded.

"Why not?"

"We had a little situation"

"We must have compromised something when we made our way in. And there's no getting out the same way we came in," Ford added.

"Why not?"

"About a half ton of rock is blocking the path."

"Jesus. You guys okay?"

"We're fine," Ford confirmed. "Shaken up, but fine."

"Do we have a Plan C?" Soto asked.

"Of course we do." Grady sounded confident. "Stand by."

"Copy," Soto and Ford said in unison.

Soto settled her gaze upon her partners. Ford looked like herself again, spent, but back. Her other partner was providing Ford comfort, helping put her back together with her kisses and nudges. Soto watched Ford wince as she mustered the energy to stand. "You got it?" Soto asked and helped steady her.

"I'm good. Thank you. Both of you. Lexy..." Ford dried her tears with her sleeve. "Thank you, girl." She ran her fingers through Lexy's fur again. "I'm sorry, Daya. So sorry."

Soto opened her backpack, fished out a water bottle, and handed it to Ford.

"Thank you."

Soto rummaged in her pack again and handed over a fistful of ginger candies. "For nausea. It's something. Eat them. All."

Ford popped several immediately followed with a swig of water. "Let's get the fuck out of this rank, fucking dead shit while we wait for Plan C."

"Does part of Plan C include Grady canceling your flight?"

"That's not important right now. We're safe. That's the main thing."

Soto nodded and inspected her jammed dart rifle aggressively, checking the chamber and turning the weapon around, muttering expletives under her breath. "Aha!" She popped out the faulty dart and picked it up, staring at it from all angles.

"You okay?"

"Better knowing I got a sure weapon with that deranged cat in here." She tossed the dart into a dark corner. Her dog's nudge at her leg, pulled her back to earth.

"I got a plan." Grady broke the silence.

CHAPTER THIRTY-THREE

Plan Sea

"We got crews working to create an outlet by the lower embankment. It's going to take time," Grady said.

They'd sent the *One-Two* home. She was all grace and they needed brawn. "And, if you are where we think you are, I'd say you have at least a twelve-to-fifteen-mile trek west." The old maps proved inaccurate. With the exception of a handful of the well locations, nothing else matched up. "We'll work together to chart the way out," he assured them. "Ditch the bag of the highest tech fucking cameras on the damn market," Grady said. "They will only slow you down." Then he added, "Plan to hunker down at least one night. If not longer."

"We're prepared," Ford replied.

"Provided we don't get buried, lost or trapped, you know, in a small room with no air," Soto added sarcastically.

"Take your time, go at it slow, and be careful," he ordered. "We'll guide you out. You worry about everything else."

"Like defending ourselves against and possibly trapping a deranged mountain lion with no visual—" Soto muttered.

"Soto?"

"Yes?"

"We got Crawly and her hounds running the show up top. She has twelve volunteers with dogs running patrols tonight. They are committed to staying on until we see the three of you again."

"Thank you, Grady," Soto said, though his assurances didn't help. Despite her years of working in precarious situations, the feeling she harbored in this moment didn't compare. "Give her our thanks too."

"We're going to proceed to the route. Stand by," Ford said.

"Copy."

"Hold it." Ford turned to her. "No one is getting trapped down here, Officer Soto, nor will anyone suffocate." Ford squeezed her shoulder. "We will be okay. You said it yourself. Now, breathe slowly." She demonstrated.

"So we can preserve precious oxygen? You predicted we would get trapped. 'Dead bodies. Can't breathe.' That's what you said. And guess what? We're trapped."

"Grady's gotten me out of worse. He will get us out of this, so let's keep moving. Okay?"

She nodded her response.

"Soto, look at me. You have my word."

"I know." She met Ford's eyes, wishing she could see the definition of the flecks of color and hope in them, but she saw enough to know Ford's promise was good. "I'm ready."

"Let's go."

They took their first steps, one foot in front of the other. One agreed upon landmark to the next. "Confirm. What next?" And "clarify the coordinates," was the extent of what they communicated as they proceeded to the route. Focusing on the facts helped settled Soto's nerves, but Ford had this annoying habit of wanting to settle other things.

"I don't understand why it didn't affect you the same way," Ford brought up, yet again. "Did you not feel anything at all?"

"No. I just heard it."

"How were you able to function?"

"I don't know. I'm at a loss too, but I don't feel like tossing theories around right now. At least be glad that one of us is able to keep a clear mind down here." Soto immediately regretted the hurtful words.

"Hey." Ford stopped, letting Soto catch up. She took Soto's hands in hers.

"I'm sorry," Soto said, closing her eyes and leaning into Ford's touch. It felt soothing and bright like it had the ability to illuminate their entire way out.

"Don't be scared, Soto."

"I'm not."

"Yes, you are. I am too. This is fucked. But look at Lex," Ford said and shone her flashlight in the distance. They spotted Lex's reflective collar. "She looks fine, doesn't she?"

"But I am scared shitless for her and for you. What was that spell you were under? You were possessed."

Ford shook her head. "I don't know."

"Can you try to explain what you do know?" She searched Ford's body language for something to go on, but found nothing to grasp.

"Premonitions. I get these feelings sometimes where random words come to me. It doesn't happen that often and usually they are more...internal thoughts. There's only one other time when it overtook me and shut me down like it did back there."

"Oregon?" Soto asked.

Ford nodded and rubbed at her dirt-streaked face. "I can't explain why, let alone rationalize the words that came out of my mouth. Usually I can piece stuff together, but..." Ford looked up and shook her head. "I can't—"

"Well I can't either. At least not right now." Soto preferred the comfort of her own mind, stirring around her own rational conclusions. "Can we just proceed to the route? Clarify more fucking coordinates? Please?"

"Fine." She started walking again.

They continued in near silence for the next hour, reverting to one-syllable responses leaving room for Lexy's snorting, gentle gruffs, and warning growls—all threats to ward off the mountain lion that was stalking them. Added to that were startling surprises of falling matter, pebbles, and other cave debris—the sounds amplifying when meeting their helmets—crunching footsteps and other reverberations, a cleverly composed soundtrack to entice morbid thoughts in Soto's imagination.

"Soto. Stop. What is that?" Ford gave ample warning, though she bumped into her anyway.

"A cut out of some sort."

Ford shone her light toward the dark opening. "I want to check it out."

"Are you sure that's wise?"

"It would be *unwise* if we didn't check it out." They ventured around the corner, illuminating each step. "Grady, we're taking a little side tour. We found something interesting." Ford gave him their coordinates. "Stand by."

"Copy."

"Whoa-ho-ho!" Ford said with glee as she passed through the opening.

"What is all this stuff?" She combined the light of her flashlight with Ford's to better light the small space.

"The find of the century," Ford said, crouching down to explore their discovery. "Old crates. Look." Ford pulled a fat bottle that looked like it held liquid at one point. "Aha! Sisters. Sisters! There were never such devoted sisters." Ford sang the tune from *White Christmas*. "The legend is true!"

"Look there," Soto said, shining her beam toward a large divot in the ground.

"Are wooden floor boards a typical geological element of this type of cave?" Ford asked upon joining her. Soto let out a laugh. "Should we open it up?"

"Go for it."

"Oh, goodie." They pried up the old boards, which didn't take much effort. If indeed they were a part of the sister's stash, they were over a hundred years old.

"Would you look at the history in here?" Soto's words echoed about the small cave.

"Old rusty revolvers, stiff leather pouches, and delicate papers," Ford said, her flashlight bouncing off various sizes and colors of glass bottles within the small box. "The ladies at the historical society would be having a hard-on right now," Ford exclaimed.

Soto laughed again, this time louder.

Ford nearly crumbled the wad of brittle paper as she sang, "Money, money, money...money."

"You sing so completely off-key!" Soto's body shook as she enjoyed herself at Ford's expense.

"Off-key?"

"Oh. Laughter really is the best medicine. That feels good." Soto snorted holding her stomach.

"Soto," Ford gasped. She picked up a wad of the brittle money, stood and wrapped her arm around Soto, holding her to her body. "Run away with me, baby. Please let's not ever look back. Here's our chance. You, me, Lex. I'll adopt her. I'll call her my own."

Soto's laughter filled her lungs with much needed positive air. "Who knew?"

"Who knew what?" Ford tossed the wad of money back onto the ground, brushed off her hands and continued to look at the old artifacts stored in the small area.

"If someone would have said to me on that first day you bulldozed your way into the center, 'See that redhead there? She's a regular comedian,' I would *not* have believed them." Soto smiled and stood. For a moment, she felt like she was back on the preserve, perhaps on that soft blanket watching the yellow warblers, lost in a kiss. She couldn't stop smiling.

"Yet here I am being funny." Ford sounded proud of herself. "Maybe I'll go on tour."

"Ford." Soto grabbed Ford's arm. "Doesn't this seem like the perfect rendezvous spot?"

Ford looked around the area taking in the stockpile of supplies and cash. "It does."

"There's got to be a way in somewhere close by," Soto said, pointing her flashlight around the room, looking for a clue.

"Whoever brought them the goods must have hiked it to here, but then where did the sisters enter?"

"I don't know." Ford shone her flashlight up and down the walls of the cave and around corners. "Come here."

"What is it?"

"Through there?"

"Let's look," Soto said and took the lead. They ventured single-file through the smaller opening. "Lexy, stay. Keep watch." Soto burrowed her way through, crouching under the low clearance until she was able to stand upright again.

"Oh, my God." Soto froze at the contents of the cave. Fear tremored through her body, overtaking the warmth she had felt moments earlier. Now, it was if she were toeing into a cold pool of water, the feeling working its way through her extremities. "Ford?"

"Right behind you. I'm not as tiny as you." She grunted. "This space…shit, is tight, as fuck." Finally. They were together. Soto watched Ford adjust to her surroundings, and then observed confusion and shock overtake her. "What in the bloody hell?" Ford threw her bag on the ground. "The cameras. These are my cameras. How?" Ford picked one up and turned it around in her hands. "Grady," she radioed.

"Go ahead."

"Camera CEW75. When was that logged stolen?"

"Um. Hold on. Last week, one of the first batch of them. Why?"

Ford locked eyes with Soto.

"You there?" Grady asked.

"Yes. Yes," Ford said. "We found it along with several others."

"What do you mean?"

"I mean we found the flippin' cameras." She waved her hand in front of her. "In a fucking small cave we discovered." She got on her knees to inspect the others.

"What in the world?"

"Or who," Soto said as she crouched to join Ford.

"Do they still work?" he asked.

Ford stared at the wall, shaking her head. "I don't think so."

Soto picked up one of the cameras and tried to turn it on. She handed it to Ford to confirm.

"No power. Totally drained," Ford radioed.

"Those batteries should last several months."

"I know."

"I wish we had eyes down there," he said. "Do they look damaged?"

"No."

"Someone or something carried these down here and carefully lined them up in a neat little row against the wall," Soto chimed in.

"Fucking freaky. How many are there?" he asked.

"Twenty-three," Ford reported.

"That's exactly the number that have been stolen."

Ford tossed her radio on the ground and slapped the top of her helmet several times. "This is fucked up," she said and paced as much as the small space allowed. She was talking to herself and wringing her hands.

"Affirmative," Soto said. It seemed like the only fitting word for the moment.

"Give me the coordinates and physically mark the area. Then get the fuck back on track," he instructed.

"Copy," Ford radioed.

"I'm serious, Special Agent Winifred Ford. Stay on track. That's an order."

"We have no intentions of doing that, do we?" Soto asked Ford.

"The way in has got to be close by," Ford said, looking around. She pressed on walls, and tried to climb one without success. "And different than through a well. Or is there a well around here that's been retrofitted with stairs or something? These cameras are in near mint condition. If that crazy cat brought those down here, they'd be crushed or have scratch markings or…"

Ford knelt and moved dirt around, shoveling it with her hands, her actions getting more aggressive as she started clawing deeper. "Why are they all here in this one spot? What the hell is the deal with this one spot? Fuck!"

"Ford, stop."

Soto placed her hand on Ford's shoulder, stilling her movement. She sat on the ground and held her head in her hands. "Come on, let's go. Back on track," Soto instructed. She watched Ford struggle to get up. "What is it?" Then she grabbed at her chest. "Talk to me, Win?" Soto crouched to support her partner. "Are you sick again?" Soto whispered as she held Ford's face in her hands and secured Ford's helmet straps.

"I'm okay," Ford assured her. "But the whispering, it's back, somewhere close by."

"Which means the cat. It's close. Time to move. Win. Seriously. Pull it together. We *cannot* get stuck in here," Soto said as she helped Ford up, found her bag, put it over her shoulder and directed Ford to the opening, nearly shoving her through. "Go, go, go."

The sound grew louder. "Grady, we are headed back to the route, however we are under threat so we may be off track."

"Copy, Soto. Clarify coordinates when you are safe. Good luck."

"Copy."

"Soto?" Ford said.

"Right behind you." She grunted as she worked herself back through the opening.

"There's something wrong with Lex. She's growling at us," Ford said, hesitating to stand upright. "Look at her."

The dog's hair was on end and her lips were curled, baring large fangs.

"She isn't growling at us."

"Is she affected?"

"She's fine. Follow her lead. Go where she tells you...slowly."

Lexy corralled them against the edge of the stone wall and inched them toward the main path. Then she directed her focus toward the room with the cameras. Gnashing jaws snapped her warning, which was more frightening than the presence of the rabid creature.

"Is this when we should be freaking out?" Ford asked, readying her dart gun.

"Probably." Soto steadied Ford's arm. "But hold up. Let me get situated." Ford gave her a nod. "You okay?"

"So that ginger chew you gave me helped tremendously," Ford said. "Do you have any more?"

"Now?" Both of them had their weapons cocked and aimed into darkness. They stood back to back, scanning for a visual.

"I think it's why you don't feel the, um, side effects. The ginger must have certain molecular properties that are countering the effects of whatever the fuck was causing me to act..."

"Possessed?"

"Yeah. Because aside from a wee bit of nausea, I'm not going down that crazy road like last time. Which is good and bad. I can't perceive anything else that might be able to help our next move. But I'm not a helpless rag doll either."

"Oh. Well. That makes sense. You know what else makes sense?"

"Running!" Ford shouted.

"On my count, six o'clock, through there," Soto said and motioned to an opening with her light. "Lexy on three!" The dog barked several times and on three, they dashed toward the small opening, through an underpass, and straight into another horde of rotting, bloody, dead animals.

"Bad idea!" Ford shouted. "Now what?"

"This way!"

They traversed through another nest of death.

"What the hell!"

They doubled back and through the room with the old crates. "We're going in circles!" Soto exclaimed as a loud crash came from behind her.

"Soto!" Ford yelled. She stopped cold and turned. Ford had stepped clean through the floorboards where the artifacts were. Her bag was the only thing preventing her from falling through the brittle wood. "Help!"

Soto pulled her up until they were on solid stone again and scrambled to their feet.

"The main path is through there. I can see it!" Soto shouted once they were upright. The whispering creature felt as if it were an arm's length away. "Lexy, hold it," Soto instructed.

"I got eyes on it, Soto. I'm darting it!"

"We got you covered!"

"I'm taking the shot in three, two, one!" Ford cocked her weapon and sent a single dart whirling through the air. "Ha!" The pained wailing receding into the abyss sounded like she had hit her mark.

"Lexy, find it!" The dog raced after a presumably injured creature. "You ready?" Soto asked as she started after Lex.

"Fuck, yeah!"

"Stay close," Soto advised. Her headlamp did little to penetrate the void. "Where are you?"

"Soto!"

"Ford! What's your position?"

"I don't know. I'm turned around!"

She sounded like she was everywhere and nowhere. Soto spotted Lexy ahead but barking into the distance. Soto caught up to see why she had stopped—a ledge. "Stop pursuit! Ford!" She was barreling straight for her. It was too late. She was moving too fast. She wrapped her arms around Ford as they collided. "Lexy, stay!" Soto yelled as they fell.

Soto came to, struggling for air, coughing up water, trying to catch her breath. Barking came from somewhere. She couldn't register amid the ringing in her ears. Something was holding her. She couldn't move. It was Ford. They were floating. Water. "Lexy!"

"Up there," Ford said. Soto grasped Ford's outstretched arm as she pointed to their canine partner sitting up on the ledge where the three had been moments ago. They were only about twenty feet, though their present situation made it feel much further.

"Hey, girl," Soto yelled. Lexy laid at the edge, peering down upon them. Her worried whines brought tears to Soto's eyes. "Are you okay?" Lexy got up and barked. She wiggled her backside in the air, looking like she wanted to jump. "Stay! Lexy. We're okay." Another bark.

"There's a sandbank up ahead. Can you make it?" Ford asked.

"I think so."

Soto dislodged herself from Ford's arms. They paddled to a small landing and flung themselves onto it. Breath-stealing coughing shook Soto's body. She gasped for air. Ford placed her hand on Soto's chest.

"Breathe." Ford removed Soto's helmet and helped her sit up. "Slowly," Ford ordered. "There you go. You good?"

Soto nodded and looked about. "Where's my rifle? My bag?" She felt the space around her. "I need my bag!" She tried to stand, but more coughing prevented that from happening. She worked her way onto all fours, moments away from being totally unraveled.

"I see them." Ford aimed her headlamp toward two objects floating in the sea of stale, murky water. "Stay put." Moments later she was back. Two thuds into the sand let Soto know the bags were safe. "I didn't see the rifle."

"I don't care about the rifle. The bag. Thank you. Thank you." Soto opened her pack and rummaged through, throwing the sopping contents—her gear, her cell phone—onto the sandbank until she finally found a plastic bag. Dog food. With a bag in hand, she stumbled about, working her way to two feet. "Here girl." She threw the bag upward to Lexy but missed. "Come on!" she yelled. "I can't get it to her." Her words were clipped and breathy, as the water in her lungs was debilitating.

"Let me try," Ford said. After a couple of attempts, Ford lobbed it within Lexy's reach.

"Open, Lex. Dinner. It's cwunch cwunch. Come on, girl." The dog worked the package open with her teeth, pulling out bits of kibble and crunching her way through it. She pulled out a bottle of water and a tube.

"What is that?" Ford asked.

"Nutrients she needs to keep her strength." She put a glob into the bottle and gave it a good shake. She handed it over. "Please. Again." Ford threw the bottle of water, nailing it on the first attempt. "Open, girl." The sounds of the dog gnawing through plastic, puncturing holes in it to get to the precious liquid, put Soto's mind at ease. "Good, girl. We're going to be okay," Soto said. She dropped with a thud. Her hands went to her head, and she worked fingers into her temples. Then she reanimated suddenly. "Where are the radios?"

"I have no clue," Ford said. "Let's sit for a second, catch our breath." Ford emptied the contents of her bag shaking away water. She was shivering badly as she pulled out a bar of some sort, broke off a piece, and handed it over. Soto reached for it, realizing her entire body was trembling too.

Soto chattered and took a bite.

"We need something to burn." Ford shoved the last bite in her mouth. "I'm going to look around. I think the room I crashed through is close by."

"What if you get lost? Ford, I can't do this alone," Soto begged.

"I promise you, I won't get lost," Ford assured her. "Lexy, I'll be right back." The dog snorted her acknowledgment. "Watch over your mom."

Soto quickly lost sight of her partner, but heard sloshing as she ventured into darkness. Soto finally noticed the details of the space where they had landed—a small strip of a sandbank against a steep rocky and jagged ledge. At the top sat her dog, everywhere else a black, gray, and muggy void. She backed against the cold stone rock while she waited for Ford.

"Holy hell." Soto couldn't believe it. Ford returned with several cuts of brittle board in her arms.

"We're not too far off track. The floor we crashed through is right over there." Ford motioned in the direction with a whip of her head. "Let's see what we got." She dropped the cuts of wood on the ground. Some of them got wet. Do you have any waterproof matches in your bag?"

"No," Soto replied, her eyes fixed on the pile of wood.

"In any of those pockets?"

"Uh...oh! Yes." Soto fished out a package.

"Perfect. Hold your lamp steady for me, please." The two worked together and got a small fire going. It lit slowly and produced a lot of thick smoke before it took.

The boards crackled aggressively as they sucked up all the air around them. Sparks and chips burst every which way, the smell of it not as inviting as she imagined it would be. "That's going to burn quickly, isn't it?"

"Looks like it," Ford said and started removing layers of clothing. "Let's see if we can dry our clothes while we have heat." The two shed their heavy, soaked clothing, wringing out each piece and hanging it onto the slowly warming wall in hopes they would all dry out before they lost their heat source.

"You have scratches all over your back." Soto lifted Ford's tank top and ran her fingers over the red, torn skin. "I tried to help you. I did, I couldn't, didn't know what to do." Soto caressed Ford's scratched hands.

"You did help me, Soto, more than you know," Ford said, though her words didn't appease Soto. "I think I got the shot."

"I think you did too. I hope it's the only one we need to take." She looked up toward her dog.

"I'm really fucking sorry. I couldn't stop my momentum."

"I shouldn't have taken off without you," Soto said. "It was dark as hell up there."

"We're lucky we fell into water. That's what? A fifteen- or twenty-foot drop?" Ford alternated looks between the water and the ledge.

"At least," Soto shivered her response. She unraveled her braid and ran her fingers through her wet hair.

"You put your life in danger for me." Ford's voice quivered.

"Do you know how many ledges and cliffs I've fallen down in my line of work?"

"How many?"

Soto looked upward.

CHAPTER THIRTY-FOUR

The Stability of the Underground

Soto took one last look at Lexy, who was lying down. Though her eyes were closed, she wasn't sleeping. Her ears were perked. She was still on guard and that settled Soto's mind significantly. "That's nearly the last of it," she whispered and edged backward, settling against the wall of radiating warmth. Tiny amber sparks crackled into the air when she tossed another chunk of the warped board. "That should last for a little longer. We can only hope. This shit burns fast, doesn't it?"

She realized she was talking to herself. Ford had fallen asleep. The steady rise and fall of Ford's chest made her jealous. Lucky her. She was able to sleep after the madness they had endured. That she was able to simply brush aside the fall and the whispering sounds and the... After a particularly dramatic head bop, she felt herself fading there too.

She was sixteen again, sneaking bottles from the vineyard, taking them to the lake and to a woman who was holding court. It was the Lake Lowell Ghost. She was divine and had a lovely singing voice. She had summoned Daya for a favor—three bottles of the finest Cab Franc, shoes made of stiff leather and a short linen skirt with seashells sewn into the hem. A door opened, a disembodied hand gave Soto a dart gun, told her to take a shot in three, two…Jammed. She looked straight into the barrel to see what was the matter…

Soto jolted awake. Her heart was racing and her dog was whining. "Do you need to go out, girl?" She rubbed her eyes and let out an unsatisfying yawn. Why did Lexy sound so far away? "Lex?" She followed the sound of her dog's voice. Where the hell was she? The caves. The water. The twenty-foot drop. Up! She followed her dog's line of sight that was fixed on something in the shadows. Soto propped herself upright to get a better look. "Oh," she moaned. Her legs were numb. Sharp needles spread from her toes, to her heels, and up her calves.

"Hello?"

She rubbed her eyes, failing to blink away faint ripples in the water. "Who's there?" Her words echoed in the small cavern. Something was floating. A large piece of wood or a board. A raft? Impossible. Odd, she thought. Why was it even out there? Where did it come from? It had to be Ford. She was looking for more wood, of course. The fire was mostly embers and their supply was low. She was so thoughtful.

But she wasn't being thoughtful at the moment. She was still sleeping. Still dreaming. Not causing ripples in the water. "Ford?" She whispered and found a flashlight, and then thought better of turning it on and drawing unwanted attention. But from whom? This was all in her head. Had to be. But a gentle slapping of water on the shore, only yards away, told her otherwise. Besides, she thought, anything could have caused it. She scooted against the wall. Drew her legs up. Closed her eyes. Her dog's continued whining forced her attention. She was thankful for two things in that moment: that her heart worked on its own, for surely it would be petrified like the rest of her most basic movements, and that Ford's weapon was within her reach—because someone was on that raft. Two people were on that raft. Three people…four people. Not people, apparitions. Faint, but clear. Hazy, but detailed. Alive, but not. Five, six, seven, eight, seemingly from nowhere they kept popping onto the raft. How was it even seaworthy? One by one. There wasn't any more room!

She tried to silence another coughing fit, holding her chest as she wheezed and sputtered—painful and sharp—as she tried to grab for air, hoping the *people* on the raft wouldn't hear her. Of course they wouldn't. They weren't even there. Coughing overtook her.

"Soto?" Ford sat up with a groan. "You okay?" She handed her a bottle of water as if *that* would help the situation. "What's wrong?"

"Nothing. Go back to sleep. Please. I'm fine. I didn't mean to wake you." She felt Ford's hand upon her back, rubbing in slow circles as she coughed and fought for air. "Please..." She shut her eyes, hoping when she opened them, everything would be gone, all of them, gone, but...nine, ten, eleven, twelve. More and more see-through people jumping on the raft, one fell off and bumped his head...

"Daya? Talk to me."

"No." She dug her hands into the sand, reaching through the cold layers looking for something real, something tangible to hold on to. Thirteen, fourteen...

Ford inched closer. "Why are you scared?"

"I'm not. I'm not," Soto said through more dry and painful coughing.

"You're lying."

"I had a bad dream." She closed her eyes again, hoping this time, when she opened them that the blooms of color and stars under her eyelids would be enough to make them disappear.

"Daya, it's me."

"I'm hallucinating." A laugh escaped her lips. It sounded odd, crazy, and not like her at all. She squinted into the darkness. "But it looks so real."

"Daya?"

"Uh-huh?"

"Come here."

"I can't."

She felt Ford scooting toward her, inching behind her, pulling her between long legs and into the warmth of her embrace.

"Don't let me go."

"I won't," Ford whispered. "What do you see?"

Soto couldn't say and shook her head to indicate as much.

"I trusted you. Now trust me."

"M-m-men, a boat. There." She couldn't bring herself to point to it and thereby confirm that it was real. "I'm going crazy."

"You're the opposite of crazy," Ford whispered into her ear.

"I hit my head when I fell."

"No, you didn't."

"Yes, I did! You don't know...How do you know?"

"Because I see it too."

"You what?" Soto squirmed between Ford's legs, trying to get up, needing to get out! "Let me go." But Ford refused to let her go. "Please," she moaned. "We need an escape route, a plan, a diversion...Let me go."

"Never," Ford whispered against her neck. She placed a couple of kisses there too.

"How?" It was worthless to hide her hysterics. Her body wasn't responding to her brain's demands anyway. "What the fuck, Ford?" she asked, through hot tears streaming down her face, her muscles rigid and cramped from fighting. "This, this is not, we are..."

"Breathe, Daya. I got you."

"I don't believe any of this fucking shit. I can't believe in this. It doesn't make sense. It's not real." And then Soto gave up. She threw holding it together out the window along with all rational explanations that were locked in her mind—out the window, over the ledge, and into oncoming traffic. "Is it real?"

"It's real. As real as you and me and Lexy and everything else you know for fact."

"No," Soto groaned.

She shut her eyes and this time made an honest-to-goodness effort in believing that, when she opened them again, the haunting images would be gone and she would wake up in her own bed in Washington State, and this case would have never appeared on her desk, and she never would have said yes. But, that would mean foregoing meeting the beautiful and intelligent Winifred Ford, currently supporting her, holding her together while she broke into fragments of her former self. Nausea boiled up from the pit of her stomach, acid at first, then violent, dry heaving, leaving her with no energy to spare, leaning fully into Ford. "It looked right at me!" She gasped. "It's coming…" She tried again to make a break for it, but Ford held her in place.

"Listen to me, Daya. What we are witnessing is a residual haunting," Ford said. "We have nothing to worry about."

"A what?"

"They aren't aware. They're residual, on a loop, like we're watching it on TV, like a broadcast."

"A broadcast?" Lexy let loose a string of barks. "She sees it too, doesn't she? Ford?"

"Without a doubt," she confirmed. "And is she freaked out?"

"No," Soto whispered.

"Look at their clothes. And their tools. They look like miners or rail workers…"

"Immigrants?"

"Maybe. God, there are so many, how many of them are there?"

"Twenty-three! I counted twenty-three."

"The same number as there were stolen cameras."

Soto didn't have a response for that comment. "Did you see that?" she asked. "It pointed over there." Lexy warned them before she took off toward the direction that the spirit had pointed. "Be careful girl…"

"They're gone. Just like that. Show over."

"I think it's just beginning," Soto said.

CHAPTER THIRTY-FIVE

Stranger Things

"What about *Stranger Things*? Have you watched that?" Soto asked.

"Not yet," Ford said and continued tickling the soft skin of Soto's arms. They hadn't moved an inch since seeing the apparitions.

"Why not? It's so good."

"Not until I'm done with *Orphan Black*. I don't want to start anything new until I finish what I'm already watching. That way I can thoroughly invest in obsessing over the characters."

"Fair enough."

Ford turned her attention to her other partner. Lexy was back, had finally stopped pacing and was lying down, though her ears were pointed, apt and ready.

"It's getting louder," Soto said.

"Is it?" Ford knew it was. Since they had seen the apparitions, the whispering *had* grown sincerer and louder, and the words clearer at times.

"I think so." Soto waved away wisps of smoke. Their fire was embers mostly.

"I can't tell for sure," she lied. She pulled Soto tighter. She didn't want to make a big deal about it. Her partner had taken that first step toward acknowledging the supernatural, but baby steps seemed more fitting a pace than delving headfirst into dissecting what it all meant. Just when she felt Soto's body relax, the whispering sounds stirred all over again, holding her hostage, her tension ebbing and flowing with the whispering. "What I do know is that we have no more than an hour before total darkness, so we should try to sleep. Luckily, I have you to hold. You're a little heat box."

"You were really good with Marnie," Soto said.

"All I said was *lit* and *shero* a couple times, and I had her in the palm of my hand. That, and she did what I asked."

"Is that how it works?" Soto turned slightly and nudged her nose against her cheek.

"For best results," Ford said, working her hands under Soto's tank to caress her stomach, to get closer.

"I remember you."

"Remember me?" Ford shook off the grogginess and let out a huge yawn.

"The Elwha Dam."

"Tell me what you remember."

"I remember thinking how in the hell is that beautiful woman traversing the rocky terrain in those heels."

Ford laughed softly. "I remember your hair and how it blew in the wind." She pressed her nose into Soto's still damp hair, then smoothed it out of the way, and placed several kisses on her neck, feeling her squirm and lean into her. "The sun was reflecting in it and it flew with the wind like black and red butterflies were dancing around you."

"That's beautiful," Soto cooed. Ford felt Soto's breathing slow, and she felt heavier against her body. "When did you realize we had seen each other before?"

Ford shook herself awake. "Hmm? Oh. When I poked around on your website and saw those photos of you and Lex."

But it had been sooner than that. It was when she held the two case files in her hands, side by side. She knew what she beheld was familiar and unique. "It's the only reason I took the case."

"The only reason?"

"It didn't have a thing to do with orders." They laughed together.

"I'm sorry you're going to miss your trip," Soto said. She lifted Ford's hand and kissed her palm.

"That is the absolute last thing on my mind, Daya." She held on even tighter to the woman in her arms. "There is no place in the world I would rather be."

"The universe did that thing where the stars align. What's that called?"

"Fate."

"Fate?" Soto asked.

"Unless you have another word for it?"

Soto shook her head that she didn't.

"There is no way in hell I could have gotten this far without you, Soto. I know I'm not the easiest to work with."

"Understatement of the year." Soto's soft laughter echoed around them. "I couldn't imagine this investigation without you either." Soto's breathing grew softer. "Can I ask you another question?"

"Anything."

"What was Grady's comment?" Soto turned slightly. "About a partner you used to have?"

"I used to have a partner, a few years ago. Make that nine years ago. She got injured in the line of duty."

"What happened?"

"The sweat lodge fuck-up in Oregon. She was in a coma for about a week, and she was in bad shape for a long time after that."

"I'm so sorry, Win."

"She blamed me entirely and wasn't shy about making it known around the bureau."

"She blamed you? Why? Did you drag her into the sweat lodge? Force her to go against her will?"

"Of course not."

"So she made her own decision?"

"Well yes. But, I outlined a pretty good argument about why we should do it. She pushed back, but I didn't respect her argument."

"That's not all on you."

"Mostly it is."

Ford had convinced herself of that long ago.

"She could have said no."

"She wasn't going to let me do it alone. Would you?"

"I don't know the answer to that, but it sounds to me like she made her own decision and when the shit hit the fan, she blamed you, and that's a problem. That's a partner who is unwilling to learn from mistakes. We all make them. That's how you learn and build trust."

"That sounds fine in theory, Soto."

"And in practicality too," Soto added. "Take me and my closest colleague, Tom Roselyn, the guy I was telling you about."

"The guy you play tricks on?"

"Yeah, him. We weren't always close. We were both green. We had recently graduated from picking up roadkill, ticketing people without fishing licenses, grunt stuff. There was no Bear Dog Program yet. We had dogs, but not like her." She looked up toward her pup. "We recently learned about this conditioning technique and had a couple of successful hard releases under our belts."

"Conditioning?"

"Yeah. When we get our hands-on wildlife, bears that have ventured into populated areas, we condition them to be scared of people, loud noises, city noises, dogs. We condition them to associate those noises with danger, to associate populated places with danger. I had one job. To keep an eye on a recently conditioned black bear. We were seconds away from the hard release. We got guys ringing bells and sounding horns, making a ton of racket. We opened the cage to let her go and she came charging right at me. Scared the shit out of me. I didn't trust my dog at the time and I freaked out, fell on my butt, and shot a dart right into Roselyn's ass."

"Oh shit," Ford laughed.

"It is funny looking back. But that dart was a cocktail made for a full-grown bear. Put Roselyn in the hospital for a week, and he had dreaded desk duty for months, walked with a limp for a while. Still does sometimes."

"Damn."

"Roselyn was livid. His wife was beyond livid. She tried to get me reassigned, tried to put me behind a desk—permanently. I could have gotten a lot of people hurt, killed."

"And he stayed with you?" Ford asked.

"It brought us closer."

"And the bear?"

"Ran past us straight into the woods. Lived a long life, had several cubs, and never saw her in town again after that."

"That's a nice ending and a forgiving partner."

"Exactly," Soto said through a yawn. "Why didn't you try again?"

"It was a two-way street, no one wanted to work with me, and the feeling was mutual." Ford's thoughts took her on a journey back in time. "I would have done anything for her. I loved her, but not like that. We were partners for years. She went with me to my parents' funerals. She was my only family after that." Ford felt a tightness in her chest, but Soto's soft kisses and her fingers upon her cheeks softened her building anxiety. "I would have given anything to have switched places," Ford said against Soto's neck.

"You would rather she wander in the woods and be held in a county psych ward and carry that stigma through her career? Because that sounds pretty damaging too."

"She had it worse. She almost stroked out. I visited her every day until… I wasn't welcome anymore."

"Why?"

"I was with her, by her side day in and day out, spending the nights. Everybody insisted that I take a break—her mother, the bureau—they ordered me to back off and get some rest. So I did. And when I went back a couple of days later, they wouldn't let me see her. She had told her mother that she couldn't heal with me around. She didn't want me anywhere near her. Ever. She had been too scared to tell me in person and rightly so. I lost it, lost my temper. Completely saw red like you wouldn't believe. I was escorted out of the fucking hospital, but they didn't need to fucking cuff me."

"I'm sorry, Win."

"No one trusted me after that. Then I turned that doubt on myself, constantly questioning my abilities, wondering if I was a good agent. 'You seek answers at the expense of others,' was the last thing she said to me. Then I turned that corner and thought, fuck them, fuck all of them. I'm the most competent and capable agent in the Bureau."

"That a girl."

"I have evolved into a complete bitch that I don't quite like anymore." She let out a self-mocking laugh. "I've been totally immersed in finding the truth, turning cases, going a hundred miles per hour. It's taken its toll on me, my relationships. Running Paranormal Investigations takes a certain type of person, and I'm not sure that's me anymore."

"Thank you for telling me, Win, and for being honest."

"And since we're being all open and honest with each other…Being outside, with you, working this case together with Lex… These past weeks have been the best fucking weeks ever."

"Me too." Soto's laughter filled the depths with warmth that worked its way into every dark corner, every cave, every void in Ford's heart.

"I've learned so much from you and from her," Ford said, motioning toward Lexy. "What I wouldn't give to have a partner like that, and like you, all the time. I'm forever changed."

"I am honored to have been able to work with you too, Ford. You are brilliant, pushy, and arrogant." She leaned into Ford and kissed her on the neck. "And I wouldn't have you any other way."

"Thank you." Ford tightened her arms around Soto. She promised herself that she would commit this moment to her memory, the feeling of this confident, smart, funny, beautiful woman in her arms. She held onto her like she would a life raft, after tossing and turning, being pounded by wave after wave, in a murky sea year after year. Now that she knew what hope felt like, she didn't want to let go. She had to hold on to see where she would land.

"I'm sorry for demeaning the things you believe and insulting your intelligence," Soto said.

"You didn't," Ford assured her. "Your perspective is valuable and has been critically important to this case. Never doubt it. I love knowing what you know. I mean, your thoughts. I want more."

She knew for a fact that she was in love with Soto—with her mind, her body, her beliefs—-all that she stood for. But voicing that she loved her was about as easy for her as it likely was for Soto to explain that she saw ghosts. Ford rested her chin on Soto's shoulder and closed her eyes. "Whatever this is, I want it."

"I crave knowing your perspective. On everything." Soto rested her head against Ford's chest. Her breathing softened and she let out a yawn. "When I'm not with you I want to be. I want to know what you're thinking all the time," Soto whispered. "I crave you more than I crave being at the top of a mountain looking down into the crystal blue water. And how I feel when I kiss you, it's all I think about. It's why I can't keep my hands off you. I don't want to stop. I know I should, but fuck that," Soto whispered. "The moment I kissed you I knew…"

Tears trickled down Ford's cheeks.

"Knew what, Daya?"

Soto's soft breathing told Ford that she had finally fallen asleep. Ford questioned what she had heard and wanted to shake the tiny woman awake to ask her to repeat it, to repeat everything, all of it, over again.

CHAPTER THIRTY-SIX

Celestial Foreplay

Waking up proved painful. Soto's entire body ached. She didn't dare shift her position. A flash, a strobe of light made its way through her heavy-lidded eyes.

"Come on!"

Whose voice was that? Then the sound of wind and barking from somewhere. She recognized *that* voice. "You tell 'em, Lex." Soto sat up with a jump, wondering where she was until she landed in the present—the yellow warblers, the *One-Two*, the historical treasure trove. The spirits! A dry cough took the wind out of her.

"You okay?" Ford asked.

Soto nodded into the darkness.

"Come on, get up."

Soto pawed around and felt outstretched arms. She grabbed a hold.

"There you go." She was pulled to a standing position. A few vertebrates audibly righted themselves. "That sounded good." Ford's voice soothed her.

"It felt horrible," Soto groaned. "Damn water tore up my lungs." She rubbed her chest while Ford rubbed her shoulders. "That feels good," Soto moaned, letting her head bob in front of her. "And you?"

"Aside from freezing, having a splitting caffeine headache, and being trapped in a dark cave, all is well in the world." Laughter filled Soto's lungs with a breath of fresh air, literally and figuratively. Then Ford went back to her knees. "Come on, light you fucker." She tried again to get the charred boards to light. "I got a plan, Soto."

"So do I." Soto had dreamed it.

"You first."

"I know what we need to do." She pulled her uniform pants off the wall, gave them a good shake, and stepped into them.

"I'm listening."

"The apparition pointed there." Soto motioned with her beam in the general direction. "That's the way we need to go. We need to go right."

"To get out?"

"To find the answers."

"Are you sure?" Ford rose quickly. She threw the charred stick into the fire pit. "Why the change of heart?"

"Chess moves," Soto said and held both her hands in front of her as if grasping her thoughts from the darkness. "Fate. The apparitions, the whispering, the cameras, the deranged animals. Whatever it is, called us down here, Win. Pulled *you* down that hole in the ground, showed *us* the wells, the sisters. Even that." She pointed upward toward the ledge. "All of it celestial chess moves to here."

"Tell me more," Ford said as they dressed.

"The apparitions looked like immigrants, right? Idaho's history isn't exactly one of open arms for immigrants."

"Not much has changed since then," Ford scoffed. "It's still a very oppressive state for a lot of people."

"Believe me, if anyone knows it's me," Soto said and held up a finger. "Chinese laborers worked on the railroad that came through here in the 1860s. I've heard stories about underground travel routes that immigrant laborers used to avoid harassment."

"Underground travel routes to where? Are we talking intrastate or something on a larger scale?"

"I don't know," Soto said, braiding her hair. "What do you know about Chinese folklore?"

"It relies heavily on numerology. Aside from that, not much, but the concepts are the same between several cultures. Some cultures believe that negative energies can manifest themselves into forces that have the ability to steal, cause disappearances, maim, and even kill."

"Terrorize wildlife?"

"Or work through them somehow."

"Why would they turn on each other?"

"Let me mull that over a bit before—what are you doing?"

Pop that was one, pop that was another. "Your buttons are off." She unruffled Ford's collar while she was at it. "Just making sure you look good in the dark."

"I'm a little bit turned on by that," Ford admitted.

"Your one-track mind." Soto grinned in delight when she felt Ford's hands squeeze her backside.

"You're one to talk!" Ford slapped her hand on Soto's bottom causing Soto to yelp.

"But I'm a little freaked out." Soto's glee was short-lived. "This could be for nothing. Coincidences. Plain and simple. There's no real science."

"I don't think so, Soto," Ford said as she pulled her closer. Soto stood on the very tips of her toes to kiss her. Her lips were dry from dehydration, their water supply totally exhausted.

"Neither do I," Soto said. Ford's touch was a welcomed distraction in the moment. "So, proceed to the route?"

"Proceed to the route," Ford said as she pulled away from a lingering kiss. "Wait. How is your uniform totally dry?"

"If there is one good thing about polyester, that's it."

"Polyester looks sexy on you, in case I haven't already said so."

"Thank you. And while we're on the topic, your reading glasses are kind of a turn on."

"Getting old and needing glasses gets you going?"

"Totally." A groan escaped Soto's lips. "I'm not sure if I should be jumping for joy at piecing things together or freaking the fuck out because we're pursuing a lead from a bunch of ghosts."

"Trust your gut. That's what I do."

"And my gut says I need to eat."

"What do we have?"

"How does soggy ginger chews and dog food sound?"

"Perfect." Their laughter echoed around the small cave.

CHAPTER THIRTY-SEVEN

Of Quartz

They had taken a right, the direction the spirit had pointed. They were basically blind and it smelled foul in places.

"You're going to fucking climb up *there*?" Ford's voice was several octaves higher than normal. She directed her flashlight upward, catching Lexy's reflective collar and her shining eyes.

"I'm going to meet her halfway." Soto dropped her bag and handed Ford her flashlight. "Light my way with this one." She scaled up the treacherous ledge. "And use the other one to help Lex out."

"Oh my God, Daya. This feels fucked," Ford said, her two beams pointed in different directions. "I feel like an air traffic controller."

"They're called wing walkers."

"What?" She broke into a sweat, making her hands feel slippery as she focused on holding steady for Soto.

"Wing walkers, not air traffic controllers, guide the planes into their gates," Soto said as she climbed upward.

"Okay, whatever." Ford's arms shook.

"Hold the light steady, please," said Soto. "It's dangerous enough as it is without you bopping the lights all willa-nilly all over the place."

"Did you say *willa-nilly?*"

"What?"

"Nothing. Nevermind. Shit, be careful. God!" Ford exclaimed, her entire body trembling. Soto was nearly there.

"Okay, Lex. Come to me."

Ford's heart raced erratically as she watched Soto's dog scaling the jagged ledge like a mountain goat, hopping sure-footed as she headed toward Soto.

"Almost here, girl. Jump!" Soto held her arms apart. "Aha!" she cried. Lexy had landed squarely in her arms. "I missed you so much. I'm so sorry we got separated," she said, kissing her dog profusely. "I couldn't stop thinking about you. Did you get enough cwunch cwunch to eat this morning?" she asked before they scaled back to ground level.

Ford's heart swelled at the reunion. The two trusted each other in a way that Ford hadn't seen between an animal and a human. She wanted that, wanted it bad.

"Hey, girl," Ford said as she crouched to her knees and greeted Lexy, who forewent licks on her fingertips for several licks on her cheeks. "I missed you too. Thanks for watching our backs last night." She gave the dog another kiss on the head then stood and looked at Soto sternly. "You. Let's not do that again. Fucking dangerous." She took Soto's face into her hands and kissed her hard on the lips before they continued their journey.

"Great. Another deceptive looking got-to-get-through-on-your-knees-through-a-tiny-pinhole-in-the-wall," Ford said.

"There's no other way unless we turn back. We can make this work."

Lexy confirmed it was possible by squeezing through the small opening.

"Besides, I'm still not a hundred percent convinced that we're not being stalked by that deranged cat. I still feel something. I want as many obstacles as possible between us and it."

"Unfortunately, I agree," Ford said. She pointed her dart gun and flashlight toward the void, a last check before she followed her partners, who had already started burrowing through the opening.

"Watch your head," Soto advised. "You're going to get wet."

"Thanks for the warning." She was upright again after yards of mostly crawling. She adjusted her stiff wet jeans. "I never thought I would envy polyester, but I do."

"Do you smell that?"

Ford inhaled a cool stream of crisp air, as if straight from an oxygen tank. "Smells fresh," she said, taking several breaths through her nose.

"Ford. Listen. What is that?" Lexy trotted to their side. "Sounds like walking. Like one distinct foot in front of the other."

"Let's keep going," Ford advised, heading onward toward the sound that grew louder. The whispers now combined with other strange noises, more footsteps, shuffling of feet, moving of objects, and metal on stone. The three of them traveled inches apart, but in the near pitch dark they might as well have been miles away from each other.

"Hold. Soto, Lex," Ford said. "What *is* this? Look. Markings on the wall. Characters of some sort...Cantonese...I think, it's too old to make out." She ran her fingers along the wall, smoothing away dirt and debris. "Fuck."

"What happened?"

"I got cut." Ford shone her light onto her hand. "The walls are fucking sharp. Glass?" She leaned in and shone her flashlight upon the area that was streaked with her blood.

"Quartz. A very big quartz vein in the stone," Soto observed.

"A very sharp quartz vein in the stone." Ford put her finger in her mouth. "Gross." She wiped her tongue on her sleeve. "Bad idea." She spat into the ground. "Sorry that's not very ladylike of me."

"Can I see your hand?" Soto asked. Ford held out her hand, blood dripping from the tip of her index finger. "You poor baby." Soto pulled the handkerchief from around her neck and wrapped it around Ford's sliced finger. "It's not very clean, but it should help."

"It feels better already." Ford squeezed the rag in her fist.

A loud clank came from the distance.

"Shit... What was that?" Ford whispered. "What in the hell is down here with us?"

"It sounds like someone is right over there."

Ford chanced a look, shining her lamp into the distance. "Holy hell, Soto. Come look. Turn your light off. It's beautiful."

Sun filtered in from fissures in the stone reflecting off the quartz, casting glimmering bits of lights. "It looks like a cave full of rubies." A shifting sun animated the space around them like a living kaleidoscope.

"The whole cave is marbled with quartz. It's rare to see it like this," Soto whispered.

"Fuck me." Ford nearly dropped to her knees. "Quartz. Of course." She pulled Marnie's lucky rock out of her pocket, rolled it between her fingers and shone her flashlight through it. "It's not agate. It's quartz." She used her nail to clean a bit of clay that made it appear marbled like an agate.

"I wish I had a camera," Soto said. "It's breathtaking. I've never seen—"

"Hello!" Ford yelled, her voice echoing around the cave and startling her partners.

"What the fuck, Ford? Sweet baby Jesus!" Soto grabbed onto her shoulder, digging into her.

"Listen." The sound of shuffling feet and whispers continued as before. "It's not a person. It's not a person! Quartz, that is, limestone quartz. Ha!" Her discovery echoed off the walls. "It makes so much sense. How stupid was I?" She leaned against the wall, her senses confused by the cool on her back paired with the ache caused by Soto's hand still gripping her shoulder.

"Ford, seriously. Keep it down. The mountain lion or another fucking deranged creature could be lurking around somewhere."

"No. I don't think so Soto. The cat, he served his purpose... all of them...served their purpose and led us to this exact spot. Of course..."

Ford continued to study her lucky rock, licking it a few times, and shining her light through it from all angles.

"Here's the thing about quartz. It can record information like events in history. When the information is released through a disturbance of some sort—in this case without a doubt, the ground breaking—a residual haunting can sometimes happen."

"Mother of Mary, warn me next time you want to yell in a dark cave." Soto was still holding on to her shoulder. "And you're going to need to repeat yourself, because I processed zero of what you said."

"I remember reading a case study once about this new community where the families were being terrorized. Seemingly out of nowhere weird things started happening. Their stuff went missing, pets acted odd, especially in one particular home. They reported noises coming from their attic—entire conversations, slamming doors, yelling, a ton of crazy shit. Only thing was, they didn't have a second level to their house and it only occurred at the same time every night and for hours at a time. Then it would stop. And again and again, every single night. The community was falling apart, fighting, and blaming each other."

"What does this have to do with quartz?"

"I'm getting there. They pulled in several experts. Mediums couldn't figure it out. The highest tech equipment didn't document a thing. It wasn't until they consulted a Wiccan expert, who was well versed in crystals, that they learned what it was. When she arrived at the property and noticed bulldozers and a massive landscaping project, she asked if the activity had started right around the time the bulldozers broke ground. It had, and it had unearthed a ton of rock that happened to be quartz."

"And?"

"It caused havoc, started playing sounds as if on a loop just like here."

"How did they stop it? Can it be destroyed?"

"No. God no. Destroying it is not recommended, and likely could cause even more aggressive reactions. I bet you two dollars that when the preserve broke ground for the new trail project, it destroyed quartz. Something happened down here that was recorded into the quartz. It's causing the animals to be severely affected by it and turn on each other."

"But why not Lex or the other dogs, the other wildlife?"

"It might only affect the animals present at the time they broke ground." Ford scratched a spot under her helmet. "I don't know."

"What did the family do?"

"After researching the property, they learned their new community was situated on a historical site where a famous battle was fought. I can't confirm what happened next, but it'll be the first fucking thing I research when we get the fuck out of here," Ford said. "My inclination is that there would need to be a dedication or a ceremony, a tribute. The victims would need to be remembered somehow."

"Remember," Soto said. "Never forget. Fuck me, Ford. Those are the words you were saying yesterday. 'Lost, cold, they are working, buried…' You were talking about those rail workers." Soto slid down against the cold rock wall. "You, Marnie, and Mrs. Richards all voiced the same things. 'Being trapped. Can't see. Remember…'"

Ford got on her knees to meet Soto at eye level. She wrapped an arm around Lexy. Then both of them looked at their partner. "What should we do?"

"What do you mean?" Soto said. She scratched her dog on the head and caressed Ford's cheek. "We find them. We proceed to the route."

"You're still in?" Ford asked, a smile on her face.

"Silly question."

"It'll be dangerous."

"I know."

Ford felt Soto's strength growing exponentially as they inched toward the answers. "But how."

"Down."

"There?"

"It's the only way."

"It's steep. As fuck."

"I think she knows." Lexy's bark confirmed it. "Lex. Find it." They stood and pointed their flashlights toward the way their partner had gone. "Ready."

"Right behind you."

They followed, seemingly in a spiral, hopefully toward answers, but each time they caught up to their fearless canine pacesetter, she would turn around yet another recess.

"Stop!" Soto said. Ford bumped into Soto's outstretched hand. She shone her light downward. "Let's not fall off this ledge."

"Been there, done that."

"Alexus Marie!" Soto yelled. Lexy was barking from the other side. "Crazy girl, you jumped it? Always got to one-up me!" Lexy's barking sounded like she was either teasing her or encouraging her. "Okay, I see how it is." Soto slipped off her backpack.

"You're going to jump that?" Ford said, her tongue felt heavy and stuck to the roof of her mouth. "That's what, six feet?"

"Hard to tell in minimal light. But if Lexy can do it, we can."

"She's got four legs!" Ford said, pacing and rubbing out a sudden growing ache in her neck. "That's a long jump for me, let alone you." Soto gave her a look. "You're a foot shorter than I am."

"I can make it."

"Jumping into darkness seems like a *really* bad idea."

"It's not that big a gap." Soto demonstrated by throwing her bag across the divide, a plopping sound a little bit away confirmed that it was solid ground on the other side. "I'm going for it."

"Wait." Ford reached out to her.

"What?"

"Nothing. Go." Ford itched the palms of her hands. "Wait!"

"What?"

"Good luck? Shit." Ford's stomach clenched.

"It'll be okay. Now…" Soto said. She placed her hands on either of Ford's shoulders, kissed her, and then pushed her against the wall, "Move, please. This will take a running start."

Soto took off, leaped, and cleared the gap. She landed with a thud. "Aha!" echoed throughout the cave, joining the shuffling and whispering sounds. "Easy! Now you."

"Have I ever told you I'm afraid of heights?" Ford shouted.

"I don't think so."

"Shit! Shit! Shit!"

"You can do it. Throw me your bag." Ford hurled it toward Soto. "Don't look down."

"Too late!"

"Watch your clearance. It's low right before the ledge," Soto advised.

"Anything else I should or shouldn't worry about?"

"One more thing…"

"Yes?"

"Try not to fall."

"Got it." Ford backed up as far as she could. "You're going to catch me, right?"

"Of course."

She took off and ran into darkness, hooking her boot right at the edge to give her the push she needed to clear the divide.

"I got you," Soto's voice floated through the dark. Ford flew right into her arms and held on tight. "Wasn't that a rush?" Soto had a huge grin on her face.

"That most certainly was *not* a rush!" Ford buried her nose in Soto's neck, listening to their combined galloping heartbeats. "I really hope we don't have to go back that way."

"Me neither."

The trio headed further into the depths toward more clues. As they approached an open expanse, a noise came from directly behind them—a clanking, sharp and harsh as if metal on stone.

"God damn it!" Soto exclaimed. They turned abruptly to see what it was. "There!" Soto shuffled toward the source. "A pick ax?" She shone her light on the object on the ground. "Where the hell did this come from?"

"Nowhere." Ford crouched and shone her light to reveal that it was coated in ages of dust. "It's been here for decades."

"The spirits were carrying tools exactly like that," Soto remarked. "Ford. This is weird. It's freezing right here. Come and feel it." Ford stood and hovered her hand atop Soto's.

"That's a good sign, depending on how you interpret it."

"How so?" Soto shone her flashlight upward inspecting the cave ceiling.

"We're close, Soto. This means—"

Soto took a step backward, which was one step too many. "Daya!"

Ford's shout was lost amidst Lexy's barking—both of their warnings coming too late. Down went Soto along with the chunk of stone where she stood seconds before. Ford's quick reaction gained her a firm grip around a single wrist. "I got you!" Ford yelled as she lay flat on her stomach, balancing her weight and Soto's. "Hold on!" Soto's cries lost in the thunder of tumbling rocks. Her flailing made it difficult for Ford to maintain her hold. The more Soto thrashed, the harder it became.

"Reach for my hand!" Ford instructed, remaining calm.

"I can't!"

Ford tried another tactic, grasping Soto's backpack to lift her out, but Ford merely pulled it off, weakening her own grip.

"Win!" Soto started to choke. "I can't breathe," she wheezed. Another coughing fit.

"I got you, Daya. Don't you worry about that. Focus on your breathing. I'll do the rest."

"I'm slipping!"

"I got you!" She found Soto's eyes, the fear in them nearly taking the air right out her own lungs. Lexy's whining and whimpering contributed to the cleaving of her heart. "Daya, listen to me. Hang on. Think about Lexy and those little birds with pretend broken wings scaring the shit out of her at the last minute. And imagine your Dad and Isa, your mother, and everyone who has ever loved you."

"Win, I can't hold on. I'm going to fall." She choked and sputtered through fits of coughing.

"Daya! Listen to me. It's all in your head. It wants you to choke, to suffocate, but you're not going to let that happen. I'm going to pull you out. We're going home and we're going to help everyone remember! Me and you! Come on, breathe for me. Daya, please!" She pleaded. "Leave her the fuck alone!" She wailed into the darkness and couldn't hold back tears, though she knew she should be strong for Soto.

As quickly as it had started, Soto's coughing fit stopped. Her breathing became more regular, clear and deep. "Reach for my hand!" Ford risked more to close the distance between them with one final stretch. Then she felt it! Soto's hand in hers. "I got you!" She grasped her hands tightly around her wrists, inching her up and back to solid ground.

"Win. Hold up. I feel something here…a ledge… I think I can…I can stand on it. Wait."

"What is it?"

"There's a ledge of some sort. I think I can slide to a landing below. Let me go."

"I'm not going to fucking let you go, Daya!"

"There's something down here. I need to see it…I think I can reach it."

"You think you can or know you can?"

"Pretty sure. I can see—"

"That's not good enough!" Ford shouted, tightening her grip on Soto's wrists.

"I'm sure, Win. Positive. There's something down here. I'm able to gain footing. Trust me."

"Not alone you're aren't."

"No. Work with Lexy. Watch my back. Please trust me."

"Fuck!" she yelled.

Soto's assurances reminded her of Oregon all those years ago. She had promised her partner that nothing was going to happen. Trust her judgment. She was as positive then as Soto sounded in this moment. But that was then and this was now. "Talk us through every fucking step, got it?"

"I will."

"Letting go now," she warned, but all she heard was a cacophony of gravel, cascading down in sheets along with Soto as she slid down into the void. Ford located both of the flashlights scattered on the ground and returned to her stomach to light Soto's way. "Lexy, please, watch our backs. Let me know if something's wrong." Ford shone her light into the depths below. The flashlight beams struggled to penetrate ancient dust and particles released into the air by Soto's descent. "What do you see?"

"Not much, but it's freezing cold."

"You're getting close. Keep going and keep talking to me," Ford ordered.

"Huge chunks of stone…more of those old tools, pieces of wood and metal…helmets and…Oh my God!"

"Soto, what the fuck is happening?"

"Bones. Human bones. Broken bodies in the gravel. This is a mass grave."

Ford shone her beam around the cave, trying to piece together what warranted this final resting place. A large part of the cavern ceiling was missing up top. "Get out of there, Soto! It's not safe. Come on, we found what we were looking for. Get out now!"

"Why were you here? Where were you going?"

"Come back up. Please, Soto."

"What are your names?"

"That's it. I'm coming down there to fucking get you."

"We need to get them out, Ford."

"We will, but you first."

"We're going to get you out! Every last one of you. Please, Ford, help me tell them, in their language…" She stuttered. "Tell them it will be okay…Tell them!"

Ford repeated after her in a dialect that she found fitting.

"We are taking you home."

She said that too.

"We will tell your story. We will remember and you are not forgotten."

After they voiced that last promise, a whispering from the depths swirled below and rose out of the depths like a freight train on the loose, through a ghost town, shaking loose every rusty hinge that had managed to hold on for over a century.

For the first time in a long time, they sat in total silence. No whispering. No clanking. No shuffling of feet. No feelings of dread or anxiety.

"Come back to us, Daya." Ford said once again.

She heard her assent before eyeing her small frame making its way out, born anew from finding the answers. Ford grabbed her wrists and pulled her the rest of the way up, wrapping her arms around her and holding her as close as she could. And they lay there on the floor of the dark cave catching their breath.

CHAPTER THIRTY-EIGHT

Tiny Traveler

"Is that what I think it is? Is that the sound of hound dogs?" Ford asked, expecting to see delight in Soto's eyes at being minutes away from fresh air. "You're right, it is a lovely sound," she added, though Soto kept walking, her gaze upon the ground. "Daya?" Ford reached for Soto's hand, halting movement. "We're almost home."

"But *they* aren't." Soto looked toward the darkness they would soon leave behind. "I want to know who they are and what their names were…their families. I want everyone to know and for *them* to be home."

"The investigation is not over. Not by a long shot. They will have their day. If I have to rip up every bit of rehabilitated sagebrush to get down there again, I will. Please trust me."

"I do trust you. With my life and with hers."

Lexy stood in between them, her hind end wiggling and her tail whapping their legs from her dancing, her ears perked at the sound of the hound dogs closing in on them. Soto kneeled and caressed her partner's furry head. "Go on, girl. Go find it," she whispered. Her dog leaped toward the daylight.

Soto stood on tiptoe to wrap her arms around Ford's neck. "It's nice to finally see you again."

"I was thinking the same thing about you too, Soto." Ford pressed her forehead against Soto's. "That and you need shower." Ford craved to see the tiny creases at the edge of Daya's chestnut eyes and the parting of her lips when she laughed softly.

"So do you, funny girl." They held each other for a while.

"Get ready!" Soto said. Lex had returned with two hound companions. They braced themselves at the happy onslaught of paws and tongues and tails that greeted them at once. "Dexter! Debbi! What good dogs you are! Where's your mom, huh? Where is she? Good pups, yes." Soto kissed the pups thoroughly.

"All we have to do is follow them out," Ford said. "You ready?"

"I'm ready."

They followed their canine leaders, sloshing their way through a giant irrigation pipe, through knee-deep water flowing fast on its way toward fresh summer air. A brush fire was burning in the distance creating a hazy pink afternoon. Then the strobing red and white lights of the first responders were in sight.

"How did they know?" Ford asked, turning to Soto who wore the same look of confusion as they looked out on a swarm of people coming toward them.

The crowd included Crawly, Grady, Gorman, Ladd, a handful of volunteers, Executive Director Jewell, Isa, and Juan Soto. Upon seeing her father, Soto ran the rest of the way straight into his open arms. Ford warmed at the sight. She stepped into the full light of high noon, bathing herself in warmth, and the knowledge that she had entered the caves as one person and come out the other side a different one.

Grady was the first to greet her. She gave him a couple of slaps on the back, shook his hand firmly, and then gave in to an embrace. "Holy shit, you are in so much trouble," he said. "I ordered you to proceed to the route, and what did you do?" He followed with a look of concern, followed by sternness and then a huge grin. "What the hell happened to you guys?"

"Fill you in later, but first how the *hell* did you know we would exit right here?" Ford asked and motioned to the irrigation pipe from which they had just emerged.

"As soon as we lost you, we scrambled like hell to find you again. We tried to get the trackers to start up again and activate the cameras, but nothing. Then we tried different frequencies on the off chance you had bugged Soto at one point, as is her modus operandi with people she likes," he said pointedly to Soto. "And…we got one." He reached toward Ford. "May I? Your bag?" he asked. Ford handed it over, confused. He inspected Ford's bag, flipping the grimy thing upside down. "Ah! There she is. It's a tiny little thing." He pulled an electronic bug off her bag. Showing everyone around them. "Isn't she a beauty?"

Ford turned to Soto. "You? "When?"

"That's classified." Soto laughed.

"You would make a fantastic special agent, Officer Soto."

"And you would make a great bear dog handler, Special Agent Ford."

"Does it come with that polyester uniform?"

"And a shiny puffy coat in the winter."

"Don't tempt me."

"What happened down there?" several volunteers asked at once. "What did you see?"

"Is it gone?" Executive Director Jewell asked. "Is the terror on our preserve over?"

"It's highly likely that the mauling of wildlife has ceased," Ford said.

"How do you know?" Jewell asked.

"There are convincing indications that the disruption of the trail project released biological components that caused the wildlife to react aggressively. We have taken initial steps to neutralize the situation."

"What does that mean?" Jewell crossed her arms.

"Until we draft our findings, that is all we're at liberty to communicate, though that isn't going to be the focus of our report."

Ford told them about the discovery of a mass grave, leaving out details like how the whispering had stopped after they made their promises to honor their memories. Everyone agreed that getting them home would be the priority of the entire community.

"The FBI is committed, I am committed, to providing support over the next few weeks and months—however long it takes—to see this project to the end." Ford found Soto's eyes before she said her next piece. "If there are no other questions, my team has a lot to do to wind down operations at the preserve…" Ford felt an overwhelming need to grab a hold of Soto and run back to the caves, just so they could be alone again one last time.

"You ready?" Grady asked, breaking Ford from her reverie.

Ford shook her head that she was. "Thank you." She followed her agents to their truck.

"Special Agent Ford." Ford turned toward Director Jewell. "I know you are very tired and have a lot to do, and the last thing you want to do is mingle with people, but a lot of them would like to thank you for everything you've done. Will you join us tonight for the auction at the vineyard? All of you? Grady? Gorman? All are welcome. Please," she said. "It would be an honor to have you all at my table."

"We will be there," Ford said as she followed Grady to their work truck and climbed in. She looked out the window to see Soto with her braid a tangled rope, dirt on her face, and her dog at her side as she fielded more questions from the crowd. They locked eyes as Ford drove away.

"You fucking stink." Grady rolled down her window. The guys agreed.

"I know," Ford said.

"You know? No 'fuck you Grady, get off my nuts'?"

She laughed. "I'm way too tired to even spar with the lot of you."

"Hasn't stopped you before. Yo, Win. You okay back there?"

"Tired."

"Whatever for," he said and made eye contact with her through the rearview mirror. "Excellent job down there. You did really good."

"Thank you, Grady. So did you." She smiled at him. "I'm not sure I ever told you that before. But you're a hell of an agent...you fucking asshole."

CHAPTER THIRTY-NINE

Highest Bidder

Lightweight black tapered dress pants, a little on the snug side, heels at her feet, and a gold sleeveless top felt wonderfully different after two days of dirty polyester. A cool breeze whipped around Soto, through her hair and caressed her skin. It felt freeing and hopeful.

The beauty of the vineyard was especially magical. Twinkling white lights on ropes zigzagged overhead, as if the stars had come down to see about life on earth. She wondered how she was able to pick up on the chirping crickets amid the festivities of the evening—their faint calls crisp and clear amid the auctioneer spinning rhymes and raising money.

Laughter and chatter abounded, the wine flowed freely, and the food was superb. Even Ford got in on the action, bidding on and winning the coveted *Ornithologist's Delight*, a gift package full of bird things, including feeders, seeds, books, binoculars and an original work of art that the Richards donated—a crudely framed eight-by-ten original photograph of a pair of yellow warblers. Not that anyone else could top her five-thousand-dollar bid.

"Hometown girl does good. Again," said Isa, joining Soto at her table. "Look what I found." She held up a bottle of red wine and two glasses. Isa worked out the cork and poured them each a glass of the vineyard's finest. "Cheers to our hometown hero. You can add that to your résumé."

"Hero?" Soto laughed. "I'll drink to that." She tipped her glass against Isa's, and then took a sip, making the toast official.

"You did amazing, and you should be proud of yourself."

"Thank you, Isa."

"I don't know how you held it together, especially after losing communications and finding the mass grave. Dear me." Isa took a sip of her wine. "I would have lost it completely."

"I'd be lying if I told you I wasn't freaked the *entire* time. And between you and me, I lost it completely on several occasions." She swirled the red liquid in her glass before taking another sip. "The things I felt down there…They burrowed inside." Soto lifted the glass to take a sip, hovering it inches from her lips. "It's hard to describe how it took a hold." She stared into her glass noticing the inkiness of the liquid and the traces of fine sediment that appeared when she swirled the wine around and around. "I thought about dad a lot, you and Ginny, my mom… and Special Agent Ford. She…"

She found Ford's gaze across the room and held it, but only momentarily, before someone stole her attention away. She took a sip of wine, enjoying the subtle notes and remembered all the subtle and not so subtle ways that Winifred Ford supported her when she was cracking. How Ford made her laugh at the right times and held her tightly when she wanted to run. How Ford's kisses guaranteed everything would be okay. "She…"

"She is a great partner and you worked well together," Isa said. "You okay?"

Soto placed her glass on the table and leaned back in her seat. "I keep thinking about the people that we found, seeing their broken bones, wondering if they died instantly or slowly."

"Those people, whoever they were, aren't suffering any more thanks to you, Lexy, and those guys over there." Isa motioned to Ford's table where she and Grady sat. "They are finally going home after all these years. Their poor souls are going to be at peace. Think about the magnitude of that for a second, huh?"

"I'll never forget it for as long as I live." Tears threatened and she closed her eyes, hoping she could hold them in for a little while longer.

"And guess what, Daya? No one else will forget either." Isa nudged Soto with her shoulder.

"You know all the right words to say." She leaned in and felt an arm around her shoulders.

"I say what I see and that's precisely why I'm right ninety-two percent of the time." Soto joined Isa in laughter and leaned into her embrace. Then she found Ford's eyes upon her again. "So, here's another résumé item for you, Officer Soto."

"What's that?"

"Animal whisperer."

"I already have that on there."

"Wild animal whisperer." Soto looked at Isa with confusion. "Very strange and wild redheaded animal whisperer," Isa clarified. "Come on kid, try to keep up." She laughed and swatted Soto's knee.

"Oh, my goodness." Soto broke out in laughter.

"I saw it the moment you watched her walk into my diner. You *so* stalked her."

"No!" Soto smiled and shifted in her chair, sitting up straight. "I did no such thing."

"You pounced on that!" Isa said.

"Oh my God!" Soto said. "No I didn't." She twirled a lock of hair around her finger and thought about all the tactics she had used to break the once wild creature. "Was it that obvious?"

"Only to me, however after tonight, probably to everyone else too. You can't keep your eyes off each other."

Soto looked at Ford sitting so elegantly. "I can't help it. She has a beautiful mind. She's not as uptight as everyone thinks."

Ford wore a pair of heels that accented the contours of her long legs. Her legs were crossed and she had the tip of her toe in her shoe and was pushing it around on the floor. She wore a classic black pencil skirt, gold belt at her waist, and an olive-colored silk blouse. Her hair was in a low and loose bun at the nape of her neck, wildfire contained for the time being.

"You should see your face."

"Whose face?" Soto asked, realizing she had been nibbling on the tip of her finger.

"Your face!"

"What about it?"

"It's telling a beautiful story, and so is hers," Isa said. "So." She slapped the table and Soto snapped her head in Isa's direction. "Rumor has it that the FBI is totally out of the center. A couple members of the team have already left. I think it's just Grady and Ford who are here."

"Oh, really?" Soto looked around the event space, confirming Isa's observation.

"You'll be okay."

Soto reminded herself to focus on her breathing as she wrestled with the fact that after tonight she wouldn't see Winifred Ford again, at least not any time soon.

"Aren't you going to say goodbye? A seat just opened up at their table. Go get it."

"I don't want to say goodbye."

"Then go and say hello. Come on, one foot in front of the other," Isa instructed and gently pushed Soto away from her.

"Isa?" Soto said as she stood.

"Yes."

"The food was superb."

"Why thank you, dear."

"And, Isa?"

"Yes, darlin'?"

"Do you think she would believe me if I told her it was love at first sight?" Soto held on to the table to steady herself.

"She probably loved you first when she met you in a dream," Isa said and gave her a smile. "X-Files, remember? Now, go on. I got dessert I need to plate." She gave Soto a little slap on the rear. "Go on. Get."

Soto navigated through the crowd of community members, volunteers, and other guests. She answered questions with grace in spite of the urgent pace her heart wanted her to travel. She kept her eyes fixed on her target as she worked her way to Ford, edging slightly whenever someone got in her line of sight.

"She got you good, Winnie. Never thought I'd see *you* get bugged," Grady said with a grin on his face.

"I was…"

"Distracted?" Grady couldn't have timed his comment any better.

"Can I join you?" Soto asked.

"Please." Grady scoot aside, making room for her between them.

"Oh my God, Ford, are you're drinking?"

"I couldn't leave without trying your family's wine."

"And?" Soto asked, watching her take a sip and swirl it in her mouth. She swallowed with a purse to her lips and a little smack at the end.

"Smoky, imaginative…" She swirled the wine in her glass again. "It's spicy."

"I believe she asked you about the wine not her backside in those pants," Grady said at the moment Ford took another sip. She sputtered and coughed and her eyes grew in shock "She's been commenting on them all night," he added while she cleared her throat before they erupted in laughter that drew onlookers.

"I like the cut," Ford said after a few clears of her throat and a slap on Grady's arm.

"Uh-huh," Grady said.

"Is that a giggle?" Soto asked her.

"That's a giggle, all right," Grady confirmed.

"It happens when I drink." Ford placed fingers over her mouth, but another one of her saucy giggles escaped.

"Who knew she had it in her?" Grady said as he stood and gave a little stretch. "As much as I would love to stay and watch Winnie get drunk, I should go. We," he looked at Ford, "have an early flight tomorrow morning." Grady held out his hand, "Officer Soto, it was hella good to work with you and Lex. You two are pretty badass. It was truly an honor," he said. Soto shook his hand then gave him a hug.

"Thank you for everything, Grady. Seriously, we couldn't have done any of it without you."

"Did you hear that, Win?" Grady patted Ford on the back. "None of this without me," he mouthed. "Give Lexy a handshake and a hug for me too, will you? She's a great dog."

"I will," She gave him one more hug before he went on his way. Soto sat again and rubbed her pinky against Ford's thigh. "You look exquisite."

"So do you."

"I only showered for two hours and flossed nine times."

"It shows."

Soto's laughter brought temporary relief. "So, tomorrow?"

"First flight of the day," Ford said and took another sip of wine.

"Are you ready?"

"Totally out of the preserve. It's back to normal and the pelts are ready for grubby hands to feel them up again." She spoke into her wineglass, swirling the red liquid around. Watching it made her dizzy. "It'll be nice to sleep in my own bed again." She met Soto's gaze and held it. "You know, be home, and all that…"

"I know the feeling," Soto said as she stood. "I'm leaving now."

"You are?" Ford stood, leaving her heart on the ground.

"To my dad's. Going up." Soto motioned toward her family home. "Up there."

"Oh, I'll…" Ford held out her hand for a shake and let Soto pull her in for a hug.

"Come and say goodbye before you leave?" Soto whispered into her ear.

"Of course," Ford said as she held Soto's hands in hers.

"Will you hurry?" Soto asked as her hands slipped out of Ford's.

Ford downed her glass of wine and nodded that she would.

CHAPTER FORTY

The Terrible Door

The house was too quiet. Feelings Soto were able to crowd out in the festive event hall were now impossible to ignore. She wasn't ready to say goodbye. It was happening too fast. She wasn't done with the woman who helped her see beyond her own stubbornness, see a world that existed in the absence of rational thinking, where blind trust overruled scientific proof.

She checked on Lex who hadn't moved from where she'd left her cuddled in her bed in the kitchen—exactly where she'd headed after two baths outside and a belly full of food. "I'm hopelessly in love, Lex."

The dog didn't have advice for her this time, though she gave her a quiet snort before curling into a tight ball. Soto headed up to her room. Each step took more effort than the last, like how it felt when she trudged through the rushing water of the Boise River. But this time it felt like she wore oversized boots made of lead, and this time, it required even more concentration to avoid being swept away. Heartache crept in again at the magnitude of their find of the century. Poor wandering souls destined for eternal rest. *Their* terror was over, but she would always wonder what other stories were waiting to be discovered.

A buzzing on her nightstand—her unusually aggressive-sounding vibrating phone was receiving an incoming text message.

Can I say goodbye?

The door is open.

Soft footsteps made their way down the hallway and then a rapping of knuckles on her bedroom door. Soto pressed her forehead against the door knowing that once Ford entered and closed the door behind her, time would pass too quickly. Another rap, this time more urgent. She let her in.

Ford stood with heels in her hand that she threw onto the floor upon crossing the threshold. Soto took Ford's hands into her own and pulled her into her arms and willed herself to hold it together even through her involuntary tears. With a slam of the door behind her, Soto pushed the tall redhead hard against it and pressed every inch of herself against Ford.

"You..." Soto whispered into wet lips that tasted like grapes and longing. "You are..." She ran her fingers through auburn hair, unclipping it so red could fall upon Ford's freckled shoulders. Her eyes, a green and gray storm, captured what words couldn't express, for there was no ensemble of words that could be crafted, no matter how cleverly arranged, that would be satisfactory.

"Tell me," Ford said, squeezing Soto's backside roughly, nearly lifting her off the floor as she pulled them closer to each other. "Tell me here." She placed honeyed kisses upon Soto's lips. "And here." Sweet kisses over each of her eyelids. "And here." She placed Soto's hand upon her chest and over her heart.

Soto pulled Ford's blouse out of her skirt so fast that she popped the buttons and ripped the fabric that slid off her shoulders and floated to the floor. Three little finger-like bruises were visible on Ford's shoulder—a reminder of their adventure in the cavern of sun-made rubies. Soto ran her tongue over each marking while she caressed the healing bruises on Ford's ribs. "You poor battered beauty," she said, inspecting other bruises on her body, all evidence of their physical commitments to the investigation.

"And what pain are you hiding?" Ford worked at a different pace, button by agonizing button to remove Soto's blouse. She ran her finger down Soto's stomach to the single button on her pants. Soto rest her hands atop Ford's, holding on to her as she unzipped them. Ford took Soto's hands in her own. She brought them to her lips and bestowed kisses upon the markings on her wrists, her purple and black bracelets—bruises made when Ford refused to let the cave claim her. She positioned Soto's hands over her own breasts.

Soto shoved Ford's bra down without unhooking it, revealing her luscious, heavy breasts, pink nipples pointing toward her. Soto took them into her mouth, kissing and raking teeth over the sensitive skin. Ford yelped and squirmed and used curses Soto had never heard before. Did she ask her to hurry? Soto would obey. She raised Ford's skirt above her waist and lifted one of her legs, pinning her against the door. That terrible door. A lingering kiss upon Ford's lips was the calm before their undoing, a calm that preceded an unraveling so vast it hadn't a unit in which to measure.

Ford's whimpers grew more insistent. She would give her whatever she wanted, needed, demanded. She shoved lace panties out of her way and gazed into glimmering green and gray eyes upon first contact. One fingertip, then two and a third swirling through sweltering hunger. She reveled in the fact that she held more than a woman in the palm of her hand. She held magic and mayhem, blind trust, and belief.

"Fuck me, please," Ford moaned against her lips. "Daya." She groaned and worked herself against Soto's palm. "I need you inside me…"

"Anything…" Soto pushed her fingers inside her, slowly at first so she could capture what Ford felt like their first time. Ford's lips curled and she uttered a pained whimper as Soto stretched her open. And she did it again, deeper this time, watching Ford mouth words and promises taken directly from her own heart. Ford wrapped her leg around her, locking her in, begging Soto to fuck her as hard as she could. Soto followed orders through slippery lust that coated her fingers and dripped down her hand and between Ford's legs, soaking…everything. Over and over until Ford couldn't breathe and ecstasy-laced tears streamed down her face. She was a mess against the door. That terrible door. Soon Ford would walk away through that terrible door.

Soto dropped onto her knees to taste what she had done. She inched Ford's panties the rest of the way down. And quickly, without warning, she took Ford into her mouth. She was still throbbing and coming and Soto lapped up the fragrant evidence—the smell of her like late harvest apples, when the fruit was sweet and crisp and ready for pressing. She lapped the precious juice, for she would never be satiated. Ford struggled on shaky footing, finally giving up and sliding down against the door.

"More," Soto said with Ford's hand in hers. She lay on her back, guiding Ford's wet heat directly onto her lips. "Use me," she demanded, brewing a storm within Ford.

Soto reached for Ford's breasts and felt Ford's hands over her own, while she pinched and teased her nipples, while her tongue spread her apart, suckling, while Ford worked herself against her mouth lightly at first and then primitive and lush, she rode the storm. A singular elated cry. Ford had come again hard and fast.

Breathless and dazed, yet acutely aware, she climbed off Soto, pulling her up. Ford held her closely, securing her possession. She ran her fingers through Soto's wild black mane and with a fist of it in her grasp, she pulled her head back and kissed her hard and rough, pushing her onto the bed. She removed the last of their clothing and took the time to fold each item despite Soto's pleas to *hurry the fuck up*, to which Ford merely smiled and told her that good things come to those who are patient.

Ford found a hair tie on Soto's nightstand and secured her red hair out of her eyes. "I saw butterflies in your hair that very first time…" Ford climbed on top of the bed and spread Soto's legs and apart. She grazed her fingertips along the soft skin there. "Then I saw you again in the center, all those years later, and I saw the butterflies again and they flew to me, surrounded me. Everywhere I looked, they...you were everywhere." She lifted Soto and pulled her onto her lap. She marveled at what lay before her. Strength, beauty, and peace. "I wanted you... Daya, so bad it hurt me here." She placed her hand over her own heart while trailing a lone finger along Soto's collarbone, down her chest over a hardened nipple and over her heart. "I didn't recognize that I needed you more than anything else." She trailed a finger through Soto's glistening center, stoking her until she was ready to combust.

"Leave me broken," Soto whispered with tears in her eyes.

"I intend to," Ford said, and she took Soto into her needy mouth.

CHAPTER FORTY-ONE

Poor Wandering Souls

It never failed. "Jingle Bells" was stuck in Ford's head. Again. It was none other than her superior knocking at her door.

"Come in, Special Agent Rankin." She removed her reading glasses and leaned back in her chair, giving in to a much-needed stretch.

"Good afternoon, Special Agent Ford." Her superior walked in with a banker box, balancing two coffees on the top, his chin ensuring they wouldn't tumble off.

She relieved him of one of the cups. "Thanks," she said after a sip of a pumpkin spice latte, her first of the fall season.

"So a couple of things—"

"First, check this out."

"UFOs?"

"Better." She swiveled her screen around so he could see. "It's called a hard release. It's a fascinating tactic." She pressed play on her laptop. The camera showed Lexy barking at the mouth of a large metal cage secured atop a flatbed trailer. "There are bears inside. They're going to release them. Watch." Ford had seen Soto's new outreach video a dozen times, learning her tactics first and then studying the woman herself. It always led to sifting through memories, her taste, her touch.

"Check it out," Ford said to Rankin.

An officer released the latch and two bears came tumbling out while bells, gunshots, loud noises and sirens sounded.

"Find it, Lexy!" Soto shouted.

"There she goes. Hot on their tails!"

Then a pan over to Roselyn and Soto with their dart rifles ready in case it didn't go as planned. "If all is successful," Soto said to the camera, "we won't see them wandering in the city ever again."

Ford pressed pause at her favorite spot, Soto looking right at her. "Isn't that so cool?" She knew she had a huge grin on her face.

"She has a very effective program. Why it's not being replicated in other states is beyond me," Rankin said.

"I have a feeling it will grow by leaps and bounds."

The discovery of the immigrants gained national attention, bringing a tremendous amount of visibility to Soto's program. "But she needs more dogs, like one for every agent. It's coming down to funding, or lack thereof."

"It always does," he added. "So, where are you with the last of your cases?" Ford was due for her leave in exactly three days—three days and three months after her originally planned departure.

"They are where I need them to be." She pointed to a couple of banker boxes in the corner of her office. "Just waiting on your signature." She mimicked signing a sheet of paper.

"Already done." He opened the box and handed her a stack of folders.

"Perfect," she said, walking them over to the boxes against the wall. "Everything is labeled and ready for storage deep in the bowels of the basement of the bureau." She slapped the top of the uppermost box.

"And the Lake Lowell Ghost?"

"I'm testifying in person tomorrow."

"Not over the phone?"

"It's important I be there," she said, sitting back down.

"Let me know how I can support," he offered. "And Blue River?"

"I'll close that one too."

"Didn't I tell you they were related?"

"You did." While she and Soto couldn't prove it empirically, they both knew in their hearts that Ford's case from nine years ago was merely the start of a chain of events that would lead them to the rail workers.

"And didn't I tell you this would be a once-in-a-lifetime opportunity?"

"You did." Ford nodded in agreement and looked back to the paused video of Soto. Rankin followed her eyes.

"And didn't I tell you that Officer Soto and you would make a great team?"

"Yes, yes, yes to all those things." Ford laughed and slapped her desktop. "You were right, Special Agent Rankin."

"Though I am sorry this took a lot longer than I had originally thought."

"We couldn't have known at the time what we would find." Their investigation had uncovered that the twenty-three men came from all over the Northwest: Idaho, Washington and Oregon. "There was a lot to piece together, and I wanted to make sure everything was completely documented before I officially closed both cases."

And it *had* taken her longer than it probably should have, but closing the cases meant filing them away—filing away moments with Daya with her collection of closed cases in the basement of the bureau.

"I appreciate your dedication, Special Agent Ford, and for sticking with it until the very end. I also want to apologize to you for another thing…"

"What?"

"I took advantage of your inability to say no. You needed to take time off and here we are three months later."

"Please, don't. I needed this. I'm glad I took this case." She took a sip of her coffee. "It was a…" Ford looked at the boxes in the corner of her office. "I learned…" She turned her focus back to the image on her laptop.

"You learned a lot over the past three months, more than you've learned in a long time, Ford." He gave her a gentle smile.

"I think you are right again," she admitted.

"Well," he said. "Now you can leave for your trip carefree, not a worry in the world."

"I can already feel the sand in between my toes."

"Then, I'll leave you to it." He stood up and picked up his banker box. "Oh. You got something." He pulled out an express-mail package. "It's from Washington State."

"Thanks," she said, and pulled the easy-open tab. A letter fell out, a postcard, and wrapped in tissue paper was a tin of magical salve. She smiled, opened the lid, and inhaled the precious scent. She offered it over to Rankin to smell.

"Oh that's nice," he said. "What is it?"

"A mix of different things…" She took another lingering whiff. "Check this out," Ford said, picking up the postcard and handing it over. "It's for the trail dedication tomorrow, which I also plan to attend *in person.*"

"It's beautiful," he said as he inspected the glossy card. "How do you pronounce this again?" Rankin looked at the handout and stumbled over the Cantonese pronunciation.

"Jide," she said. "Pronounced JEE-day. It means *remember.*" Ford winced as he tried again to pronounce the word. "Better. But try to say it with more feeling next time."

"Not everyone speaks as many languages as you."

"I'll try to remember that next time I berate someone for not pronouncing something as eloquently as myself."

"So, will you see Officer Soto and Lexy?"

"I think so," said Ford. "Officer Soto said they would be there." She and Soto talked with each other almost daily, but their last interaction had been over two and a half weeks ago via a text.

I'll be investigating an intense poaching case over the next few weeks," Soto had texted. *I'll be out in the field a lot with no reception.*

I'll be thinking about you," Ford had texted.

"I can't stop thinking about you," was Soto's response.

"Tell her hello for us." He stood. "And send me the final reports when you're done and I'll send them to storage."

"Thank you, Rankin." She stood to see him out.

"Care to take some reading material on your trip?"

"Like what?"

Rankin slid a folder over. "It's an interesting one, right up your alley. Apparently there is a never-ending road in Ely, Nevada." In her time with Soto, Ford learned that it wasn't about finding answers. It was the stories in between and finding common ground along the way. "I'll leave it on your desk."

"Don't even think about it."

Rankin laughed and picked it back up. "Send me a postcard. Better send one to Grady too. He gets jealous."

"I will," she said as he headed out the door. As soon as she heard it latch, she grabbed the card from Daya and tore it open. The image on the front showed that it was from someplace called Leavenworth, Washington. The cover displayed girls in dirndls holding large beer steins. She was utterly confused. Last she looked, Leavenworth was a penitentiary in Kansas not a German-themed town.

Winifred,

Nobody writes cards anymore. That and I am in between phones. Mine is at the bottom of Lake Chelan. That was my sixth phone this year! Like last time, my number will be the same, but I won't have a new one again until a few days from now. My case looks on track to wrap up in the next couple of days. I still plan to testify in person and attend the trail opening. The dedication card turned out nice, huh? The photos I saw look even better. I am proud of what we accomplished together.

I've missed you these past few weeks. It's been hell pretending to laugh at other people's jokes. I hope we can have lunch or something when we see each other? I have some exciting news to share!

See you soon,

Daya and Lexy

CHAPTER FORTY-TWO

Jide

"Hey, Isa." Daya picked up after the third ring, using her hands-free setup as she traveled down the interstate.

"Where are you?" Isa asked.

"I just crossed the Idaho border."

Today was the day that she and Winifred would give their testimonies and also the day of the trail opening and dedication.

"Rumor has it there's a pushy federal agent in town."

"She's there?" Daya asked. Her insides clenched at being so close to the woman she loved. "Where?"

"She just had breakfast at the diner," said Isa. "Left a big tip. I told her she didn't need to pay, but did she listen to—"

"How was she?" Daya asked, finally picking up on the din of the diner in the background.

"Skinny. Too skinny. I fed her good, though. Aside from that she looked good. Asked about fifty Daya-related questions."

Daya squeezed the steering wheel and hoped that a few in-through-the-nose-and-out-through-the-mouth breaths would help calm her nerves.

"You there?"

"Yeah, I'm here. A little anxious."

"Don't be."

"I can't help it. I'm a mess. Couldn't sleep a friggin' wink in like three weeks! I feel like crap and probably look—" Then a pain seared her chest that she tried to soothe away. She rubbed her hand over her heart.

"Stop. If it makes you feel any better, she was a wreck too." Isa laughed. "Goodness gracious, young budding love..." she added. "When will we see you?"

"I'm headed to the bureau to testify and then straight to the dedication this afternoon."

"Drive safely, okay?"

"I will."

"And pay attention!" Isa ended the call.

"Oh, Lexy." Daya said, making eye contact with her dog sitting patiently in the backseat. "How are you *so* calm?" she asked and looked to the growing pink morning sky. She opened her window all the way, hoping the fresh winter air would bring clarity and help calm her angst. She and Winifred exchanged very few words that last night they were together, instead leaving it to the power of touch to express themselves. During the past few months they had exchanged almost daily phone calls, emails, and text messages that included teasing and sexually charged subject matter. But they had skirted their true feelings, discussing facts about the case and leaving the most important stuff unsaid.

Twenty-three men, twenty-three people, representing those who migrated to our state to work and to contribute.

Daya was standing with her family and friends at the preserve for the dedication. It was an elegant installation that incorporated the massive quartz rocks and educational components, dedicated to those who had died—restless souls lost in a mass grave. The town's mayor was giving the dedication, joined by members of the Hsu Family Foundation, representatives from the local chapter of the Human Rights Coalition, and Executive Director Jewell.

A great shame is upon us and our treatment of them, our abusive and discriminatory laws that framed them as lesser human beings.

Daya was running on fumes after a grueling half-day question-and-answer session. She had relayed the facts as she knew them. She didn't have a logical explanation to back most of it up, but she communicated what she believed to be true.

We've come a long way since then, but not far enough. We still cannot say that all men, all women, all people are treated equally. We say as much through our local laws and nationally at our airports and our borders—families are being ripped apart all in the name of the law. Our workload is enormous…

She had seen Win briefly in between their respective turns in front of the federal panel. Win wore an exquisite suit that hugged her every curve in a way that only something tailored could do. She had also seen her long enough to notice that her fingernails were perfectly manicured. Daya on the other hand was flailing—a nervous, fidgeting force.

Jide, which means remember. We will never forget the immigrants who died here under our preserve in darkness because they couldn't live with respect in the light of the day. Where they were going, we can only speculate. May future generations to come enjoy Jide Trail so named in their memory and may all who visit Deer Flat know them by name.

And after each of the twenty-three names were spoken and a moment of silence, oversized scissors cut the ceremonial ribbon followed by a round of applause. As much as the dedication meant to Daya, one person meant more. She gave Lexy the go-ahead to say hello first. Her pup darted as fast as her four legs could take her, like an agility contender in competition through the crowd of people toward her goal. With a little encouragement from Isa, Ginny, and her father, Daya too followed in her dog's footsteps toward their target.

"Are you making out with my dog?" Daya asked with a smile on her face. She watched her partner and her former partner make up for lost time. Daya offered Winifred a hand and pulled her into her arms. Finally peace.

"Guilty," said Ford.

"You look…" Daya said, justifying a reason to take her in from head to toe. She leaned in for another embrace and slipped her arms inside of Winifred's long wool coat. This time they held on longer.

"So do you," Win whispered in Daya's ear and finally pulled away. Her hands went into her coat pockets. "Love your puffy coat."

"It's standard issue." Soto laughed softly. "Hi," she whispered.

"Hi." They held each other's gaze. Daya watched Win carefully for things her eyes would tell her. "How are you?"

"Good. Great. Thank you for the card. That was a wonderful treat."

"And the salve too?" Daya asked. Winifred's response, a flush of pink creeping slowly up her cheeks. "I missed seeing that." Daya smiled.

"I missed you doing that to me." Win tucked a lock of hair behind her ear. "And your poaching case?"

"Straight forward. Solved in record time, thanks to Lex." She patted her dog on the head. "People think they can bury their transgressions, but not with this little lady on the case."

"So what is your exciting news?" Win asked. "I'm dying to know."

"Come, let's chat." The three navigated through the crowd and shuffled their way through brittle brown, gold, and magenta fallen leaves toward a covered shelter. "I've been wanting to tell you…Well, I only recently found out." She sat close, hoping to absorb Winifred's heat in the early winter elements. "I'm having a baby!" she said, watching Win turn ash white and her eyes grow large, opening her mouth and nothing intelligible coming out.

"Wait? Who? Wait, what? You?"

She laughed and enjoyed the look on Win's face as she visibly tried to make sense of her announcement. "My program got approval for another dog thanks to a donation from the Hsu Family Foundation." She laughed, took her dog's face in her hand, and kissed her on the head.

"Oh! My goodness. You! Jesus!" Color returned to Winifred's face. "I guess congratulations are in order. I'm so happy for you, for both of you and your program. You more than deserve it."

"Thank you. We're due any day now."

"Is it a boy or a girl?"

"Don't know yet. After these dogs are born, the breeder puts them through testing and suggests the best-suited ones. I'm beyond excited, even if it's just one more dog, it'll be a tremendous help."

"I have no doubt, especially if they're as dedicated as this one." Win scratched Lexy behind her ears. The dog looked up to her with a huge grin on her face.

"What about you? It feels like forever since…" Daya looked into the distance to a shimmering lake and to a fog that settled upon it, and to bare trees that once held leaves while they searched for answers. "When do you leave on your exciting vacation?" Soto rest her hand upon Ford's knee and let it linger there. She was pleased that her touch still held its ability to arrest Ford's most basic movements.

"Day after tomorrow, then sandy beaches all day long…"

"It sounds relaxing." She tried to sound peppy. She felt conflicted and selfish for wanting Win to stay and be hers. "Are you looking forward to eating tropical fruit all day and swimming in the ocean?"

"I was ready all those months ago. But now…" Ford ran her hand over hers, still upon her knee. "I don't think I can bear it." Win whispered and leaned into Daya. "My bags are packed. They're in the trunk of my rental, but I'm not ready."

"You are more than ready, Win. You need to go. You need to rest and recharge, think about what you want…what you need."

"No…" Her voice started to crack.

"Where are you staying?"

"In Boise at the—"

"Stay with me, at the vineyard. Please." It was out before Daya had an opportunity to truly evaluate what she was asking and what the toll on her emotions would be.

And just like the last time, the time together went way too fast. And just like last time, they exchanged very few words, preferring to show each other how they felt while wallowing in their circumstances of the forthcoming time apart.

Daya thought Win's leaving the first time was painful, but seeing her again after so long and having to say goodbye again after such a short time, took everything she had that was holding her together, out of her. "Winifred?" Soto asked.

Ford zipped her belongings into her suitcase. "Yes?"

"I'm in love with you," is what Daya imagined herself saying. "Have fun," is what she said. Instead she let Ford go again without voicing those words. When she finally found her courage a few hours later, she told herself that wasn't the kind of thing she should text or say to Ford over the phone.

CHAPTER FORTY-THREE

Alternate Ending

"Officer Soto." Knuckles rapped her door.

"Come in, Captain. Have a seat." Daya cleared one of the chairs. Since their work on the Lake Lowell Ghost, public presentation requests had skyrocketed. Other enforcement agencies from across the nation were interested in learning more about her program. She had even done interviews on *Animal Planet*. Coupled with the end of winter and planning for the spring, she was knee-deep in work. Her superior held a handful of file folders likely meant for her.

"How's the training going with the little one?" Captain Fox asked.

"Mercedes," or Sades, as Daya and the others on the force had started calling her, "is doing really well. Lexy is a great with her. She's a better teacher than I am, but, as much as I want Roselyn to have this partner, I'm not sure their temperaments are right for each other. Sades is much too high-strung for him. He tells her one thing and she does the opposite. She's stubborn beyond measure. She's going to need an *uber* alpha. We don't want to force it."

"Good call, Officer Soto. And aside from that?"

"Later this month we're taking them out to that orchard in Enumclaw, that one with all the deer problems, to see what she can do and get her more field work."

"You better get that on social media," Fox advised.

"Oh I will."

"Well, don't feel too bad about Roselyn. I have a feeling that he will get a perfect partner sooner than you think."

"It only took us three years to get a second dog. What's another three?" Regretting her bluntness in front of her superior, she quickly said, "So. What can we do for you, ma'am?"

"I think you better sit down."

"Okay." Lexy got out of her office bed and joined the duo for the news. "What is this all about?

"Your program got a gift." Fox handed her the folder she was carrying.

"Cool." She opened it expecting to see a few donation checks or gift certificates for dog food. That wasn't uncommon, especially after all the national attention.

"Six more dogs," Fox blurted, before Daya had time to read the contents. Sitting wasn't the wisest suggestion. Daya almost fell off her chair.

"Come again? How? When? Who? When do I get them? Oh my God! I got to know." She felt herself hyperventilating and took a deep breath.

"An anonymous donor made a *significant* contribution to your program. The details are all there inside that folder. It outlined that the gift would pay for everything from vet care to food." She opened it again, her hands trembling. She couldn't read! Captain Fox was smiling at her reaction.

"Lexy, six brothers and sisters!" Her four-legged partner danced about at her master's jubilation. "Where will they train? I can hardly manage the two we have with the budget I got now. Between me and Roselyn, we're maxed out!"

"There's more."

"Okay." Daya sat back down and held on to the armrests of her chair.

"The gift includes funding for a training facility."

Daya stood up, then sat back down, and then stood up again. "Are you kidding me?"

"I wouldn't do that to you Soto."

"Holy mother of Mary." She slapped the sides of her face again to ensure she wasn't dreaming.

"There's also an increase of three more dogs every other year for the next three years." Soto rummaged through folders and papers on her desk, spilling them on the ground in search of her phone. She had to call her dad. She had to call Roselyn. She wanted to talk to Win!

"You okay over there?" Fox was grinning.

"I'm stunned. Elated. I'm not sure what to do." She ran her hand through her hair and rubbed her forehead trying to keep it together.

"You have a good program, Soto, and I'm sorry we could never find it in the budget to get you this far."

"I totally understand." Daya wrapped her arms around her dog while she worked hard to contain tears of joy. Failing, she let them flow into her dog's soft fur.

"One more thing."

"Oh my God." She sniffled and blotted her eyes with a handkerchief.

"Mostly regular stuff is what I got now." Fox handed her two file folders. "Three new recruits starting this spring."

"Fantastic. This I can process." Daya laughed. "What do we have?" She thumbed through the folders.

"Two agents both assigned in the coastal region."

"That will be a huge help. And the third?"

"The third is a little…" Fox slapped the last folder in the palm of her hand. "Needs to be treated differently."

"How so?"

"This one is the cream of the crop."

"Great."

"And she indicated a strong interest in working with dogs, even has a little experience too. This particular recruit made a good case as to why she should be fast-tracked to the Bear Dog Program."

"I look forward to training—"

"She will report to Officer Roselyn."

"What? Why? I mean, I'm all for sharing the load, but he has his hands full with his team."

"He can make room for one more. You can help train, of course. You are the expert, this is your program, but this one needs to report to Roselyn. This isn't negotiable."

"I don't get it," Daya said, shaking her head.

"It's a lateral shift from the FBI."

"Oh," Daya said. "What territory?"

"North Olympic."

Daya ran through the counties within, Dungeness, Morse Creek, South Sequim Bay, Elwha... A smile grew on her face and more tears filled her eyes. "What's the recruit's name, ma'am?"

"Ford. It's Winifred Ford," said Fox, and she handed Daya her the file.

"I see," she said. Finding her phone. Dialing. "Will you give me a moment?" she asked Fox. "I need to call someone." She smiled, thinking about her elegant redheaded lover wearing work boots and polyester.